WHAT
SHE
DID

BOOKS BY CARLA KOVACH

GINA HARTE SERIES
The Next Girl
Her Final Hour
Her Pretty Bones
The Liar's House
Her Dark Heart
Her Last Mistake
Their Silent Graves
The Broken Ones
One Left Behind

WHAT SHE DID

CARLA KOVACH

Bookouture

Published by Bookouture in 2021

An imprint of Storyfire Ltd.
Carmelite House
50 Victoria Embankment
London EC4Y 0DZ

www.bookouture.com

ISBN: 978-1-80019-967-5
eBook ISBN: 978-1-80019-966-8

I dedicate *What She Did* to anyone who is struggling with a traumatic past, and I also have to give people who sleepwalk a thought too. It sounds like a tough condition to live with.

I'd also like to offer some of this dedication to my husband, Nigel Buckley, who is always incredibly supportive of my writing.

CHAPTER ONE

To finally know and understand who I am is a powerful thing. The polythene that covers this room is there to hide the real me from the rest of the world. This is where I get to hold a person's life in my hands.

Let's hope I choose my next move wisely. This knife fits so comfortably in my clenched fist.

Live or die. Live or die.

Let me see…

CHAPTER TWO

Twenty-three years ago

It's not red enough. The apple is meant to be red and I want the smiley worm to be blue. I ruined it with green and then changed my mind. As I press the pencil crayon harder into the colouring book, the tip breaks and pings off the table leg. 'I broke it, Mummy. I broke my pencil.' I sniffle a couple of times and wipe my nose on my sleeve. I'm five years old now so I know I can do better. Mummy won't let me use the sharpener even though I know I can sharpen pencils really well. She says they're dangerous.

'It's okay, baby girl. Mummy will sharpen it for you.' Her hands shake as she takes the red pencil from me. I don't know why she's staring at my picture so hard.

'Mummy, don't cry. I'm making it for you so that you can be happy.'

Her black hair drops forward as she kneels on the edge of the rug. She hands the sharpened pencil back to me then does my chunky cardigan buttons up before kissing me on the forehead. I lie there, mouth open in concentration as I try not to colour over the lines. Pressing harder and harder with the pencil, I try to make the apple redder but the green still won't go. The pencil snaps and I've made a tiny hole in the page. This won't make Mummy happy. Now I'll have to start again and colour another picture.

As my bottom lip trembles I look away. Mummy will know I'm sad if she sees me and it will make her sad. There is a bang at the door and it makes me jump.

Mummy holds her finger to her lips and creeps towards the door. She stares through the spyhole so that she can see who is there. I shuffle out of the way as she takes a few steps back. 'Mummy, you nearly trodded on me.'

'Shush.' She places her finger over my lips and stares at me for a second.

'I know you're in there.' It's a man's voice.

It's the bad man. Mummy grabs me up in her arms. I go to shout but her hand covers my mouth. I can't breathe and I'm frightened so I try to wriggle out of her grip. She drags me into the bedroom, keeping her hand clasped over my mouth as she bends over. Another little cry escapes my mouth.

'You can't make a noise, baby girl. Promise me and I'll take my hand away.' She is crying too and red blotches spread across her light brown cheeks.

My heart flutters; it feels funny and I can't stop shaking. 'Mummy, I'm scared.'

'Shush. What mustn't you do?'

I reply in a whisper. 'Make a noise. I mustn't make a noise, Mummy.' My knees almost knock as I grip the blunt pencil. I need to wee but I can't tell Mummy now.

'That's right.' I can only just hear what she says as her warm breath finds my ear. 'It's like a game. You're going to hide under the bed and you can't come out until I say. Okay? Promise?'

I nod as a tear trickles down my cheek. I know I'll upset Mummy more now that she's seen me cry but I can't help it. She kisses me on the head, pulls me onto my belly and slides me along the shiny wood until I'm under our big bed. She pulls the blanket over the end but it doesn't quite reach the floor. I peer through the gap as she almost slips in her thick black tights. She picks up the colouring book but my apple picture slips out. I ripped it out of the book so that she could keep it. She snatches that up too and throws it into a drawer. The bad man shouts from outside the door and the next bang makes me flinch.

'Just go away. I've called the police.' I know Mummy hasn't called anyone. She has no money and her phone doesn't make calls at the moment, that's what she keeps saying. I lift up the blanket and watch as she reaches for the sideboard and grabs the shiny blue and yellow glass globe that she told me is called a paperweight.

'You thought I'd never find you, but I did. You know what I've come for.' As he finishes talking, the door bursts open and I wet myself a little.

My mouth dries, then my throat. I wonder, if I called her, would I make a frog noise? I want to cough or swallow but I can't. Mummy said not to make any noise and I promised. My nose fills up and I'm shivery cold. The floor is like ice and I can barely feel my fingertips. My teeth begin to chatter and I can't wiggle my toes. Mummy told me to keep my socks on but I was playing with them. I wanted to see how long they could stretch. I wish I'd left them on then my toes would be warm.

I peer through the gap. Mummy's eyes look so wide. She lifts the paperweight with her shaky hand. 'Please just leave me alone.'

His laughter fills the air followed by a loud footstep. He's coming for me. I drop the blanket and lay my head on the floor but all I can see is feet and a long shadow. Now there are two shadows and a pair of black boots, not like Mummy's – they're flat. I flinch at the loud thud. Has Mummy hit the bad man?

I hold my hand over my mouth to stop myself crying out as Mummy falls to the floor. The paperweight rolls to a stop at the blanket's fringe. I hold in my tears. The bad man will get me if I cry.

I won't make a noise, I promised. I mouth the word Mummy then everything is silent, except for the ticking of the wall clock.

The booted man is silent for a few moments, then he laughs. Stepping away from Mummy, he starts to empty the sideboard drawers before taking a few items, then he stomps to our kitchen.

I hear the neighbours below, shouting. They always shout. Everyone around here shouts. Mummy gets upset living here and she tells me of a house we'll have one day, one surrounded by pretty flowers with a garden gate, just like the one we used to live in. I want to go back to the cottage where we lived before so I hope that's where she means.

I slide along the floor, peering under the blanket. 'Mummy,' I whisper as another tear runs down my cheek. She doesn't move. I slide a bit further, just like a snake, until I've cleared the blanket. The man in boots still opens and closes drawers in the kitchen. I have to get out and get help for Mummy while she sleeps. As I stand, my trembling knees almost buckle.

I see Scarecrow, the knitted toy that used to be Mummy's when she was little. He always sits on the chest of drawers until bedtime, then he sleeps next to me. I grip Scarecrow and hold him to my chest. The stomping halts and my bottom lip trembles.

'What have you done with her? I will find her, you mark my words.' As he hurries back into the lounge, I fall to the floor and slide back under the bed, squeezing my eyes together. This is hide and seek, that's all it is. I'm hiding and he can't find me. My heart bangs hard so I grip Scarecrow closer.

As I open an eye, just a little, the man steps into the bedroom, standing at the end of the bed that Mummy and I share. He smells funny, like chips.

One of Scarecrow's button eyes must have fallen off as it's at the bad man's feet. As he bends down and reaches for the button, I hold my breath. My chest hurts; I need to breathe. As he scoops up the button and leaves the room, I gasp. The front door bounces back and forth, banging away until it finally stops. Has he gone or is it a trick? It's hide and seek, I must stay under the bed and not make a sound. I promised Mummy.

I look at her. A single tear had run from her closed eye.

I want to come out from under the bed. I want to shake her, to wake her up but I can't. I can't move. My legs are numb and I can't look any more. I scrunch my eyes closed and cling to Scarecrow as I lie in a wet puddle and silently weep. Mummy will tell me when to come out and I promised her I wouldn't make a noise, so I won't.

I'll be quiet, Mummy. I'm being a good girl.

CHAPTER THREE

Now

I grab the blouse with the broderie anglaise strip along the cuff then I run my fingers over the smooth pearlescent buttons. It's perfect for my meeting; professional but stylish. My phone alarm rings, its shrill racket piercing my thoughts as it buzzes along the chest of drawers. Mr Ben Forge, my nine o'clock appointment, will be here in fifteen minutes and my heart flutters away. Since first meeting him at his office, I've been thinking about him – a lot. He's charming and good looking. I shake those thoughts away. He's a potential client, which means I need to forget how he makes me feel and concentrate on getting more business. The extra money would definitely come in handy.

It's rare that I invite clients to my home but he was keen to see where I work. I glance around at my spare bedroom that has been kitted out into an office. All is in place and I'm ready to receive my visitor.

The office is ready for his arrival, and so am I. One last mirror check confirms that I don't have a hair out of place. My light brown skin is clear of blemishes and I look alert; yes, I'm as ready as I can be. I bite my lip and smile, reminding myself that I can do this.

I've just got time to run downstairs to collect my post, so I grab my keys and head out the apartment door. As I reach the bottom of the stairs, I grab the three letters from my post box. One from the council, a water bill, and a white envelope with no name on the front; simply addressed to the resident at apartment number twenty-seven.

Mr Forge makes me jump as he presses his nose against the glass of the main door and waves through the wet glass. I push the door open for him, letting in the freezing cold December air. The stray cat that always loiters pushes through, trying to escape the rain. His scraggy black fur is drenched and he starts brushing his head against my trouser leg, depositing hairs everywhere. I stroke him before popping him back outside and brushing my leg down. Swallowing, I feel a little guilty. I'll put some food out for the cat later.

My client smiles. 'Morning, Marissa. What a day. Sorry I'm early.'

'Ah, Mr Forge, please come in. It's really lovely to see you again.'

'Please, call me Ben. No one calls me Mr Forge except the bank manager.'

I feel my heart rate picking up a little. He's taken me by surprise by being early and I realise I haven't even got the coffee pot on, and I really wanted to impress him. 'I'm not quite ready but follow me up. I'll get a hot drink on the go. It's so cold today. I bet you're freezing.' I glance back as I lead the way up.

'It's lovely and warm in here though.' He smiles as our gazes meet for a second, then he brushes his hand through his head of blond hair which is slightly greying around the sides.

I hope that he can't tell I'm nervous. Right, I don't want to look like I haven't done my research. What do I need to remember? He has twelve offices around the Midlands. His main office is in the centre of Birmingham. He bases himself at his Stratford-upon-Avon office, employs around seventy people and he's won numerous awards. I also know that he's divorced and I swallow, wondering if he's single at the moment. My cheeks start to burn and I hope he doesn't notice. I shouldn't think like this but I can't help that I find him attractive.

'Nice apartments.'

I know he's being polite as they look a bit shabby. Number twenty-four's dogs begin to yap as we pass their apartment and continue up the stairs. 'Sorry about the noise.'

'That's okay, I love dogs. Are they yours?'

'No, I'd like a dog one day though but not in the apartment.' I feel a sense of shame as we reach my floor. The communal area looks scuffed and the carpet gives off a musty smell. A cleaner hasn't attended for months and a couple of the bulbs flicker. This is when I wonder if my home office set-up is enough to get me the more lucrative business I need to move forward.

He smiles as I unlock my door. 'Please come through and make yourself at home. My office is in the first room on the right. Coffee or tea?'

'Coffee would be great. I take it black, no sugar and make it strong, I need to perk up a bit.'

'You're in luck, I make great coffee.' I hurry through to the kitchen and pop a filter into the cafetière and hurry to make the drinks.

He looks up with a smile as I pass him the coffee. 'Two coffees.' I take a sip, enjoying the richness. We both like our coffee black; that's one thing we have in common. 'I forgot to ask the other day, how did you come across my details?' It's a question I need answering as I have no idea.

He looks up as if trying to remember. 'My financial adviser is retiring and Justine Delaney gave me your number. She said that you arrange mortgages and insurances for her clients which is exactly the type of person I desperately need right now.'

He reminds me that I need to call or message Justine, we're definitely due a night of wine very soon. 'Yes, Justine. I've been working with her for years. Are you looking for a similar arrangement to the one I have with her?'

He nodded as his shoulders relaxed. For a moment, he looks like he's thinking about something other than our conversation and our gazes meet again. I know that my thoughts are totally unprofessional but I felt this chemistry between us the moment I saw him. I clear my throat and break the silence, knowing that he wouldn't be interested in a wallflower like me. He's here to do business and I'm being an idiot.

He's poised with his pen, ready to take notes. 'Tell me a bit more about your set-up.'

'Of course. I work from home and I visit the clients as and when needed. What you see here is me; well, I mean this is it and I love working from home, for myself.' My nerves are really showing now as I waffle on. I look like a silly schoolgirl who has a crush on the popular boy, the way I'm biting my bottom lip and looking up at him. I open my tablet case hoping that he can't see the redness creeping up my neck and I wait for the gadget to light up. 'Can I have your card, please? I didn't take one the other day.'

He passes one to me, then I click onto my email and forward some documents to him.

'I've just forwarded my terms and conditions and contract, which is what we spoke about before. I'd really love to work with you and if you'd like to work with me, I'll need you to sign the paperwork before we get started.'

'Whoa, fast mover.' I think I saw him wink. Is he flirting with me? No, he can't be. I'm Marissa; the woman that goes unnoticed. I dress to blend in. If people don't see you, they sure as hell won't want to hurt you.

'I didn't mean it to feel like that.' A pathetic little titter slips through my lips and I relax, feeling my anxiety subside. 'Sorry. Would you like more coffee?' Idiot. He hasn't drunk the one he has in his hand.

'I'm good, thank you. If I line another one of these up, I'll be wired and I have more meetings this morning. Let's hope this is the start of something great, I mean I hope it is. I'll get the paperwork emailed back to you this afternoon. It's lovely to see where you work, Marissa. It's just as I pictured it in my head when you told me you worked at home. Everything is so neat, like you.' He checks out the rows of filing cabinets that are stacked up behind my desk, all locked and shiny. There's not a piece of paper out of order in this room and my collar and cuffs are neatly starched. They are as precise as my office, my cupboards, and my life. That's the image I like to give off. Behind the façade, everything is in disarray; but I'm working on that at the moment. One day my interior will be as tidy as my exterior, I think, as my stomach does a little dance.

'Is there anything else you'd like to ask or need to know?' I'm a little confused as to why he wanted to visit me at my home office. No one else has ever wanted to. I can only think that he likes me; and I like him. He must be in his mid-forties, about twenty years older than me but that doesn't matter, not to me anyway.

He shakes his head, swigs the rest of the coffee down in one and stands. 'No, that was it really. I wanted to see where you worked and now I have. All looks fine so everything is great.'

As I go to stand, he reaches for my wrist, hurting me with his grip. I open and close my mouth, not quite able to get my words out. His fingers press so hard into my skin I feel my hand start to tingle so I begin to pull away. I know he can feel me trembling. After a few seconds, he lets go.

He grabs his coat and puts it back on. 'I'm sorry.' He smiles warmly. 'I was just trying to find the words to ask you out for dinner and…' He cups my chin. 'I know you want to go out with me. I can see what's happening between us and I know under that innocent pretence you can too. I didn't come here today to check out your home office. I came here to check you out and I like what I see. Come on, say yes as I don't take rejection well.' His smile reverses into an over-exaggerated frown. 'I'm a man who's used to getting what he wants.'

'Erm…' I step back and he releases my chin.

I don't like the way he grabbed me. It was as if he owned me. He steps in front of the door and my heart starts to pound. I feel trapped in my apartment and he's still making that face as he waits for my answer.

I feel a prickle of sweat forming at the nape of my neck.

'Right, I best get on.' He pauses and his smile is back as if nothing happened as he moves away from the door. 'Are you okay? You don't look so well.'

'I'm fine, honestly.' I swallow, forcing a smile.

'You're shaking. Probably best not to have any more of that coffee. It's really strong and it'll keep you awake at night. So, what about dinner?'

'Err, yes, you're right about the coffee. Can I let you know later, about dinner?' The best thing I can do is think this through properly. I also can't work out if something weird just happened or if it was just me making something out of nothing? Maybe I'm blowing it all up into something huge when all he did was ask me out. So he grabbed my wrist but he probably didn't mean to pinch so hard, but I still feel trapped.

'Of course, you have my number. It's just dinner. We can get to know each other a little better, that's all. Have a think about it and get back to me.'

I open the front door, my heart now pounding. 'Of course, I'll call you.' I hope he doesn't hear the crackle in my voice.

'You know, I only live a few streets away which is why I suggested dropping by for this meeting.' He buttons up his coat. 'I'm a nice guy, I promise, and I know how to treat a lady.' He steps towards the door and I feel my heart slowing down a little. He throws his bag over his shoulder and stops for a second too long. What he doesn't know is that I have a paring knife behind the sunset picture that I'm leaning against. The main reason for it being there is I'm scared; in fact I'm petrified of someone bursting into my home and hurting me, just like when that man killed my mother. It's there to grab should I need to defend myself from a murderous intruder.

'It was lovely to see you again. I'll message you, I promise,' I say with a little squeak.

'And I'll read and sign the contract. Speak later.' He smiles one last time before leaving.

Idiot. Idiot. Idiot. I handled all that ridiculously. He asked me out, held my wrist and romantically cupped my chin. I read too much into everything. Hurrying to the kitchen with the dirty cups, I place them in the sink before picking up the post again. I open the mystery letter. It's an invite to a residents' meeting to discuss the demise of the estate and I'm invited to attend, along with everyone else. I throw it onto the worktop.

My phone flashes and rings but I ignore Ben. I'll have to call him later or tomorrow when I'm feeling less confused about what just happened. When he stood in front of my door trapping me in, that sense of powerlessness freaked me out as if it was yesterday. My mother's murder is something I'll never forget.

I grab my phone and press Justine's number. She answers immediately. 'Hiya, it's Marissa.'

'I know who it is, silly. Your name comes up. 'Bout time you got back to me, I've missed you and I have vino in the fridge. We badly need that catch up.' She laughs. 'Everything okay?'

'Yes, just realised we haven't spoken for ages and I wondered if you wanted to do something later today or this evening.' Maybe I need to let my hair down and all will seem clear when I've had the chance to unwind with a friend. A few glasses of wine will help.

Packing my work away, I realise it's getting on a bit and I don't want to be late for Justine. I dash around my bedroom, doing my hair and make-up, ready to head out into the frosty winter's evening. Tonight I will put Ben and his dinner invite to the back of my mind and have a good time with my friend. Grabbing the bottle of red that I keep for times like this, I secrete it in my large shoulder bag.

I don't change from my shirt and grey trousers even though I know Justine will have made an effort. My face flushes as I check my phone again. I never did get back to Ben on whether I would go to dinner with him. I might do it later, maybe when I've sunk a couple of glasses of wine and gained some perspective. Dating a potential client probably isn't a good idea but I'm making an effort to get out and meet new people. My therapy is over but I need to continue doing the work if I'm to develop trusting relationships in life. Not everyone is out to hurt me or let me down. The past is the past and only I can make positive steps to build the future I deserve. I do one last mirror check and smile. That's better. Keep positive and happy and everything else will fall into place.

As I grab my handbag and the bag of scraps for the cat, the fire door outside my apartment barges open, making my door creak in turn. I look through the spyhole. *Hello new neighbour in a denim jacket.* I close one eye to get a better look. He turns and I see his mottled face, the look finished with a grey goatee. There's something about him, he's taking in his surroundings and checking over his shoulder. Who exactly is he expecting to be close behind him? His dark beady eyes remind me of an eagle preparing to swoop. Oh well, the apartment couldn't stay vacant forever. I should introduce myself and say hi. I swallow, wondering if he will turn out to be as awful as the stoner neighbours that left a month ago.

I haven't had the best experiences with neighbours, which is why I dread new people moving in. Why couldn't the mature lady who owned the apartment stay there forever? Why did she have to move abroad and rent it out to just anyone? I was in a really happy place when she lived opposite.

There I go again. I'm already jumping to conclusions. How do I know this man is out to cause neighbourly havoc? He might be the best neighbour ever; maybe I should give him a chance. The man stares at my door for a few seconds making me shudder. It's silly for me to be nervous. He must be as curious about me as I am about him.

Two more bodies stomp up the last flight of stairs and then the two hooded teen boys appear at his side. The lad with the nose and lip piercings turns to look at my door. I want to swallow but I fear he might hear.

'Wonder who lives here.' He takes a couple of steps towards my door and clamps his eye over the other side of my spyhole.

I gasp for breath and lean out of the way, hoping that he didn't see me. Maybe he heard me shuffling behind the door. I don't know why he's trying to peer into my apartment. My stomach begins to turn a little. I stare at the sunset picture on my wall knowing that if I'm attacked I have some protection. Taking a long deep breath, I count to five. I'm being ridiculous. Not everyone is out to hurt me, certainly not a curious teenage boy. I've worked through this irrational fear and right at this moment, all I'm doing is taking a step back in my recovery.

They've gone quiet. I can't hear anything but the boy might still be there. Carefully. I kneel and try to look through the miniscule gap under the door and I can see a shadow where his feet are planted and I tremble as I remember the boots from behind the blanket all those years ago. My mother's lifeless body flashes through my mind; my lovely mother. Now is not the time for those thoughts. I'm going to see Justine and it's going to be fun. Pushing that image out of my head, I stand. They mean me no harm. They're just people going about their business of moving into a new apartment.

The older man grunts as I hear the key turning in the door opposite. 'So, boys, you'll be able to stay with your old dad when you want to now. Let's check out your room.'

With a gentle click, I turn the lock and smile at the pierced youth. 'Hi, you must be the new neighbours.' I maintain my smile even though my heart threatens to explode from my chest. I step out, accidentally treading on the end of the boy's toe.

'Sorry—'

'Bloody hell! You just trod on me, you dick.'

His aggression takes the air out of my lungs and I don't know what to say. It was an accident and the hostility has taken me aback. 'I didn't mean…' I open my mouth to say more but the words aren't coming out.

The mature man wearing the denim jacket steps in. 'You just hurt him. Apologise.'

'Look, I didn't mean anything. I only wanted to say welcome to the block and—' Shutting up is my best option. I can see that none of them want me to speak.

The other boy doesn't know where to look as he pulls his long curtained fringe over his eyes. 'Dad, just leave it.'

'Maybe I will. It's probably best that we keep out of each other's way. What do you say?' He's so close I can smell the beer on his breath.

With a turning stomach, I know that I need to stick up for myself. I don't know what his problem is but it can't be me, or the fact that I accidentally stood on his son's toe. 'Actually, I agree. It will be a pleasure to stay out of your way.' The booming in my chest feels as though it might escape and the shortness in my breath is showing.

The boys' father grins and stares at me. The slight twitch on the corner of his left eye keeps me glued to the floor, wondering if I'm dismissed. I should walk away, push him aside, but I can't. The fear that I felt as a child is keeping me stationary.

'Dad, seriously, just leave it, my toe's fine now. Let's just get settled.' The taller lad begins to twist his lip piercing.

I force a smile. 'I'm glad it's okay. Right, I have to go. Sorry we all got off on the wrong foot.' I grab my bag from the hall floor and lock my front door. The father refuses to move so I have no choice but to knock into him as I pass. His arms are like steel and his position, firm. How hard is it in life to stay away from trouble? Very, it follows me everywhere. My heart pounds as I hurry down the stairs noting that I'm almost running late. Justine is cooking us dinner and I'll probably end up ruining it.

As I burst through the communal door, the cat runs over. With trembling hands, I empty the bag of chicken bits onto the pavement and it starts to gobble the food straight away. Leaning over, I gently scratch its ears.

The winter sun is gone and I button my coat up, warding off the chill as I start the twenty-minute walk to my friend's house. I glance back up at the apartment and see that the father is staring right at me from what must be his kitchen window and I shiver. Picking up the pace, I run, needing to get out of his line of sight. As soon as I turn a corner, I stop and place a hand over my chest, feeling my banging heart and hoping that it will calm down. As it returns to normal, I glance back down the road. My new neighbour has gone and the cat sits outside the block, licking its paws. As I walk to Justine's, I'm haunted by a memory from my past; a memory I never would have had if my mother hadn't been taken from me.

I remember being in my bedroom. I think it was around November when I was ten years old. It was so chilly that winter. I remember the panes of my bedroom window being frozen on the inside at Aunt Caroline and Uncle Simon's old farmhouse that sat in the middle of nowhere in Herefordshire. The sound of the chickens clucking always gave me the creeps; their bodies always fighting for the tiniest dot of floor space, sometimes even fighting to the death.

Aunt Caroline had taken the heater from my room as it was too expensive to run and all she ever did was go on about my mother. 'Your mother mixed with the wrong men and look what happened. One of them killed her and now I'm stuck with a kid…

I never wanted kids… Life is so unfair. That's why you'll never give me any trouble. Do you hear me?' I'd nodded, knowing exactly where I stood from day one.

On this particular night, Simon's snoring came to a halt. Him waking in the night was what I'd dreaded the most back then.

Pulling the quilt over my face, I waited and hoped that he wouldn't come anywhere near me. My mother and Aunt Caroline grew up in the care system and he'd tell me that if I was a naughty girl and didn't do as I was told, I'd have to go there too and it would be horrible. I'd been petrified that he'd send me away to the scary place.

I can't remember Mum that well but Aunt Caroline reminded me of her. We all shared the same light brown skin tone and lithe frame. We all had black hair and brown eyes. Then, I'd heard a creak. I remember pulling the bedcovers further over me as my body stiffened. All I hoped was that Simon wasn't coming to my room. If I thought back then that begging him to leave me alone would have worked, I'd have begged with all I had. At that moment, I wished I had Scarecrow with me, but he'd been banished to the attic with all my other childish toys.

After I'd inhaled my own breath for a minute, I needed fresh air or I knew I'd pass out. It had seemed hot and I remember trembling that much, I couldn't grip the blanket any more.

As soon as I'd gasped and looked up, I saw that my visitor was Riffy, the cat. I remembered feeling relieved that it hadn't been Simon. The fluffy cat was my best friend back then. He'd purr in my ear and leave generous clumps of grey fur on my clothes and bed. I'd stroke him and he'd stay with me, protecting me from the monster that was my uncle.

Then I remembered hearing a shuffling noise coming from the corner of the dark room. The quarter moon wasn't giving off any light as the clouds blew by. I was convinced Uncle Simon was coming for me. Again, if my mother was still around, she'd never have allowed Simon to lay his grubby hands on me.

I shake that memory away and scurry up the road to Justine's house, shivering as I think of what happened to my mother. I've managed to keep my focus off that terrifying day for so long now but today was hard. It's amazing how a simple moment and feeling can bring everything back. The fear that ran through me when Ben was blocking my only route out has made me uneasy all day. Then, there was the altercation with my neighbour. I still don't know what that was about or how it started. Never do I want to feel that scared and trapped again. I still miss my mother every single day, though, and the fact that her murderer has never been caught makes it all the harder. I still live in fear, wondering if he'll come for me; the only witness to his crime. It's not that I saw his face, or have any idea who he is, but that thought is always at the back of my mind. Staying invisible is what I have to do.

CHAPTER FOUR

The security light flashes on, illuminating the long drive that leads to Justine's grand mock Georgian house. Conifers line the neighbour's border and her new Mercedes sits on the drive like a big shiny red prize. She oozes self-made success and I want to be her. If there was anyone I idolised, it was Justine. I'm not sure how we became friends. She's bubbly and can quite happily sashay into a party. Me, I fear a scene where all eyes are on me. I fall over and stumble for words.

I go to knock but she beats me to the door, opening it as my hand was about to rap on the wood. 'Marissa, come in. Take a seat at the table. Food's nearly done. I'm just having a game getting Sam to bed. I'll be with you in a minute. Oh, and help yourself to a drink, lovey.'

I follow her through the hall. She runs back up the stairs, leaving me on my own. The kitchen is homely and smells of garlic and cheese. My mouth waters but my stomach still churns from the encounter with my new neighbour. Maybe he was having a bad day. Perhaps I just have to put it behind me and next time I see him, we'll start again with a proper introduction. I take out my bottle of red and leave it on the granite worktop. I'm sure that Justine will drink it in front of the telly one night. It's definitely not as nice as the wine I see before me.

As I pour some of the open bottle of Chardonnay into a glass, I think back to the night in my room when Riffy had jumped onto my bed. Terrified that it might be Simon, my hands had been shaking when I reached for my lamp switch. At first I freaked when I saw that dying mouse but it had been a relief moment. It wasn't Simon but there is still one thing that makes me shudder as I sip the cold crisp wine; it was that feeling. I had it again today with Ben and tonight with my neighbour. A fear of the unknown is often worse than what actually happens and I'm scared.

'Right, I best get the garlic bread in.'

Glass shatters on the tiled floor, the sound echoing through the vacuous space. The glass of wine slipped out of my hand and I'd barely felt it go as I'd been so consumed with my thoughts. 'Sorry, Justine. I broke one of your glasses.' For a moment I cower like she might shout at me.

Grabbing a dustpan and brush, she shrugs. 'No bother. Just grab another.'

Again, my heart races and I can't get my words out. As she pushes the fragments into the dustpan, I shakily pour another glass and take the longest swig I can. I'm not a drinker but I need something to calm me down. The clash with my neighbour has set me on edge.

'So, how's things?' She pours the glass into the bin.

'Good. Sorry, I haven't been in touch for ages. Things have been manic.'

Justine rolls her eyes. 'I know what you mean. I think the property market around here is going berserk. That takes me to my next announcement. When you called earlier, I was thrilled. No longer am I celebrating alone.'

I smile and take another swig of wine. 'Tell me more.'

'I have sold, not one, but two of the large country houses on our books this week. Both around the one point five million mark. It's been phenomenal and you'll find out soon because the financial stuff will be heading your way. So, like I said, we are celebrating tonight. Look, I treated myself.' She holds up a handbag. 'I couldn't resist.'

'Oh, wow! It's stunning.' I stare at the bag, knowing that my knowledge on designers is lacking. The most I ever spend on a bag is thirty pounds.

'It's only the Jimmy Choo Madeline Top Handle Bag. I've wanted it for so long and I thought today's the day. It's time to put me first for a change. I'm always buying things for Samuel or the house. I had a total me day. Notice anything else?' She fluffs up her hair and pouts.

I peer at her face, then her clothes. Her long straight red hair shines in the kitchen light and she looks ten years younger than her forty years. I've seen the leopard print dress she's wearing before so that isn't new. 'You've done something with your make-up.'

'Yes, I had a makeover. Anyway, that's me. What's happening in Marissa's world?'

'I had a meeting this morning and I have to thank you.'

'Thank me.'

'Ben Forge. He hasn't signed the contract yet, but I think I'll be sorting all his mortgages and insurances out for his estate agencies. It could be huge for me.'

'Ahh, Ben Forge. He's quite the charmer too. Yes, I saw him at a networking breakfast and he mentioned that his financial adviser was retiring so I gave him your card. He's the competition really. I shouldn't have been helping him.' She let out a devilish laugh. 'It's okay though. I know my agency is the best. I'm not at all threatened by the others. Was he okay?'

'Yes, well, I think so. He didn't stay long. What's he like?' What I really want to know is, should I go out for dinner with him but I don't want to tell Justine that he asked me.

'Erm, I know he's good to work for. His staff stick around. He has a lot of offices.'

'I did my research.'

'Just be careful of him.' Justine's smile has dropped and her brows furrow.

'What do you mean?'

'Nothing. Just like I said. He can seem charming.' She looks distantly beyond me for a few seconds and smiles, then she nudges me as she tops up her wine. 'It's all going to be great. You with your new work coming up, me with the big sales.' She calls out a command to the glowing cylindrical assistant and tells it to play eighties music. 'Going back to Ben, I think you'll be able to make a lot of money out of the work he'll give you and I know you said you were saving up so I thought great, Marissa would be brilliant for him. I gave you the best reference ever. If he doesn't use you, he's an idiot.'

'Well, thanks again. And you're right. I'd like to move at some point but I just need to save more to get what I want. It's so expensive around here. Bloody Shakespeare, keeping the prices high.' I let out a laugh.

'You're telling me. It took a lot of hard work to get this house but it was worth every minute. You'll get your dream home soon, I know it. You absolutely deserve it.' She grabbed a bottle of champagne from the fridge. 'As this is a celebration, we need bubbles.' As it popped, a fizz and dribble spilled over the bottle. 'Here's to riches and success.'

She passes me a glass and I drink that down, enjoying the bubbles in my throat and nose. I let out a hiccup and giggle. Warmth seeps up my neck and across my face as Justine opens the oven to reveal a big dish topped with crispy cheese. I do love her food.

'Cheers. Let's eat this lasagne. When Sam goes to his dad's next, we'll hit the town and celebrate properly. What do you say?'

'Definitely. I can't wait.'

I want to go back to asking about Ben Forge but she's moved on. Dancing around the kitchen to Whitney Houston, she passes me a plate and tells me to sit. Then there's more champagne and more wine. It's no good, I have to ask her again so I shout above the music. 'Jus, please tell me what you meant when you said I should be careful of Ben. Why would you say that? Is there something I should know?'

She stops dancing and puts her glass on the table. 'It really doesn't matter. Just save him for business, nothing more and you can't go wrong.' She staggers to the window, pulls the curtain slightly and peers out. 'I'm probably being paranoid but he seems far too sure of himself.' She pulls the curtains closed again.

'You and he aren't... you know?' I don't know why I can't just ask her if she's sleeping with him.

'No...' She grabs her glass and drinks again. 'No way. Don't be daft. Here, have a top up and forget him. Take his work and money and don't get involved, that's all I'm saying.'

I've already had too much to drink as the room is swaying but I don't care so I join her in yet another glass of wine. 'But...'

'Shush. No more work talk.'

CHAPTER FIVE

Damn! I fell asleep on Justine's settee. The fire crackles and three empty bottles sit on the coffee table of the snug. The illumination from her garden lamp is disorientating, swaying across the room as the tree branches outside are blowing around. I'm not used to waking up in a strange room. Double strange. My throat feels dry and a sickly taste hits the back of my throat. I think it's just acid from the wine and the lingering garlic from the food. Justine must have gone to bed as her house is in silence. I wonder for a second if I made a fool of myself. I remember slurring and going on about Ben but I can't remember what she said. It's all a drunken blur. I know she was holding back on me though.

I place a bare foot on the wooden floor and follow that with the other then I knock over the bucket. Justine obviously left it next to me just in case I threw up. Gently, I rise hoping that I won't wake Justine or Sam. I reach over and grab my coat and socks before scurrying into the hallway. Where are my shoes? I can't find them. Damn. I see that Justine has a few pairs lined up by the door but she's two sizes bigger than me. What an embarrassment I am. It's best that I leave and go home. Knowing that I struggle to hold my drink, I shouldn't have got so carried away with the wine and champagne but she kept topping me up and we were dancing around the living room. There, I spot one of my shoes. Putting it on, I glance around, looking for the other in the orange glowing room. The fire crackles before simpering. I guess I'll have to make do with one shoe.

As I quietly leave, I take in a breath of cold wintery air and with wavering vision, I start the short trek home, knowing it will take me twice the usual time. My toes are already numb as I walk with a one-shoed limp, crunching on the layer of frost below.

I need to sober up a little and the walking is helping. Stopping, I lean over a bush, convinced I'm going to vomit but after pausing for a minute, I'm fine. I should hurry home but I want to see the cottage first so a diversion is in order. I need to grab that feeling of home before I go to my own bed and this will work, it always does. I keep walking, no longer able to feel my shoeless foot, but it doesn't matter. It was a good night. Smiling, I enjoy the quietness of the usually busy streets. The Royal Shakespeare Company is nothing more than a dark outline in the night sky. I pass the pub at the other side of the bridge that goes over the River Avon and I keep walking for a further twenty minutes until I reach the cottage.

The old two-up two-down building sits at the end of a terrace. It has a cutesy little gate and a wishing well in the front garden. The skeletal branches of the trees and shrubs conceal the side of the house. In the summer, they bloom and blossom, a mixture of pinks, whites and lusciously thick foliage. In winter, they remind me of the bony fingers of the dead as they try to claw their way out of hell. I blow into my hands. I will just stand for a moment until the need to be here passes. Behind the house is a good-sized patch of woodland. If I lived here, I'd have to get a pet or start jogging.

My heart judders as the gazing pair of eyes in the top left window meet mine. Someone has bought the cottage. I can't look away or move. I'm sure they have a clear view of me but all I can see is an outline of their head. The wine is well and truly wearing off and the cold is working its way through my body. The occupier's icy stare stays on me and I feel exposed. I could just walk away, run, but it's as if the watcher has a hold on me.

He or she steps back into the darkness and I'm left shivering alone in the street, wondering if they still have their eyes on me.

My safe place feels tainted now. This cottage was meant to always be filled with happiness and love. It's where I lived with my mum in happier times and I want it back more than anything, but now it's gone. The beautiful cottage that should be mine is no longer available and I missed my chance. I'm unwelcome here, especially now that the new owner has seen me. I should have put in an offer, bought it, but I felt that my apartment wouldn't easily sell given that there are problems with the maintenance of our estate. I need more money too which is why I needed that work from Ben. I'd lost the cottage – again. All I want is to feel close to my mum and now that has been taken from me.

As I reach my apartment block, I hear the booming of 'A View to a Kill' by Duran Duran spilling from the open upstairs window and the drone of many unwelcome voices that stiffen my body. If I wasn't sober a minute ago, I am now. The new neighbour hasn't even properly moved in and already he's having a party. I remember that the flat was being rented as furnished. He'd have only needed his clothes, a few bits and a bag of shopping to get started. He certainly hasn't wasted a moment in arranging the house-warming bash.

These apartments aren't built for parties. The noise travels and the walls are pretty thin. The other neighbour's three dogs begin to bark. I hate it here and I'm now pining for the cottage more than ever. It's worse now I know I can't have it. I need to get out of this apartment soon but I feel I'll be stuck here forever. The estate is in dispute with the management company over poor and overpriced services and I'm stuck until it is all resolved. No one would want to buy this place while there is a dispute going on and I can't afford to pay for two homes. I don't have the luxury of being able to rent it out while buying somewhere else. It's up to me to ensure that the estate doesn't get into any more trouble. In fact, I need to fix things, make it all better.

I climb half of the stairs and a body gripping a bottle of cider is curled up on the landing. A man of about fifty wearing a Santa hat. His jeans are wet around the crotch and a string of spit is dribbling from the corner of his mouth as he snores.

Taking two steps at a time, I scurry towards my apartment. The neighbour's door is wide open and several people spill out filling the landing with the scent of sweat, cheap perfume and beer. A glassy-eyed woman starts staring at me before shifting her gaze to my one shoe. There are too many people and they're all drunk. I don't know what to do. I want to cry, hit something, or curl up in a corner.

'Oi, you! Want a beer?' My less than delightful neighbour holds out a bottle. 'We got off on the wrong foot earlier.'

I shake my head. 'No… thank you. When's the party finishing as I'm quite tired?'

He twists the point of his goatee with his other hand and stares at me. I don't want his beer. I want them all to go. I want the place to be tidy and I don't want all these drunks and stoners littering the outside of my apartment. I want to be able to sell this place one day. A man pushes past with an unlit joint dangling from his lips. The nauseating smell of weed is giving me a bit of a thick head.

'Whatever.' My neighbour pulls the beer away. 'I'll just drink it myself.' He steps forward, his widening grin exposing a gappy set of nicotine-stained teeth. 'My beer not good enough for you? Looks like you've already been partying tonight.' He glances down at my socked foot. I'm sure my eyes are glassy and I probably smell of stale wine. He takes another step closer. I can smell stale whisky on his breath and the layers of cruddy sweat oozing from his pits. My stomach churns as he grabs the shoulder of my coat. He leans in a little. 'You smell so good, like old cheese.'

The other partygoers aren't taking much notice. Two men belly laugh and the woman I saw when I came up the stairs is trying to fit her head out of the small top window while repeating that the green air is possessing her.

Clenching my collar, he pushes me against my door, pressing on my neck with his knuckles. 'Ooh, little neighbour wants us to finish up with the party. What shall we do?'

I'm hot and my vision prickles. I need to get him off me, get away, but I'm trapped under his strength. He's going to hurt me, I know he is.

'Come on, Dan, just leave it. She's just trying to be a party-killing bitch.' His friend places his beer on the window ledge next to Miss Possessed, then he drags Dan away from me. That escalated quickly! Gasping for breath, I move away from the wall.

So, his name is Dan. That doesn't give me much to research. Dan what? Dan from where? Dan has two sons and – without a doubt – a failed marriage or relationship. I can see why. 'No wonder you're living here alone. Did your wife have enough of living like this?' I don't know what came over me. Keeping my mouth shut would have been the best strategy but he doesn't argue my statement. He had or still has a wife. I've taken both him and me by surprise and I don't know what's going to happen. It feels as though something is stuck in my throat as I wait for the fireworks.

He exhales flecks of spit through the gaps in his teeth as his friend pulls him back. He's no longer trapped in a red mist; I see sadness wash over him. I shouldn't have said anything. For a moment, I think he might cry. He knocks his friend's hand away and hurries back into his flat. 'I want you all to leave. Just go,' he yells. The music stops as '99 Red Balloons' has just started playing.

Several people clasping glasses and bottles stagger out.

'Come on, Amy, you're not possessed.' The last man drags the woman towards the stairwell.

As Amy goes to turn, she glares at me like I've ruined her life and I shudder. I think she's on something strong. She mutters that I'm Satan.

Tension oozes out of my body and it's replaced with a tremor as I unlock my front door. I was lucky; things could have been much worse than they were if everyone had been as unreasonable as Dan.

This is turning into a war and he's been living here less than a day. I kick my one shoe off in the hallway and wiggle the toes of my frozen foot. The feeling is coming back now and the sole of my foot is sore.

Who knows what the morning will bring. After locking up, I drop my keys on the worktop, next to the letter. There will come a time when I'll need help with my neighbour, so I should go to the residents' meeting. I could really do with someone on my side should this thing with Dan next door escalate.

I rub the point where the hollow in my neck reaches my breastbone and I can still feel the pressure of his knuckles where he'd pinned me against the wall. The ice is about to crack and I can't be the one to drown. I've come too far to have a major setback. Dan will not beat me. I now feel just as sober as I did before I went to Justine's. The cold, the confrontation; everything has brought me back to reality.

RSVP. Sure thing. I send an email confirming my attendance to the residents' meeting. For now, I should keep out of Dan's way. Hopefully there will be no more parties. Now the people have left, the dogs at number twenty-four finally stop barking and all I hear is an occasional whimper. A heaviness washes over me as I take a glass of water to bed.

As I drift off and fall, deeper and deeper into the abyss, my body relaxes until I'm gone.

*

I awaken with a start, sweating, itching and shivering and all I can think of is my mother's murder. Am I awake? An icy breeze almost freezes my naked body and my jumbled dream fades into confusion.

I jerk up and gasp. I'm not in bed. Where am I? Reaching for anything, I crawl across the floor, bumping into furniture, scratching my knees on the wooden grain below. Finally, I reach a lamp. As I click it on and drag the cord with my arm, the contents of my in tray slip out and cascade over my head. How did I get to my study? I cower under my desk and try to rub away the goosebumps on my arms. I go to close my eyes and still, all I can see is my dead mother. I wish my mum was still alive, I'd never have been sent to live with Simon and Caroline. We'd have gone back to that cottage forever and we'd have been happy. A tear slips from the corner of my eye. I look up and see that the window is open. Standing, I pull the window shut. It's happening again. The professionals said that the sleepwalking could come back if I got stressed. I just want it to go away.

CHAPTER SIX

Eighteen years ago

'Come here, Riffy.' Lifting him up, legs dangling below my elbows, the cat doesn't struggle. No one else can pick him up like this without getting a claw across their face. I kiss his head and stroke it before sitting on a stool at the breakfast bar. He purrs and meows so I pull one of his tuna cat treats from my pocket and hand-feed him. He brushes me with his paw, his way of asking for another.

The front door slams. My heart flips as Riffy scratches my arm and escapes out of the cat flap. I grab the biscuits from the table and shove them into my pocket as I'm not allowed to help myself to food. One of them falls to the floor so I stand in front of it with a second to spare, as Aunt Caroline enters with several bags of shopping. 'Don't just stand there, child. This is your food too so go and grab some bags.'

It wasn't my food. I ate what they gave me, nothing more; nothing less and more often than not, I got the leftovers after they'd finished eating in front of me. Hurrying along the hall and out through the door, I shudder as a blast of hail hits my face. I begin to pull the Christmas tree from the boot of her filthy four-wheel drive but it's stuck. I tug and tug until I tear off a branch and with flailing arms, I fall, cracking the ice of a large puddle with my head. For a moment, the grey clouds turn black. The black sky then turns into a grey swirl and I'm pulled into a vortex where I swirl and twist, my arms being shredded by the flying debris as I fight to remain conscious. I'm lost and I feel odd. My head, it hurts.

'Marissa? What the hell are you doing? You broke the tree!' Aunt Caroline is fussing around its branches, swearing each time she is pricked by a needle. Her anger builds and she kicks the tree.

How did I get from lying in the puddle by the car to standing at the edge of the drive? I sleepwalk now and again and this felt similar. Blood trickles from the side of my head and a slither drips onto my mucky hand – red mixing with murky brown. In the distance, Riffy jumps from one of the outbuilding roofs onto a fence post and stares right at me. The chickens begin to cluck in unison. Riffy knows if he comes over, Aunt Caroline will punish him too. I blink and he blinks back. 'She scares me too, Riffy,' I whisper.

Spinning around with the weight of Aunt Caroline's yank of my sleeve, I flinch and rub my head. 'What on earth, you've messed your clothes up. All I asked you to do was to bring some shopping in but, no, you broke the tree. You can't do one simple thing, can you?'

The hail slows down and I wipe the drizzle, blood and dirt from my face. There's no point expecting any sympathy from Aunt Caroline and I've learnt my lesson. *Look okay, say you're okay, be quiet and be invisible.* I shake my head, agreeing with her that I'm useless. It's best that way.

The landscape ahead of me sways like I'm on a boat in stormy seas and if I can't go inside soon, I might fall over. I really hurt my head when I fell. 'Can I go and get cleaned up?' Another blast of hail falls from the sky and it's not letting up. Aunt Caroline's dark hair is frizzing up and looks like it's full of dandruff boulders.

'What's this?' She opens her hand to reveal the biscuit that I'd dropped on the floor.

'I don't know.'

'It was on my kitchen floor and when I came home you were in the kitchen.'

She places it in her pocket. 'We'll talk about this with Uncle Simon. Stealing food is not okay. For now, you must be punished. I swear you're not normal. Stupid, crazy child.' She drags me across the potholed drive towards the house. As she drags me to the door, I catch sight of a dark figure right at the end of the barn. When I glance again, whoever was there has gone.

Aunt Caroline flings me into the cellar and slams the door closed.

There's no light in here. I can't breathe. Tears stream down my face and I resist the urge to pound on the door. There's no point. In darkness, I cling to the handrail and take one step at a time. There are a pile of sacks under the stairs, I can pull those over me and wait, like I've done before.

I can't feel my fingers as I try to grip another sack. Riffy meows at the cellar door. Aunt Caroline shouts at him. I flinch as he yelps. She's jealous that he loves me more than he loves her. Cliff Richard blasts from the radio and the house is filled with the sounds of 'Mistletoe and Wine'. It's the one Simon plays a lot and all I see is his grin. I can't bear it. I hold my hands over my ears and sob. She turns the volume up even more and plays more Christmas songs. My nose and eyes fill up as I grip the sack and cry like I've never cried before.

CHAPTER SEVEN

Now

I slip on my knee length grey woollen dress and sweep my hair into a clip, which emphasises my cheekbones. I'd tried to call Justine to thank her for her hospitality but I hadn't managed to get hold of her. I made a mental note to try again later, hoping that she wasn't avoiding me because of something I said when I was drunk.

It's been three days and I still haven't seen my nuisance neighbour since his party. There is a smell that seeps from under his door, a mixture of mould, chip fat and cigarettes. There's something about that smell. It gives me the shivers as it takes me back to the night my mother was murdered, the night when all I saw was booted feet from under the bed as I gripped Scarecrow. I know I could smell chips or grease.

There's a slam in the hallway. I bound over to the front door and peer through my spyhole. Dressed in a stained vest and some torn jeans, the party animal is leaving his flat. His reddened eyelids tell a story of drunkenness as does his sallow dehydrated-looking skin. The yellowish tinge to his eyeballs tells me he drinks far too much. I wonder if cirrhosis is starting to slowly take him as he goes about his business every day.

Now would be a good time to go out there and face him. Maybe I could grab my rubbish and hurry after him; after all, I can't avoid him forever.

My fingers stroke the door handle. I can't remain hidden behind this door any longer. We need to air what happened the other night so I run to the kitchen and grab the small bag of recycling out of the cupboard, then I hurry onto the landing. His heavy footsteps pound from the ground floor. He's coming back up.

Back straight, head held high, I stride along the corridor inhaling the stale smell that he left on his way down until I reach the middle set of stairs. He stops and looks up, no grin this time. Maybe I hurt him when I mentioned his wife. I want to ask him, to probe him further, but I won't. Most of all, I want him to understand that other people live in this block and that we all need to get on. I'm sure I can do that without causing an argument. It might be different now he's sober. 'Morning. Can we talk?' I soften my request with a slight smile.

He hurries past, nudging my arm with his as he passes. 'You can fuck right off.' He stomps up a few more stairs then turns. I can feel the weight of his stare on my back and I turn as he bellows out what he has to say. 'It must be lovely being you, sucking the life out of everyone around. I bet you wouldn't know pleasure if it slapped you in the face.' His grin widens. This is nothing more than a game to him. My hands tense. He's wrong. I do know pleasure but in different ways to him. What I don't enjoy is knowing that I'm really upsetting other people with my presence. That reminds me, I still haven't answered Ben and he hasn't contacted me either. That's another thing I need to sort out. Why are there so many complicated things to sort out?

'Look, Dan.'

'Don't Dan me. Dan is for my friends.' He scratches his chin and meets my stare. 'Mr Pritchard, that's what you can call me.'

'Mr Pritchard. I'll be straight with you.' I wish I hadn't just said that to him. It's made me sound confrontational again. All I want to do is make him realise how I feel, not antagonise him.

'Do. I love a bit of straight-talking.' He beams a false smile while stroking a few bits of dried skin from his goatee.

I almost want to heave as I watch them land on his dark jumper. 'We all have to live in this block and the other night, the party, the drunk man on the landing, it's too much. I don't want to ruin your fun, I just ask that you be mindful of your neighbours.' That's it; I said it and I kept my calm. I'm almost proud of how I'm handling myself.

He takes a few steps closer and looks down on me from the top step. 'You're a little troublemaker too. Don't think that I can't see what you're doing. It felt like you were goading me. You'd love it if I hurt you. You could run to the police and tell them about the big bad neighbour.' He held his calloused hands up in a gripping motion. 'If I wanted to strangle you, I could.' He began to whisper. 'I'd grip your scrawny little neck and squeeze and I'd laugh as you took your last breath. Nobody, I repeat, nobody, tells me what to do ever again. My wife tried and she failed. I cared for her far more than I care for you. Are we clear?'

'Clear?' My speech comes out like a squeak. I'm numb and hurt that my attempt at diplomacy hasn't worked, not even a little.

'I will have friends around when I want. I will do what I want and you will shove off into your poxy flat and mind your own business.' He drops the grin and points two fingers at his eyes then back at me. 'I'm watching you. Just stay away and stay out of my life—'

'Or what? I mean, what, err…' I don't know where this is going. Keeping my mouth shut would have been the better thing to do. I seriously wonder if I have a death wish.

'You don't want to find out.' As he turns, the man from number twenty-two appears at the top of the flight we're blocking. 'Morning.'

A bag of clothes flies from behind the fire door and a woman appears in a half-dressed state. 'And don't come back.' They narrowly miss my head before dispersing all over the stairs.

'Sorry about that.' The man clears his throat, his cheeks red.

They argue all the time, day and night, and I guess I feel a bit sorry for him as he's always the one to leave. He'll be gone today and back tomorrow and it will all start again. I grip my bag of rubbish as the man hurries past, grabbing his clothes as he leaves. It's just me and Mr Dan Pritchard again. Why won't he go? He's standing there and for some reason I can't move. It's like my feet are stuck or I'm waiting for permission to leave. He can see he holds the power, which is why he's keeping me here.

He laughs as he takes a step back. 'I see you with your pathetic little life. Don't push me.' I have no time to answer him. He's already gone. My fingers are rigid and shaking. Did he see the fear in my stark stare? I know he did. I pass the urine stain that has been left to dry out on the stairs. I pound my hand onto the wall and press a palm into my thick head.

Exhaling, I continue with my day and hope that all will be calm in the building for a while now but deep down, I know it won't. Dan is testing my limits and that's not healthy. I fling the rubbish into the bin and slam the lid so hard the plastic cracks, then I kick it once and then again. All I want is good neighbours. Respectful, clean people who don't make a noise. I want to leave this place but I can't. The cat runs over and purrs at my feet so I bend over to stroke its gritty coat. 'Hello, puss. I wish I had a treat for you. Maybe later.' I go to lift it up like I used to with Riffy but the cat struggles and goes to claw me so I drop it on the pavement. 'Sorry, cat.' He isn't ready for me to get any friendlier yet. Maybe in time the cat will trust me.

As I go back in I see a piece of paper sticking out of my post box. Someone has scrawled the word 'bitch' in red marker pen across the page. I feel slightly light-headed as I glance around to see if he's watching, but he's not there. It had to be Dan. He's the only person who seems to hate me enough to do something like this.

CHAPTER EIGHT

Thoughts of that note have upset me all day which is why I needed to get out so what better place to come than the cottage. I need to find out who's now living there but I can't let them see me, not after the other night.

It's dark and I'm wearing my black coat in the hope that I blend into the night. An image flashes through my mind. My young mother and me as a child. It's all so familiar, I can see the layout in my head. I would walk on my chubby legs into the front door and be faced with the stairs, which seemed big at the time. It's a long narrow house. I'd walk through a lounge, then a tiny dining room and off that there would be a galley kitchen with a bathroom at the far end. That's how I imagine it still to be.

A flake of snow lands on my nose, a perfect little flake. As it melts, I feel another land on my cheek. I walk into the white mist that I've exhaled and follow the path alongside the cottage that leads to some woodland out the back. The cottage is in total darkness, which would suggest that no one is in. Maybe the person I saw at the window hasn't moved in yet. I catch sight of the old lady who lives next door but I don't think she saw me. Her little dog jumps up at the window just before she pulls the curtains.

I reach the back of the house and push through the brambles behind the fence at the back of the garden, then I spot the hole in the panel. That hole has always been there, that's how I know I have the right house. I bend over, close one eye and gaze through, trying to peer through the overgrown garden and into the windows. An old swing rattles each time the breeze picks up. The trees have long since taken the frame as their own. Branches entwine around the rusty frame, winding and winding, strangling the cracking metal. It's so clear above that I can see stars. It's not like where I live in a light polluted area. There's nothing much to see from my window except street lighting and headlamps as cars come and go.

I catch a glint of light in one of the bedroom windows, like a flickering match as it burns down. The hand that holds it moves it nearer to their face. I can make out the outline of a chin. There is someone there, living in the cottage. I try to get a clearer look but their face is too far away. As the wind picks up, eerie branch fingers reach across, obscuring my view. I grapple with my scarf to try and keep warm. A twig snaps behind me and my heart begins to boom.

The light in the window has gone.

The figure has gone.

I swallow and catch my sleeve on a thorn as I turn.

Battling with the brambles, I wade through, whimpering each time I hear another cracking sound. Someone knows I'm here and they're coming for me. My memories of living here are vague but I remember that my mother seemed scared all the time.

I glance back and the cracking noise I heard in the woodland reveals itself. The fox remains still as a flurry of snow lands on its red coat. Its ears and nose are highlighted by the moon's milky light. It too is here looking for something but I know we're not both looking for the same thing. I reach out to touch it but it scarpers into the thicket.

The banging of the back door makes me flinch. Whatever my mother was scared of back then was real. This is real, and the person in the cottage is moving ever closer to me. I push through the thorns and branches, getting caught and slapped as I dart back to the path. I have to pass the house if I head up the path.

Instead I follow the path that winds deeper into the woodland and I hide behind a tree as I catch my breath.

My phone lights up, beeping to tell me I have a message. I silence it and gaze down.

Sorry this is all taking so long, I've had a few personal issues to deal with. I will read and sign the contract but I wondered if we could discuss it further over dinner. Sorry if I'm being pushy about the dinner, I just thought it would be nice and it's just business. Ben Forge.

I turn my phone onto airplane mode as I hear footsteps catching up with me. Leaning into a rough tree trunk, I hold my breath as I press my cheek against the bark. How did the person in the house know I was watching? That hole in the fence was my secret – mine. No one knew it was there and I was well hidden. The footsteps stop. I'm hot, so hot. I'm burning to the point of nausea. I need to undo my coat, scratch my skin and breathe. A burst of icy sleet hits my cheek, providing some relief from the feverish feeling that's come over me.

My mind flashes to Dan Pritchard and I feel trapped. Has he followed me? Holding my breath, I peer around the corner and just as a glint of moonlight catches my pursuer's nose, my heart is in my mouth as I stay hidden. This can't be happening. Why him and why now? My world feels like it's about to crash. The new owner is the man who has haunted my dreams for almost my entire life.

CHAPTER NINE

Eighteen years ago

'Go away! Go away! Go away!' I wake up at the bottom of the cellar stairs and what I thought was a shaft of light from the moon is daylight coming in through the tiny high up window. Gasping for breath, I run right back to the pile of sacks in the corner and snuggle underneath them. I press hard to dull the pain where I hurt my head yesterday. I'd been sleepwalking again.

Lying there, I hear the lock on the cellar door turn but no footsteps follow.

'You need to get up now. Get a move on.' Aunt Caroline's voice gets quieter the further away she gets.

A patter of footsteps comes closer and Riffy meows as he pushes my arm up so that he can snuggle against me. I stroke him, kissing his head and stealing his heat. I'm cold, so cold and damp. It's time to face the day, whatever that might entail.

As I reach the top of the stairs, I see that Aunt Caroline has laid the table with cereals, milk and toast. 'Grab some breakfast.' She smiles as she grips her coffee. Something isn't right.

I pull my tangled hair over the side of my head covering the sore from my fall. I sit at the table and wait to be told to eat.

'Eat then.' That was an order. Her smile drops. 'I do my best to look after you since what happened with your mother and sometimes... I don't think you appreciate me. Your mother's dead. Your father's dead. All you have is us. Simon and I have had to sacrifice so much for you.'

He walks in and goes to the sink, clearing his throat as he pulls his pyjama bottoms up higher over the crack of his bottom. Aunt Caroline passes him a coffee, then both of them stare at me.

Uncle Simon points at me. 'She's right you know. Yesterday, you ruined the Christmas tree. That tree was to make things better for you. It was meant to make the place homely and special, and now it's broken because of *you*.'

'It was an accident.'

Aunt Caroline tosses her hair back and tuts. 'Like everything is an accident? You wander around in the night, breaking things, causing trouble with every move. Most people would have put you in a home for your weird sleepwalking, but we're not most people. We care. Look at the breakfast I've made you. I've done it because I care.'

'We care.' Simon places a loving arm over her shoulder and grabs a piece of toast and bites into it. A trail of butter oozes down his chin.

I'm speechless. I don't know what to say. This is out of character for them. Something's going on.

'We have a visitor in an hour. I want you looking your best and to be on your best behaviour. Remember what we did for you. Never forget it. Like Aunt Caroline said, without us you'd be in a home and you know how awful that would be. All those bullies and beatings. You wouldn't like that would you?' He winks. 'Remember I told you about my friend.'

I nod.

'He got beaten up every day for four years. I saw his bruises, his broken bones. Anyway, let's not think about all those horrible things because you are loved and happy and our visitor will be here soon.'

Who was the visitor that he spoke of? I let my mind wander. There's a woman who visits now and again. She sits at the table for a short while and asks me questions while Aunt Caroline sits by me brandishing a false smile.

'The kids in those homes are brutal. Just imagine it. In the middle of the night, you lie under your bed, hiding.'

An image comes back to me. I'm gripping Scarecrow and then there's my mother. I can't go there. I can't go into a home.

'You don't want that, do you?' He kneels down in front of me. I can smell the coffee on his breath as he places my hair tidily behind my ear. His touch fills me with a crawling sensation. I don't want to stay here but I don't want to go to the home he speaks of either. I just want to grow up and leave. I have to keep my head down, try to be good and maybe, just maybe, they will grow to love me.

Shaking my head, I wipe a tear away.

'Don't cry, Marissa. We won't let you go anywhere. You can stay right here with us forever.' He stares at my sore, just by my ear. 'What have you done to your head?'

'I fell over yesterday.'

He drags Aunt Caroline out of the room and they hurry to the lounge, closing all doors behind them. I hear muffled shouting and a loud 'we need the child benefit payments' and moments later they come back in. She pulls out a make-up kit from the kitchen drawer and begins to pat some skin-coloured cream over the edge of my face, rubbing over my sore skin. I almost cry as she pushes it harder into my scratch. 'There, all sorted.' She pulls a bit of my hair forward. 'There. Covered it even more. Wear your hair down today. You can't see it at all now.' She grabs a piece of toast and places it into my hand. 'Eat your toast, honey, before the nice lady gets here. I'll go and pick out your best top and jeans.' She leaves me there, with him.

The wooden chair creaks as he falls into it and takes another piece of toast. 'Eat up.'

I can't eat. I don't want to eat. If I eat, I'll throw up.

He leans over, grabs my hand and pushes it towards my mouth until the toast touches my lips. I take a bite and chew. He turns to face the window. I spit it out into my hand and place it in my pocket, along with a bit more of the toast. He looks back and I pretend to chew.

'That's a good girl. Can't have you wasting away.' He places his hand over mine and tickles it. I want to remove it but I'm frozen to the chair.

Breaking the silence, Aunt Caroline returns with the clothes I'm not allowed to wear on a normal day. 'Come on, we best get you cleaned up.'

I follow her up the stairs and wonder if I should say something. The lady who visits seems really nice. Petula who smells of petals. She always brings with her the aroma of a summer garden and wears her glasses on the end of her nose. She's clad in bright colours and chunky jewellery. Would she really lead me into harm if I spoke up?

I'm going to do it. I'm going to tell her. I wonder what my mum would want me to do.

Aunt Caroline stops me outside my bedroom. I shiver as a chill is carried through the air. 'Whatever you're thinking, let it go.' Her stare bores into mine and I look down. She knows. I can't even think in front of her any more. 'Here you go. Get changed and paste a big smile on that pretty face. You know you can and you know you will.'

Don't think. Don't think. Don't think. My mind is clear. She looks puzzled. She can't read me. I take the clothes and return the smile she's expecting. Her shoulders sag with relief.

A short while later, Petula gets out of her little Volkswagen and slams the door. With a folder held over her head to stop her hair getting wet, she dashes across the uneven drive as she hurries. Glancing through the kitchen window, she sees me. I hold my hand up in a half attempt at a wave.

Aunt Caroline grabs my shoulder. 'Don't you dare embarrass me. Do you understand? We're happy, aren't we? One perfect little family.' She glances up at Uncle Simon and his sickly grin makes me shiver. I'm not happy. Not one bit but the alternative scares me more.

Petula knocks on the door. Uncle Simon holds his finger to his lips and bends down to my level, his breath almost making me heave.

As the door opens, I hear the chickens clucking in the distance. The trapped birds are making themselves heard to our visitor, hoping to be saved from their deadly fate. No one will save them just like no one will save me. Riffy follows Petula through the front door and shakes his sodden fur on the mat.

'Hello, Marissa. Don't you look well? It's so lovely to see you again.'

Was it? Or did she say that to all the kids she checks on? It feels lovely to hear though so I smile back.

'Say hello, Marissa. Don't be rude.' Aunt Caroline gives me a nudge and smiles.

'It's okay, you've always been a shy girl, haven't you? May I sit?'

I bite the skin on the inside of my mouth.

'Of course, please do.' Aunt Caroline smiles and moves out of the way so that their visitor can get in.

Petula removes her coat and places it over the back of the kitchen chair and sits as Aunt Caroline puts the kettle on. 'As you know, this is just a visit to see how you are. It's been a long time since my last visit but you do look well.' She smacks her lips and pauses. 'I've spoken to your teacher at school.' She smiles widely. 'They're really pleased with how you're doing. Apparently, you're excelling in maths and history. It's so wonderful to see you flourishing.' Her chunky blue bangle taps on the table every time she moves. She pops her glasses on and scans the wad of paperwork in front of her. 'That's better. I'd be blind without them.'

Uncle Simon takes a seat at one end of the table and Aunt Caroline places a tray of coffees down. She passes one to Petula who helps herself to a dash of milk from the carton. Petula's hair is different from last time. She's dyed it a deep red colour and it's frizzy. It was brown and greying before.

'So, how are you all getting on?'

Aunt Caroline clears her throat. 'We're doing really well.' She pauses. 'We wondered what had prompted this visit. Marissa has lived with us for years now. We're a cosy little family, aren't we, darling?'

She kisses my head and pulls me close to her. This doesn't feel natural at all.

'Marissa? We're happy, aren't we?'

I feel her pinching the skin on my knee under the table. 'Yes.' I smile as best I can. 'We're getting ready for Christmas. We have a tree.' She lets go of my skin and I exhale silently.

'Oh, how wonderful. That's so good to hear.'

I can smell Petula. Today she smells of roses. I wonder if she has children. If she has, they are the luckiest children ever. I bet her home is full of love and games and fun. In my mind they bake a lot and do arts and crafts. I open my mouth to speak but Riffy enters, meowing as he runs over to his empty food bowl. My friend, my best and only friend. I close my mouth. If I leave for a life of uncertainty, I leave Riffy behind and who knows what they'll do to him when I'm not around. I've seen Uncle Simon kick him when he's drunk so I have to protect him.

'Tell me about school.'

I shrug. 'It's okay. I like my teachers.'

'You like Mrs Alcott, don't you?' Petula has been talking to my teacher. I wonder what they talk about. As far as I know, I fit in. I don't speak much and I'm no trouble. I glance to the side, maybe I'm too quiet.

Nodding, I fidget away from Aunt Caroline. Finally, she's loosened her grip on me. Uncle Simon cuts me a glance that makes me shiver.

'Tell me a little bit about school. Do you have any friends?' Her pink lipstick has imprinted itself on her two front teeth and the coffee cup.

'A few. Can I go to the toilet?'

All three adults nod. I hurry out of the room and push the door closed as I leave, escaping Petula's questions so that I can think. Now is my time to come clean, to tell her everything and get out of this house. I could burst through the door and tell her that Uncle Simon comes to my room at night, that he touches me. Petula would take me away immediately. Turning, I stand outside the closed door and place my hand on the handle, ready to burst back in. My fingers tremble. My heart beats in an irregular way and I'm scared that I'll choke on my words, that my voice will be silent as I attempt to blurt it all out. I can't do it. Not like this. I creep up the stairs and stand in the bathroom for a few seconds as I mull it over. What do I say? How do I bring Uncle Simon and Aunt Caroline up when they're sitting at the same table? I'm spending too long in the bathroom and I don't want Uncle Simon to come up. I flush the toilet and creep back down the stairs. Their voices are getting louder behind the door so I listen.

'She's a quiet girl, that's all.' Aunt Caroline is trying to explain that everything is okay; that my home life is loving and caring.

I glance through to the living room at the wonky tree and I catch sight of the blue baubles covered in white glittery snowflakes that used to be my mother's. What would my mother want me to do?

Petula pauses, then continues. 'Her teachers are worried. What happened back then would be traumatic for any child and we need to keep an eye on her, make sure things don't escalate. Here's what we have in the report. She was caught scratching her arm with a pencil. There is also another concern, the other kids' bully her over what happened with her mother. I know, I know, kids can be cruel. The reports of self-harm have prompted me to visit today. We all want to be here to support her and I need you both on board. I need you to keep me up to date on how she is and I'll be liaising with the school too.'

I sit on the stairs as they continue talking about me, not knowing that I can hear everything. Jane at school shouldn't have told the other kids about my mother's murder. How can anyone laugh at what happened to me? I trusted her when I told her my secret. That's why I don't trust anyone.

'Are we under review? We've done everything we can for her. We love her like she's our own. Well, she is our own. She's my dead sister's child which makes her my flesh and blood too.'

'No one's saying you're under review. I'm just saying that Marissa is displaying a few signs that her past trauma is affecting her and we want to keep an eye on her, make sure she's developing okay. Her safety and well-being are everything to us.' Petula's voice is warm and sensible as always. I'm not safe, not from Simon, Caroline or Jane. No one is on my side, except Riffy. No wonder I'm not happy. If my mother was here, she'd be on my side. I swallow, trying not to well up. If I think too hard about Mum, I'll cry and I can't let them see me like that.

Simon pipes up. 'It's okay, my love. We knew that this could happen and we'll continue to love and nurture Marissa like we always do. Petula, like us, just wants what's best for her.'

I hear Aunt Caroline sniffling. 'Of course. I'm sorry for my overreaction. She's everything to us and it hurts to hear that she's struggling. She's been fine at home though. No issues here.'

I hear Petula's bangle tapping on the table again. 'Glad to hear it. I'll ask her about the self-harm, then I'll be on my way.'

I brush my clothes down and neaten my hair as I enter. They don't look like they've missed my presence at all.

Petula removes her glasses and places them on her folder. 'Marissa, do you mind if we have a little chat?'

Shaking my head, I take my place at the table. Aunt Caroline smiles at me like she loves me. For a second, I see my mother in her. It's weird, too weird. Uncle Simon tilts his head and gives me a look of sympathy. 'No,' I say. Simon grabs Riffy and places his hands around the cat's neck. I know what he's saying. If I talk, he will kill Riffy.

'Can I see your arms, sweetie?'

I roll up my sleeves. There is only one faded scar from weeks ago.

'Okay, you can pull them down. Are you having any problems at school or home that you want to talk about? The teacher said you'd cut yourself with a pencil.'

'It was just a silly accident. I was trying to draw on my arm.'

'Are you sure? You can talk to me about anything.'

'I'm fine, I'm really happy.'

'Is there anything else you'd like to share with me?'

Riffy cries as Simon grips harder, then the cat drops with a thud onto the floor after wriggling out of Simon's arms.

Shaking my head, I stand and swallow. 'Can I go now? I want to finish helping with the Christmas decorations.'

'Of course.' The woman smiled but I could see she wanted me to say more. I wanted to say more. I wanted to shout about how angry I was that my mum had been killed, that I was stuck with two people who hated me and my best friend was a cat. I wanted to tell her that Mummy and I were going to live in our rose-framed cottage with a little gate, that we were meant to go home and then she'd been killed. It hit me. I now knew that I would never feel the warmth of home. Right now, I had to leave the kitchen, if not I would cry in front of her and Simon would hurt Riffy. I couldn't talk today, or ever. Calmly placing my chair under the table, I smile and leave. Once again, I'm standing outside the door.

'As I said, we'll keep an eye on how things go at home and school and we'll take it from there. Any problems, call me straight away.'

The chairs scraped on the stone floor. I dart to the living room and stand by the Christmas tree. Battered decorations of Christmas past are a token effort on Aunt Caroline's part, except for the snowflake baubles. I pick one off the tree and hold it close to my body.

One day, I'm going to live in a cottage and it'll be all my own and I won't have to share it with anyone else and I'll take Riffy with me.

CHAPTER TEN

Now

I can't stop thinking about the person at the cottage the other night and it chills me right to the core. My mind is elsewhere as Justine chats away to me on the phone, talking non-stop about her huge house sales. Ordinarily I'd be super thrilled for her but my mind isn't on our conversation and I didn't get the chance to speak to her properly about Ben as she quickly brushed over what I was asking. There's definitely something she's not telling me.

Sleet lands on my nose. I look up, watching it fall from the black night sky as I try not to slip on the path. I'm running late which isn't like me but I will make the residents' meeting. I've committed now. Justine carries on talking and laughing. 'You were so funny the other night, lovey. I can't believe you walked home wearing one shoe. I don't know what came over you.'

I'm definitely stupid, that's for sure. After the greeting I received from my new neighbour, I wish I'd just stayed on Justine's settee like any normal person would have. 'Me neither. Must have been having a half-drunken moment. Thank you again for inviting me over. Dinner was fantastic as usual. It was just what I needed. I have to go, I've just arrived at the pub.'

'Well, I hope he's a hottie.'

'It's not a date.'

'It's definitely a date. You put it in your diary. We've yet to see if it's a romantic date.'

'Leave it out. It's a residents' meeting, that's all.' I giggle as she continues talking. 'Right, got to go. Call you soon.'

As I walk through the pub door, I see the roaring fire and the huge Christmas tree up the far end. Then I spot a man sitting alone and I wonder if it's him who I'm meant to be meeting. He waves and catches my eye with a warm smile.

'I'm Glen. Please say you're here for the residents' meeting.'

'I am.' He offers me his hand so I shake it. The man shows me to a seat in the back room and gives me a copy of the agenda. The neighbourhood meeting I'd considered not attending has become more important after my run-ins with Dan Pritchard. I've found myself creeping past his flat so that I don't alert him to my presence. Each time I have to pass his door, my heart is in my mouth. A crowd roars from the other room, the one I know contains the dartboard and pool table. I hear a clanking of balls and another round of whoops.

'What do I call you?' His eyes look a little creased around the edges. I guess he's in his late fifties, maybe sixty at a push. He has a modern haircut for his age, shaven at the sides and brushed back on the top, light brown specked with grey. His jeans, shirt and pumps make him look younger than his years, maybe I have his age wrong. Maybe he's early fifties.

'I don't think I've seen you around before on the estate?' Looking at him, I try to picture the people I see on the estate, at their cars, out walking, but I don't even vaguely recognise the man in front of me. For a moment that makes me nervous.

'I think that's half the problem with this estate. No one knows anyone. It's so impersonal. Coffee or something stronger? It's my shout, after all, I got you here.' He stands at the bar waiting to be served.

I shake my head. 'It's okay, thank you. I'll get my own in a minute.' He isn't coming across as a sleaze but the last thing I want to do is give him the wrong impression. Allowing him to buy me a drink might just do that. I'm suddenly nervous in his presence. Too many bad things have happened to me and I don't need any more complications in my life at the moment.

He rolls his eyes. 'Suit yourself. But it's just a drink. Nothing more. I don't expect anything in return.'

He's right and I'm being silly so I smile. 'I'm sorry, I'm Marissa and I'd love a coffee, black, no sugar, thank you.'

He gets the attention of the young man behind the bar and orders a gin and tonic for himself and a coffee for me. 'Shall we start again? I'm glad someone turned up. It's always the same. Last time I only had a couple turn up. I'm surprised they're not here now, they seemed so keen to get involved in making our estate a better place to live.' He shrugs as he pays for the drinks. 'There's still time for more residents to come along and I'm a total optimist. We'll give it five more minutes.'

I glance at my watch. I was five minutes late. Although Glen seems lovely, I wish I wasn't here. This man in front of me isn't going to be able to help with my problem neighbour, he looks too nice to take on the problems that I foresee coming with Dan. An army of two against someone like my neighbour isn't going to cut it. I hope he's not just about litter picks and moaning about the state of the communal areas. Antisocial behaviour is the real problem. Maybe dog muck will be at the top of his agenda. He's not well built or even strong looking. I think of Dan, again. When I bumped into him, he had arms of steel.

Glen places the coffee in front of me.

'Thank you. What happens if no one else comes?'

'I guess we carry on like the troopers that we are. Two people fighting to make the estate a better place to live is better than none. Are you in?' He holds up his drink and smiles before guzzling the clear bubbly liquid.

'You haven't lived here long, have you?' I can tell straight away. He's so happy. When he's lived here as long as I have, he'll realise that this estate has always been littered with neighbour problems. At first I thought Dan would be just another neighbour problem to resolve but he's different. He scares me.

Glen shakes his head. 'I've been in my flat six months. I live off the main road.'

'So you get the traffic noises and the pubs at the weekends. I live at the other end.' I place a hand on the back of my neck and rub the tension away. The hoppy smell coming from the bar is making me scrunch my nose. It's not a smell I'm fond of. It reminds me of Simon's beer that he used to brew in the shed, a smell that lingered on him when he used to come to my room in the night.

'Okay, that's a start. How long have you lived in your flat?'

'Sorry, I have to ask, how do you know I live in a flat?' There were a fair few houses on the estate, not as many as the flats but enough. Immediately, I feel a chill run through me.

'Don't look so worried. I don't stand around in the dark spying on people. When you confirmed your attendance, you gave me your address and I know it to be a flat. I make it my business to know who is coming and as you were the only confirmation, it didn't take me long to do my research. The only thing you didn't give me was your name.' He presses his lips together, then takes another sip of his drink. His eyes sparkle with enthusiasm. 'People in flats often experience different problems to people who live in houses and I wanted to be ready to talk about anything. That's all.'

I exhale and try to relax the muscles in my face. Not everyone is out to get me and I know I could do with someone to open up to. 'I've lived here too long. I thought about moving but a cottage I like has just been sold. That'll teach me to hang around when something comes up that I'm interested in.' That wasn't entirely true. So many things have held me back, including the state of the estate. I made no effort at all to secure the cottage and that was my biggest regret. As I work in the industry, I could have at least put in an offer and tried to secure a mortgage but deep down, I knew I couldn't quite afford it. If only I'd got this extra work earlier, I could have maybe been in a position to buy my dream home.

I pull up at the cottage regularly, always at night so that I can stare at the windows where I take in the house, not whoever might live in it. Then I saw *him* from my hiding place. I shake that thought away for now.

An uncomfortable silence hangs in the air and the door opens letting in with it a gust of wind and I shiver.

'Have you come for the meeting?' Glen walks over to the young couple, obviously delighted that someone else had arrived to break up the uncomfortable moments that were passing between us. I'm not good at socialising with people I don't know. It takes me ages to build a relationship like the one I have with Justine.

'Sorry, mate, we've just come for a drink.' They hurry past and make their way to the bar, removing gloves and rubbing their cold hands together.

Glen sits back down. 'Wishful thinking. We might as well start properly. How are you finding living here?'

I shrug. 'Where do I begin?'

'I'm a good listener.' His smile is warm and inviting. Maybe I should give him a chance. I could do with a friend on the estate. A redness spreads across his cheeks as he takes a longer swig of his gin and tonic. 'You'll have to excuse me, this is my second and I'm not a huge drinker. I thought it might lighten the meeting up, you know? I felt it was good not just to air problems but to make friends. After all, we all have to live together on this estate. It's nice to know that we can help each other.' He rips up the agenda and places it on the wooden table. 'I don't think we need this.'

I smile, feeling infected by his warmth and friendliness. 'Okay. I'll go first. Over the years that I've lived here, people have come and gone. Slowly, slowly, the estate has got rowdier. People don't tend to stay and they tend to bring with them noise and problems. I think I've just had a bad run of neighbours. First the stoners and now the party animal.' I lean back a little, worried that I'm sounding miserable. 'Antisocial behaviour is the biggest problem. People want parties in flats. The corridors stink of weed and people get drunk and make a mess of the communal areas. I also paid a lot for that apartment and I'm worried that it's losing value.' I stop to think. The last thing I want to say to him is how scared I am when things get rowdy and that Dan Pritchard has taken my fear to a whole new level.

'Wow! That was a good opener. I'm new so I haven't experienced much of that. We have problems in the bin store. People can be right dipshits sometimes. What is it you do?'

I knew it was only a matter of time before the conversation moved to something more personal. He can't help me with Dan. Just one look at him tells me that. Glen doesn't come across as assertive in any way. He gazes back at me and smiles. I can feel his warmth from across the small table. 'I'm a financial adviser, mostly mortgages and insurances. I work from home. How about you?'

'Electrician. I wire up new-build estates mostly, a bit like ours.' He finishes his drink.

'Can I get you a drink this time?'

'Another gin and tonic?' He grimaces, like he's asking for too much.

Smiling as I stand, I take my purse to the bar and I glance back. He's messaging someone on his phone and grinning. Maybe he has a girlfriend or it's a friend. He chuckles like he's just read a joke.

'What can I get you?' The server stands waiting.

'Two gin and tonics, plain tonic, double gins.' I need something. Maybe then I can loosen up enough to tell Glen about my real problems with Dan. I know I shouldn't really drink too much. I can't hold it that well and there's a chance I could make a fool of myself like I did with Justine, leaving my shoe behind at her house.

The young server's Iron Maiden T-shirt is creased and his Christmas hat looks like it's about to fall from his head. I play with a strand of hair as I wait. He smiles as he places the drinks down and I tap my card on the machine. 'Thank you.'

Glen looks at me like he's weighing me up. I clunk the glasses onto the table, breaking the moment.

'You had a real drink?'

I nod.

He reaches for his glass and holds it up. 'Let's make a toast to new friendships. I think I'm going to like living near you, Marissa.' I join in, clanging my glass against his. I'm not sure though. There is such a thing as moving too fast and I know this is only a friendship, but still. I'm wary about who I let into my life and I don't really know Glen. My heart skips a beat and not in a good way. I sip the gin and break our eye contact.

'You're not used to going out, are you? I can tell.'

How does he know these things? I'm invisible and people can't see me. I sit up straight, my smile gone, not wanting to tell him any more. I've already shared too much. 'I'd rather talk about the estate if that's okay.' I don't know him well enough yet but I'd like to get to know him better.

'Sorry, I didn't mean to upset you, I'm just being my awkward, friendly self. Sometimes, I should keep my thoughts and questions in here.' He points to his head then he nervously taps his fingers on the table.

But he still would have wanted to ask those questions. Is it better that he vocalises what he's thinking or hides his thoughts from me? I surmise that it's better I know. Sometimes guessing at what people think or mean isn't easy and it isn't accurate, but then again, sometimes they lie. I clear my throat, knowing that pushing away his attempt at friendliness is setting back my progress. Not everyone is out to hurt or abuse me like Uncle Simon did. It's best I don't go there, not even in the tiniest of thoughts. 'No,

I'm sorry. You're right. I spend a lot of time alone. I work from home and don't have any family close by.'

'And I'm new here. I don't have any family close by either. So let's drink to that. Friends?'

I hold up my gin and feel its warmth working through my veins. My cheeks flush. 'Friends.'

'Something specific is bothering you, isn't it? That's why you came tonight. I've run these kind of meetings before when I've lived in other places and, most of the time, people only turn up when they have something going on that they can't handle alone.' He pauses. 'What is it that you can't handle alone?'

I lean back. Glen can't see me as the person who wakes up in the night somewhere other than my bed after a stress sleepwalking episode. He can't see the me that keeps knives secreted everywhere out of fear of being attacked or hurt in my own home. He can't see my weakness, my vulnerability, the abuse I've suffered or the dead stare of my mother's corpse that I keep replaying in my head. He can't see any of that. Hiding them is what I've always done. 'My new neighbour is deliberately antagonising me with his parties and rudeness and it's getting out of hand. I'm scared of him, scared that he will hurt me.' I think back to that note in my letter box the other day. Nothing but the word 'bitch' written on it in red pen. Red is such an angry colour. Why red? Dan is trying to scare me. That's all.

'Sounds like you've got yourself a real problem in him.'

'He had a party the other night. Everyone was spilling out on the landing, all drunk and high, the music blaring out and I ended up arguing with him over it. We live in flats. He's scary and intimidating, as are his sons and his friends.' I pause. 'It's not that I'm anti-party, I've been through similar things before with previous neighbours and it escalates. I just know where it's going and I'd like to feel safe and happy in my own home.' I glance out of the window at the falling snow. Beautiful perfect little flakes piling on the outside sill.

'I can see your point. People can drive you mad. They nip away at you until you can't take any more and they can force you to act out of character, but be wary when confronting him, especially if he's drunk. It's always better to tackle these things the day after, when the person concerned isn't reacting in the heat of the moment.' For the first time that evening, he looks deadly serious. 'I can see why you're upset.'

Finally, for the first time in my life, I feel at home and it's all down to this stranger sitting in front of me. He understands.

'I want to help you. Next time you have any trouble, or you just want some support, call me. Don't go out there and tackle him alone. I'll back you up.' He writes his number on the back of one of his torn up agendas and passes it to me. 'Call anytime. I'm determined to be a good neighbour and that means I'm here to help you if you need me. Besides, I have to work on keeping my only friend around here.' He takes another swig of his drink and swishes it around in his mouth like he's swilling out with mouthwash, then he swallows it minus the gargle.

I'm moved by his concern and his genuine nature. A rowdy crowd enter and one of them walks up to the jukebox holding a pint and feeds a pile of silver coins into it. 'Mistletoe and Wine' plays, reminding me of Simon and Caroline. I have to get out. My heart is going to burst from my chest. I'm hot and my hands tremble. Blood pumps through the veins in my head and I'm suddenly woozy.

'Marissa, are you okay? You look ill.'

'Sorry.' I do my coat up knowing that my anxiety is taking over. 'I have to go.' That song makes me feel like I did as that little girl locked in the cellar all those years ago. I grab my bag and run out into the night. The cold air doesn't cool me down. I still feel hot and sick, and I just want to be back in my apartment. My head is whooshing a little and I'm tipsy. Having the gin was a huge mistake, as was getting so drunk the other night. The only thing it does for me is make me more anxious. I almost slip on an icy puddle as I hurry through the houses and along the path.

I burst through the main door and run up the stairs. Dan is waiting outside his door and I sense he's waiting for me. Taking a deep breath, I slow down my pace. He can't see the terror that wells inside me. Keys gripped in hand, I get closer, hoping that I don't have to try to defend myself with them. He sucks on his weed roll-up and blows it in my face while gripping his phone in the other hand. All I can hear is sniggering, the howling of mocking laughter emanating from his mouth as I fumble with my key in the lock – and turn. I'm in. I slam the door and feel a stream of tears escape. Dan's door slams and I flinch, then my home phone rings.

My hands are clammy. I don't use this phone for private calls. It's my business line but most people still call me on my mobile instead. I stumble to the living room in the dark, the ringing getting louder and louder, like a wasp that's entered my ear. I need to stop it. I need to shut it up. I grab the receiver. 'Hello.' Whoever is on the other end doesn't speak. I glance out of the living room window, spooked by my caller. 'Hello. Who is this?' The call ends.

I end the call and press 1471 but the caller's number is private. I grab the snuggle blanket off the settee and I wrap it around my shivering body, trying hard to get warm, but I know I'm going to struggle to sleep. That song and seeing Simon living at my cottage when he knew it was one of the only places on Earth that I held close to my heart… I wonder if it's him calling. My life was going fine. All was on track and I was recovering from my past, that was until he came back.

CHAPTER ELEVEN

'Leave me alone!' I scream until I wake myself. Blood drips down my arm. It's the middle of the night. I'm confused in my half-awake state. I was dreaming of the cottage and my mother was telling me that we had to leave as the bad man was coming. Is that what made me sleepwalk onto the car park? I shiver as a frosty breeze whistles by. The last I remember was getting home from the neighbourhood meeting and being so woozy and tired, I fell asleep on the settee, scared of my silent caller. I'd had an anxiety attack in front of Glen at the pub. That song had come on.

I move and the security light comes on, putting me in the spotlight. I pull a tissue from my pocket and wipe the blood specks away. There's something bulky in my other pocket. I reach in and pull out the smashed blue snowflake bauble. That's what I cut my arm with. Shaking my head, I worry that I have zero recollection of what happened in my sleepwalking state.

A car pulls in and parks. It's the neighbour I saw on the stairs after his partner had thrown him out. He grabs an overnight bag from the back seat and glances at the blood smear on my hand.

'Are you okay?'

Smiling, I point to the mess in my pocket. 'I had an accident with a Christmas bauble. Nothing to worry about. Thank you for asking.'

His brows furrow. I glance at the time. It's three in the morning. I look down and I'm wearing my pyjamas.

'It's okay. I just popped to the garage for some chocolate, couldn't sleep. I had this thing in my car and it was rolling around being a nuisance. I went to pick it up and put my finger through it. They're so fragile.' I'm not sure if he believes my strange tale.

He nods and returns my smile. 'All good then. Take care of yourself... err...' He pauses. 'I don't think we've ever properly spoken.'

'Marissa.' I smile, trying not to stand out any more than I already am. I'm the weird one here. He's just returning home to make up with his girlfriend, obviously. I pictured them both sending 'I miss you' messages all night and he, in a bold romantic gesture, tells her that he's coming home right now.

'Well take care, Marissa. By the way, your new neighbour is an arsehole. Me and the missus were arguing the other night over him. Should we say something or shouldn't we? Hopefully he's had his house-warming and now he'll behave. This place... it gets to you after a while. Anyway, she's waiting for me. I get the big homecoming. Go me.' He raises his eyebrows and winks like he's on a promise. Seconds after finishing his sentence, he's through the communal back door and the lights flicker on, one by one, triggered by his movement. I glance up, waiting for him to go before I head up, then I see Dan staring down from the window of our corridor. The light flicks off and a plume of smoke catches the light of a street lamp as he blows it out of the window and continues to watch me.

I can't stay in the car park all night and I know he'll wait as long as it takes for me to return. Wiping my hand again, I know I still look a mess but I have to try to clean the blood away properly. My hair is half stuck to my face and my muscles ache like I've been in a fight. I glance down and see another stream of blood oozing out from under my sleeve. Pulling it back, I see the line across the top of my arm. 'Shit.' I pull my sleeve back down, hoping to keep my scratch concealed until I reach my apartment.

With every step, I sink into the cold mush until I feel the gravelly tarmac underneath. The cat appears from under a car and jumps on a car bonnet, looking to me for fuss or food. On a normal day, I'd stroke its fur and talk in a silly voice but not now. The darkness feels like it's enveloping me and blood pumps through my body, whooshing at my ears. I'm confused. I only normally sleepwalk around my apartment but this time, I've been out and I don't know why. My vision prickles – I can't faint, not now. I lean on my car and glance up, another plume of smoke. I'm so cold but I don't want to go up while he's there.

The communal light comes back on. Dan flicks the nub end out of the window and slams the window shut before he turns to go. I hurry across the car park and I open the door and climb the stairs, a thudding beat coming from my floor. Entering through the fire door, it's Dan – again. His door is wedged open with the communal fire extinguisher and he's talking loudly on the phone about how he's loving his new flat and that they should come over to have a drink with him. I can't take this any more. Slamming my door, I lean against it, feeling the beat of the bass spreading across my back as the music bangs away. Since he moved in, it feels like all my problems are coming back.

I think of Glen. Maybe I don't have to be alone with my problems this time. I like Glen. Maybe for once I can trust someone to help me and maybe it can be him. I also have Justine but she does all the talking most of the time, although I do like her a lot.

Right now though, I'm alone here. There's not one person I can call at three in the morning. Not Glen or Justine. I have no one to talk to about Simon either. I seriously need to consider counselling again. I thought I was past all these feelings. We'd worked through them and I'd become a stronger person. No one could have predicted things could get this bad, this fast. I go to bed in my dirty pyjamas and pull a pillow over my ears as I try to drown out my neighbour's music.

I glance once more at the cracked bauble; one of a set that used to belong to my mother; one of the many things that Caroline took for the farm. Something strange has happened because I haven't seen these baubles since I left Simon and Caroline's farm all those years ago. I don't own any baubles like this, yet I have one in my hands and it's covered in blood. I'd meant to take one with me when I left, but I never packed it.

CHAPTER TWELVE

The winter sun glints off my microwave, filling the day with hope. Whatever happened when I was out in my sleep wasn't serious. I got home safely and avoided a confrontation with Dan. I pull the sleeves of my jumper down, covering last night's scratch on my arm. It's getting a little chilly even though my heating is set on full. In the background, I hear my printer chugging away with the six mortgage illustrations that I'll be posting out. Another six done, another six closer to getting paid for, another six happy clients who are another step closer to moving into their dream homes. That element of my job makes me happy. I like the thought of people moving towards an exciting new chapter in their life. One day I'm going to be that excited woman moving into her dream home.

Last night was bad, I know it was, but today is another day and I feel that to avoid going backwards, I need to start with a clean slate. I'm just stressed, that's all. Stressed that Simon has taken my cottage, stressed that Dan is playing a sinister game with me, and stressed that I'm so active in my sleep. The stress will pass. Nothing ever stays the same. Things always get better and this situation is no different. As for the bauble, I must have taken one when I left the farm all those years ago. There's no way I could have had it in my hands last night if I hadn't. It's impossible, so I reason that I must have had one all along. I cover it up with a piece of kitchen roll and push it into the corner of the worktop, out of sight for now.

As the kettle boils, I press the remote control and the television kicks into life. Maybe I'll take a short break, have my coffee and get back to work after that. Lifting my sleeve, I rub the line that I must have etched along the top of my arm with the broken up Christmas bauble. Grabbing my coffee, I push my cushions aside and slump back as I try to recall the events of last night.

I remember lying on the settee thinking that I'd never get to sleep. Then, I woke a little while later, changed into my pyjamas and went to bed, then I slipped into my dream world. What were those dreams? I close my eyes, inhaling the fresh coffee smell and tried to think back. Nothing was coming to mind. One minute I was in bed, the next, I'm in the car park wiping blood off my arm. Where did I go? There were only a couple of places I think I'd go to.

I remember dreaming about the cottage; Mum and I lived there before we had to flee to that crumby flat. My phone might hold the answers to my whereabouts. I check to see if I sent or received any messages late last night and I haven't.

My phone flashes with a message and Ben Forge's name flashes up. That's another thing I failed to do. I never got back to him, but then again, I'm still not sure about him. He scared me and that's something I can't put aside, despite how attractive I originally found him. I'm not so sure now. I open it and read.

> *Hi Marissa, I thought I should let you know I've signed the contract. You should get it any minute. We need to get together soon to chat. If we're going to be forming a working relationship, I'd like to get to know you a little better and possibly pass you a few files over to start on. Are you free for lunch today at one? You never did message or call to accept my dinner invite. It's on me! Forge.*

He signs his name Forge. Not Ben but Forge. My coffee is cooler so I take a sip, savouring its smoothness and comforting warmth. The more I think about it, the more I feel I should accept his invite to lunch and he's right, I can pick up some work at the same time. Was my own fear playing with my head? Besides, we'll be eating in a public place so no harm can come to me. Justine never really told me why I should be careful of him, just citing that he was a charmer. If that's all he is, then I'm sure I can handle things.

> *Yes, a lunch meeting would be lovely. I'm keen to start the work too. Marissa.*

I place my phone on the table and sink back into the cushions feeling a deep weariness consuming me. My muscles relax and I'd love nothing more than to put my feet up and have a nap to make up for my disturbed night. The newsreader on the television talks about how the seasons are affected by climate change and that demonstrators are preparing to disrupt Londoners outside tube stations over the coming week. As I'm about to drift, the national news ends and the music for the local news begins. I lean back and half listen, then my neck begins to prickle. A murder in Stratford-upon-Avon. I'm sitting rigid and wide awake, all sense of tiredness gone. Glancing at the screen, I hear of the stabbing. The victim – male. A cottage that is cordoned off by police tape fills the screen. That's my cottage. My cottage – mine. And, now it's a murder scene. What did I do last night?

CHAPTER THIRTEEN

Twelve years ago

Aunt Caroline's funeral.

The service had been a no expense spared one and my life was a little better by the time I was sixteen. I'd threatened to tell my teachers and the police what Simon had been doing to me and, just like that, he'd stayed away from me.

In the week running up to her funeral, Uncle Simon did nothing but drink and that worried me to begin with. I thought he'd come to my room like he used to but instead he never even made it upstairs at night. He'd pee out of the front door and in the kitchen sink, too drunk to get around.

On the day of the funeral, I mimed to 'All Things Bright and Beautiful' – apparently this was Aunt Caroline's favourite hymn. There was nothing bright or beautiful about Caroline. When she was around everything was ugly. I hated my mother for being murdered. Why did she have to leave me with this shower of shite? Then my father. I never knew him but Caroline told me he was dead too, even though she claimed she never knew him. They never did tell me his name.

During the service, Simon sang 'All Things Bright and Beautiful' out of tune with the faint smell of whisky oozing through his stinking clogged pores. He'd glanced down as if to say, sing. But he didn't have Riffy in his arms to make me do as he said. I'd also found a way to keep both me and Riffy safe from Simon. I'd been crushing half of one of Aunt Caroline's sleeping tablets into his beer on nights when he wasn't drinking enough.

CHAPTER FOURTEEN

Now

That cottage is one of the only places I would have gone to last night. I must have walked there in my pyjamas to watch the house. Maybe I saw the murderer in my sleepy state or maybe I got into an altercation with them; that might explain the scratch on my arm. I only wish I could remember.

A picture of Simon flashes up. He's the victim. The coffee I drank is working its way up my gullet. I run to the sink and throw up, shaking as I heave the little bit of liquid from my stomach, then I heave again but nothing else comes up. Wiping my mouth with a sheet of kitchen roll, I steady myself against the worktop.

He was stabbed to death. I check behind my picture, the knife is still there and it's clean. I check under the settee – that knife is still there too. Everything is where it should be. Who killed Simon? I need to try to recall the events of last night, which sounds easy. I barely ever recall what I see when I'm sleepwalking but I need to try. Not only that, this could easily be pinned on me. I have motive and I certainly had opportunity, but it wasn't me, I know it wasn't. Maybe the killer saw me there, watching through one of the holes in the fence or staring up at the windows. The old lady next door, she's sometimes nosing too. Normally I keep out of her line of sight. Would I have been that careful in my sleep?

I stare at Simon's face until the local sports news begins. An image of the cracked bauble flashes through my mind.

Simon is dead and even though I don't remember a thing, I know I must have seen everything. They're coming for me next, I know they are. I'm a loose end that needs exterminating.

It's only a matter of time before the police come here to tell me of his death and what do I tell them? I may have sleepwalked over to his house in the night, just at the time he was murdered. That's going to make them focus on me and I know it wasn't me. I have to find out who did this before everything is my fault.

Simon's face fills my television screen along with the cottage – the murder house. Not content with seeing the news on one channel, I'd switched to another to see it all again, watching obsessively to see if the media reveal more clues. Something had to trigger my memories.

I tremble as I think about the old lady in the cottage next door. I know she's seen me before. If she reports seeing me last night, I've had it. Then again, I'm only guessing that I was there. One lousy bauble doesn't prove a thing. I know I couldn't have killed Simon, despite what he did to me, but no one would believe me. That thought won't leave me alone. My heart is nearly in my mouth. When I was behind that tree, it had been Simon chasing me into the woodland. He knew about that cottage and what it meant to me. He even taunted me with how much of a filthy little hole it was that my mother used to live in. It was never filthy and it wasn't a hole. It was part of my childhood, the happier early years I can barely remember; only tainted by the occasional visit from the bad man.

Once it had come up for sale, he bought it, knowing that he'd taken the last thing I ever cared about. His revenge for how I left him all those years ago. I think about the day I left that farmhouse and I know Simon would have been out for revenge. Buying the cottage had been the most hurtful thing he could do to me and he would have known that.

A number flashes across the screen. It is the police appealing for witnesses to come forward. The victim was known as Simon Ferris, fifty-five years old and had moved in only a few days before.

I began to wobble a little and placed my palm on the wall for support. The scratch on my arm could have been the result of a struggle. Around another little scratch in the centre of my hand were a couple of tiny sores. They could have been made from the cracking bauble or was I involved in an altercation? Was that altercation with the murderer or Simon? Too many questions and I have no answers.

Grabbing the remote, I turn off the television. It's not helping me to remember anything but it may be planting images into my head as I hear more about the case. I could do without that if I want to recall the truth. The home phone rings and I stare at it. My silent caller could be on the other end of that line. Did that even happen or was I in the throes of a nightmare? I'm confused about everything. Shaking my head, I hurry to the phone and pick it up. There's always the chance that it could be a client and I don't want to let anyone down. 'Hello, MB Financial Services.' I pause and wait – nothing. 'Hello.'

The line makes a hissing noise, which clears after a few seconds. 'Hello?'

It sounds like a coffee percolator is spitting away in the background.

'Hello.' I swallow. As I go to place the receiver down someone speaks.

'Ah, Marissa. That lunch meeting. I was just wondering if we could move it to one thirty instead of one today. I have a meeting I can't get out of and, after discussing it with my client, I fear it will run over. Hope you don't mind. I'll bring all the work with me, as promised.'

It's Ben. I grab my mobile and look at the message he sent me requesting a lunch meet up. My head is fuzzy from the gin I'd drunk last night and my episode. I don't know why I feel so bad and why I was so out of it when I came around in the car park. It's as if I reached a deeper level of sleep, deeper than ever before. Mostly, my head is full of the news of Simon's murder. This is stupid. I'm jumping to every conclusion going. Simon probably had enemies that I don't know about. That bauble is just a stupid bauble that I must have had secreted in my apartment. No, too much of a coincidence. I have to act normal until I work things out. 'Of course. One thirty will be fine by me.' My voice is croaky. I can't seem to clear it.

'With the paperwork signed we're good to go. I'll bring some of the client files with me and I'll email you everything else you'll need in the meantime.' He paused. 'I didn't think you'd answer that message but I'm glad you did. I'm looking forward to our lunch date. I know you'll enjoy it.'

I don't think I'm going to enjoy anything, ever again; or at least until I know who killed Simon. As for Ben, something isn't sitting well with me. *He knows I'll enjoy it.* The presumption is making me feel uncomfortable just like when he said he doesn't take rejection well. I wish I wasn't going to lunch with him but I have to. I have to collect my work and act like everything is normal. 'I'll see you then and no worries about our meeting being later.' I really wish I could stay in all day where I could monitor the news and hide from the world.

'Shall we meet at the Drunken Duck opposite the river? It has a good Wi-Fi signal and the coffee is good. It's generally where I suggest having meetings.'

'Great, I'm really looking forward to seeing you again.'

I turn off the television. Maybe I'm overthinking all this. Nothing happened last night, I'm just stressed and I wandered down to the car park. End of.

'The Drunken Duck it is. See you there, Marissa.' With that, he ended the call.

After taking the fastest shower ever, I select my warmest black jumper and a pair of boot-cut grey trousers and my flat boots. I make sure my hair is clipped up and my glasses are clean. I don't need glasses but if I feel the need to hide behind them, I can. In my mind, they'll help to conceal my thoughts of last night. My hands jitter as I mull over my episode. I have no idea how I'm going to get through lunch.

My mobile rings. 'Hi, Justine. You okay?'

'Yes, lovey. I was just wondering if you wanted to do lunch. I have a bit more work for you.'

I check my watch. 'Damn. I've committed to meeting our mutual friend, Ben, for a business lunch. Can I call you later, when I've finished?'

'Of course.' She pauses.

'Are you okay, Justine?'

'It's just… be a bit careful of Ben. He's a bit of a charmer. I know what a sweetheart you are so I'm just warning you.'

'Justine, I'm okay honestly. It's business, that's all. I'm not five.'

'I know you're not but you're my friend. I'm looking out for you. Anyway, how did your date last night go?'

'It wasn't a date.'

'Or whatever.'

'The residents' meeting went well. I know I touched on my horrible neighbour the other night. It helped to talk to someone that lives around here and who's trying to get things done. I feel better about it all now.' I pause. Who am I kidding?

'You sound a bit nervous.'

'Well, I'm about to go to a meeting where there's lots of new work involved. You'd be nervous too.'

'Okay. I best let you go. Call me later and remember what I said about Ben. Keep your distance, he only loves himself.'

That gets me wondering. She tells me to be wary of him and keep my distance but she fails to say much more. 'Have you and Ben—'

'God no. I get around, you know at these networking events. It's a small world. Ignore me, I'm just being over the top. Go to lunch, have fun and get loads of business. But remember, the work I give you comes first because I'm definitely special. More special than Forge.'

I laugh at her joke, momentarily putting all my worries aside. 'You definitely are. You're my number one estate agent and friend, Justine. Got to go and get ready for my lunch meeting. Bye.' I end the call, knowing that I need to see if I can retrace last night's steps. I have a bit of time before meeting Ben. Maybe being where I woke up might trigger a memory. It's worth a try. I need to know before the police come looking for answers.

Running down the stairs and out into the sleet-filled air, I stand there and close my eyes, picturing myself standing right in this spot last night.

A shiver passes through my body as the sleet begins to seep through my jumper. It's no good, nothing's coming back.

Had Simon ever mentioned to anyone how I left the farm all those years ago? I gaze around, half expecting the police to be parked up and coming for me. I have no idea how long it will take them to find out about me, his adopted daughter. If they delve into Simon's past it might put me on their radar, but then again, I haven't been in his life for years now. The sound of the chickens begin to fill my head and I want to curl up into a ball and cry like a scared child. Once again, I feel the weight of my past crushing on my chest and I can't escape. Gasping, I lean against my car and catch Dan's face reflecting in the bonnet from the window above.

The music goes on. 'Always Look on the Bright Side of Life'. I glance up and he's grinning at me. I need him to shut up, to shut the music off. I can't cope. Worst of all, he knows that I'll be heading back up those stairs in a minute and he'll be waiting. For a moment, my vision prickles and the heat begins to crawl up my neck. I select the name of the only person who will understand in my phone and I press his number. 'Glen, can you help me, please?' There's no way I'm going back into my apartment alone.

CHAPTER FIFTEEN

Ten years ago

I worked on a neighbouring farm throughout the summer after finishing my A levels and I managed to save a whopping fifteen hundred pounds. Day after day, I picked strawberries, and came back to my room every night with an aching back. When I pull the banknotes from the box under my bed, I smell freedom. I have my savings and my battered old car so as a new adult, I'm ready to enter the big wide world.

Simon still doesn't venture upstairs. He tends to the chickens and then he drinks and sleeps. I still drug him sometimes but I don't need to do that so much any more. He's slowly giving up.

Grabbing the only photo I have of Riffy, I pack that in my memory box along with a few other bits and bobs that I've kept all these years. I'm just missing Scarecrow. Glancing down at the photo of my grey-haired cat, a tear slides down my cheek. After caring for him as he slowly withered and died of old age, I'd buried my head in my studies to take my mind off everything. At least I did my best for Riffy by filling his life with my love.

I listen and I can hear Simon's loud snores. That sound once filled me with fear but now I'm in control of when he sleeps and when he wakes, I feel reassured that I'm safe. I grab the stepladder from the junk room at the end of the old house. Each floorboard creaks as I head back to the loft hatch and I crash the ladder into the wall. The dripping tap in the bathroom echoes.

As I climb up the steps, my heart rate hums away. I haven't seen Scarecrow for over ten years and he's the only thing I have of my mother's. If Caroline was telling the truth, he is in the loft somewhere. I just hope he's easy to find. At eighteen, I shouldn't be pining for a raggedy old toy but I am. I want to smell it and to hold it close while I breathe the smell of my mother in.

The hatch resists as I push so I slam the palm of my hand into it, making a crashing noise. I hold my breath and listen. Simon still snores so I'm okay for now. Exhaling, I step further up and shift the loft hatch out of the way before pulling my body up onto a wooden beam. A mesh of cobwebs hit my face as I turn and I wave my hands to fight them away. Flicking on the loft light, I gaze around, not knowing where to start. Boxes upon boxes fill the space and not one of them is labelled up. I swallow as I see the Christmas box. Rats have gnawed at the edge and the snowflake baubles spill out. I grab onto a rafter and pull myself up. It was going to be a long evening.

An hour later, I open one of the boxes on the bottom row. Caroline and Simon had kept so much junk. Paperwork spanning back over ten years and old clothes that were now moth-eaten. The box I'm staring into is different. I recognise that A-line denim skirt. It's the one my mother always wore, come rain or shine. It would be with bare legs in the summer and thick opaque tights and boots in the winter. I lift it away and the smell hits me. My mother's hairspray. I lift the black jumper up and hold it to my nose and inhale. Another tear trickles down my cheek. There's a large, yellowing envelope that has come apart along one of the edges. I place the jumper down and open it, the contents spilling in my lap.

I remove the elastic from the batch of photos and squint to clearly see each one in the dim light. They are of my mother as a young child and she's with Caroline. They're both sitting on a bench with a smiley woman with similar features. I know that to be the grandmother I never met. I never got to hear of how she spent her childhood living in North Africa. If only she'd lived for long enough and brought both my mother and Caroline up together, maybe things would have turned out better. I flick through the old baby photos and those of the three of them having a picnic, then I come to a photo of my mother holding me. She looks sad. There is a man standing next to her but his face has been cut out. Did he kill my mother or was he a lover she wanted to forget? Maybe he was my dead father.

Shaking, I throw the photos back in the envelope – apart from one of me and my mother – then I pick up the old newspaper clippings. My mother's murder was huge news and I had been mostly protected from all this when I moved in with Simon and Caroline. I always thought that when the police came and pulled me from under the bed, my nightmare was over but in reality, it had only just started.

They never caught my mother's killer.

I throw everything back in the envelope. The case was now as cold as I was. I lift the lid on another little box and there he is, the toy I'd come looking for. Scarecrow has unwound and is mostly a mass of tangled wool. His shape still exists but the features have gone. I hold him close to my chest and smile through my tears. It's as if I'm back there, hiding under the bed while my mother's blood pools in front of me.

I stop crying as a grunt fills the house. Something clatters below. I grab the things I want to keep, including one of my mum's baubles, and throw them into an old beach bag and hurry down the stepladder, replacing the hatch. Simon's not likely to come upstairs but he might. The smell of urine hits me as I lean over the bannister. This is how the place always smells now but I don't care because I'm finally escaping this hellhole.

Hurrying to my room, I throw all my personal treasures into the large holdall and creep down the stairs. He's in the kitchen. Maybe I should wait in my room.

He's stomping around slamming cupboards and running the tap. I itch to run back into my room and close the door. Maybe I should drag my chest of drawers in front of it so that he can't get in. He's meant to be asleep. I popped a whole crushed up tablet into his can of beer.

Something's not right and I have to face this. I don't want to hide any more after promising myself that I would leave tonight. If I stay, I'll die, I know I will. If not in body, in spirit and once I lose the will to fight, I'll be stuck here forever. No – he will not scare me any more.

'I'm not scared,' I whisper under my breath. That's a lie but if I tell myself often enough, I might actually believe it. 'I'm not scared. I'm not scared. He is weak and I am strong.' Leaving my bag at the bottom of the stairs, I creep towards the kitchen.

'You bitch.' The table has gone over along with everything on it. That'll be all the empty bottles, all the sauces and the vinegar. The unopened letters and the pile of newspapers.

Swallowing, I step into view and his wide-eyed stare fixes on me, then he charges forward, taking me down right outside the front door. My breath goes and I can't breathe. He's so heavy, it feels as though my ribs are breaking and my lungs are being crushed. I retch at the stench that spills from his body as my hand comes up and jabs him in the eye with my nail. 'Get off me.'

His hand instantly goes to his face and to the blood that trickles down his cheek. He can't see. I bring my other arm over and slam my fist into his nose and push him with everything I have. He moves off me, while calling me every name possible. I'm the slut, the whore's child, the ungrateful little bitch, Lolita – that was his favourite – like the abuse he put me through was my fault, just like Lolita's wasn't either. I kick him in the groin and manage to wriggle out of his grip and go into the only room I can safely escape into, which is the kitchen.

Slamming the door shut, I lean against it to get my breath back. Had I really just hurt him like that? He's pounding on the door. I bounce as he slams his body into the old wood and a huge crack appears above my head. His rage is fuelling him and he seems to be getting stronger. I almost slip on all the fallen newspapers and broken plates. My heart pounds when I see the bottle of sleeping pills on the side, the ones prescribed to me, which I used on him and now he knows. That's maybe why he didn't drink that last can of beer that I left next to him while he was sleeping. I've been busted. It's game over.

His fist slams through the rest of the door taking the whole panel out. I step back, falling into the range cooker. Reaching behind me as he lunges towards me, I slip my hands around the first thing I can grab; the vegetable knife, and in one swift movement, I bring it forward and plunge it into his shoulder. He grips it, his mouth opening and closing as the realisation hits him.

Staring at the phone on the wall, I wonder if I should call an ambulance. He slips to the floor, landing on all the debris while he swears at me. I walk to the phone and lift it out of the cradle, my stare never leaving his as I go to press the buttons.

'You bitch, you absolute bitch.' I was going to call an ambulance but now I know this is my only chance to get away, especially as I won't be able to drug him any more. I'd never be safe here.

'Wait until they all find out that you stabbed me. They'll put you in prison.'

'And then they'll all know what a filthy, dirty paedophile you are. I'll make sure my story comes out to the world.' I'm shaking so hard, I feel as though I may break a bone. He looks away and screams as he fiddles with the knife in his shoulder before dropping it to the floor. He groans in pain, defeated and unable to move.

I place the phone back in its cradle. There's no way I'm calling help for him. I need to get out of here. Instead, I run to the cupboard under the stairs. There is a recess in the wall that looks like it is a part of the wall. I pull the frontage away and see that Simon's money is still there in his hiding place.

'What are you doing? Bring that back now, bitch!'

That's it. I'm out of that house and I never have to listen to another one of Simon's words again.

As I throw my bag in the car, I feel high. He might call the police, he might not. All I know is that I am never going back to that house ever again. There's just one thing I have to do before I go. I run to the large building that houses all the chickens in the dark enclosure. They cluck and jump on each other. I open every pen and leave the main door open, letting each and every one of them escape as I half sob and half laugh in the chilly night. 'Run chickens, run. Your freedom awaits you.'

I put my key into the ignition not knowing what waited ahead but I had to be prepared for this to catch up with me one day.

I'm sure I catch a glimpse of a figure beside one of the outbuildings but when I glance back, it's gone. My imagination is playing up, that's all. There's no one else at the farm apart from Simon and I can still see his shadow bouncing around in the kitchen as he struggles to get up.

As I drive through the winding roads out of the area, I shake as I wonder what my future will bring.

CHAPTER SIXTEEN

Now

Taking a deep breath, I put the kettle on. Now I feel stupid and I hate that I've asked Glen for help but when I saw Dan Pritchard, I couldn't face coming up those stairs and facing him alone, especially as I feel giddy at the day's news. Glen had hurried over almost immediately to help.

'Bloody hell. He's really taking the piss. When you said the music was loud, I thought you were exaggerating.' Glen sits in the chair under the window and moves the cushion aside, the grey speckles in his hair twinkling slightly as he fidgets to get comfortable.

Flinching, a sting comes from my hand as I pour the drinks.

'Are you okay? Your hand is bleeding through the plaster.' He stands and hurries over to the kitchen.

I step back and hold my other hand out in front of him. My heart bangs against my chest as he breaches my tiny kitchen area, trapping me in. Clearing my throat, I try to hide the tremble in my body but my quivering voice is a giveaway. 'I'm fine, honestly. My hand, I mean. My hand's fine. I just cut it when I was doing the washing-up. What I should do is wash the knives separately. Sit back down, I'll bring the coffee over.' The bauble lies on the worktop, wrapped in kitchen roll. I don't want Glen to get too close to me and I don't want him to see the part of me that is represented by that bauble on the worktop.

He gives me a pitiful look as he moves back towards the chair, sensing my fear.

'I'm okay, really.' I pass him the cup with my other hand. I check my watch. It's a while before I need to leave to meet up with Ben. I wish I hadn't called Glen now as I feel really stupid, but sometimes a person needs a friend. I wonder for a second if I should tell him about what happened last night.

He takes the coffee. 'Sorry, I didn't mean to scare you just then.'

'I'm not scared.' That mantra repeats itself in my head. Who am I kidding? No one has ever been in here to drink a coffee that I've made for them, except Justine, once. I mostly go to her house. And recently Ben Forge, of course. I'm scared of what's happened to Simon and every time I hear a bang in the building, I'm scared that the police are coming to talk to me or worse, take me away. The madwoman who came home bleeding and can't remember a thing. I swallow.

He sips the coffee, then smiles. 'That's good, because I'd be really upset if I thought that I scared you. I was just trying to help with your hand but I should have thought first. You don't really know me and I'm literally a stranger in your apartment.'

His concern touches me and feel a tear welling up in the corner of my eye. I blink it back. 'You're not a stranger any more. We bonded over a gin and tonic and you're here helping me. I should be a little less nervy. It should be me who's sorry. Can we start again?' I glance at the bottom of the sofa, right where I'm about to rest my ankles when I sit. There's a knife secreted right under me. I grab a thick wad of kitchen roll and wrap it around my hand before joining him in the lounge area. The music played by my horrible neighbour is turned up and booms through the walls.

'Okay, so you invited me over to talk about him opposite. I can see why you're fed up and you say this happens at all hours?'

I nod. 'Three in the morning too, that's when it started today and it went on for three or four songs.'

'The first thing you will need to do is keep a diary.' He sips the coffee. 'Could I have some milk, please?'

'Sorry, of course. I take it black. It's silly of me to think everyone likes it that way. I keep some milk in for when I have breakfast.' I open the fridge and take out the small bottle and leave it on the coffee table where he helps himself. 'I should have thought to keep a diary. I'll start today. What happens after that?'

'I think you'd need to contact the noise people at the council. They'll probably want to install a gadget that records sound levels in your apartment to measure how loud it is but it all starts with a diary. I suppose we may be able to contact the owner of his property as he's definitely in breach of his tenancy agreement, but who knows what good that will do. It's hard and costly to get rid of a nuisance tenant and if he's paying rent without any trouble, they might not do much.' He pauses as if in thought. 'Have you spoken to the other neighbours? If there's more of you, it might be a case of power in numbers when it comes to approaching the council.'

'I haven't yet but I know the man who lives at number twenty-two argues with his girlfriend over the noise. Maybe he'd be prepared to join forces. In all honesty, I don't know anyone in this block and I've lived here for ages.' I pause. 'I think Dan is making this personal. He's getting at me, personally?'

'Why would you think that?'

I don't know whether to open up as Glen is so easy to talk to. He leans back and doesn't speak, respectfully waiting for me to offload my problems. 'He stares at me out of the communal window, blowing smoke into the darkness when the light has flicked off. He sneers at me and is always standing in the corridor when I go out or arrive home. I found a note in my post box, written in red pen with the word "bitch" scrawled across it.' I swallow, knowing that I must fill him in a little more. 'It feels like I've made an enemy of him by complaining about his party on the first night.'

'And you had every right to complain. Why should you just shrink and take it all from him? Just be careful though. For your own safety it's probably not wise to get too confrontational and be prepared to call the police if things get bad. He could be dangerous.' He drinks his coffee down while steam is still coming from my cup. It's seemed like forever since anyone has ever been concerned about me and I feel slightly emotional, especially with what happened last night. For now, though, I can't share that with anyone.

I take a sip of my coffee and nearly take the skin off my lips as it burns. The music abruptly stops and Dan's door slams, followed by the fire door. 'I guess it's over for now.' Shivering, I grab a snuggle blanket from the back of the sofa and wrap it around my shoulders. I'm aware I look vulnerable now; cut hand; shivery; wrapped up in a blanket. I really am allowing Glen into my world. 'Thank you for coming. I didn't know who else to call.'

'You're welcome. If anything like this happens again, call me. Remember, I'm a witness. I'll keep a diary too. Everything that happened today, I can corroborate.'

It makes me feel feeble to have to involve someone else in my battle but at the same time, I feel that the whole thing is less of a burden. Glen's eyes are so warm and he's a good person, I can tell. 'I have a meeting soon but I'm really grateful for all that you've done.' I go to tell him about Simon, about the local murder but then I stop.

'Did you want to say something?'

I smile and shake my head. 'No, just, thank you.'

He stands. 'Right, it's my day off so I think I'm going to go shopping or I won't have anything for dinner later.' He places the coffee cup on the table and turns to face me. 'If you're at a loose end this evening, you're more than welcome to join me for supper. We can formulate a plan of attack. Sort that dodgy neighbour out once and for all.'

'Dinner?'

'You know. That stuff you eat that keeps you alive. Food. Nothing special, just fish and chips or cottage pie. Those are the only things I cook. Everything else comes in a microwavable box. As I said, nothing special so don't expect Michelin Star style food.'

'Okay.' Did I just say that? I'll be fine with him, I can feel it. I like him and I could do with a friend around here. Glen seems like a lovely person. He spends his time trying to make our area better for everyone and no one turns up to help and now he's helping me. I owe him a bit of friendship. I best make sure I have a light lunch with Ben.

'Great. I live at number sixty-six. I eat about six – that's an easy one to remember. All the sixes.' He laughs a little. 'That okay for you? It's nice to finally meet someone friendly around here.'

For a moment, I enjoy being referred to as friendly. For all my trying, I've never managed to befriend anyone on the estate and I want to meet more people. I smile, the pain in my hand easing. I don't have to continue living like a hermit. 'Likewise.' Did I just reply with that cheesy word and a slight smile?

Walking towards the door, he leaves with a little wave. 'See you later.' And with that, he's gone.

I remove the kitchen roll now that the bleeding has stopped. My eyes water a little as I swill it under the tap. Did I really just agree to go to someone else's home for dinner? Justine doesn't count. With all that's going on, I need to get out otherwise I'll spend all evening thinking about Simon. I think I need to let the memories of last night come back in their own time. Trying to force them to appear isn't working. I swallow. I might not have time if someone saw me at the cottage. Glancing out of the window, I wonder if the killer knows where I live or followed me home. I don't see anyone loitering but that doesn't mean I'm safe.

I place a large plaster on my hand and check the time. It's midday. I have to finish getting ready to go out.

A flashback to the night before suddenly fills my head. *I'm crying as I walk but I'm vacant. It's like I'm in a haze. The path ahead looks as real as ever as it leads from the cottage but then it's longer and the proportions aren't quite right. It's like I can never reach the end and I remember tasting something metallic. I'm bleeding.*

I open my eyes and the tap is still running. The bowl has filled and is spilling over. I turn the tap off and listen to the water gurgling down the plughole as I stare out of my window at the car park below, wondering exactly what I did last night. The flashback could be nothing more than a dream. Closing my eyes again, I try to recapture what I'd just been feeling. Go back to the path and see if I can see anyone else, but it's no good. I can't. It's gone.

CHAPTER SEVENTEEN

As I pass the gift shop next to the Drunken Duck, I check my reflection one last time. What I see is the professional person I normally look like but inside my stomach churns away. I can't get what happened to Simon out of my mind and I still haven't worked out what I did last night. Again, my best advice to myself is to act normally until I can work out what went on. I can't afford to lose this work so I have no choice.

The day is dull and small flakes of snow have settled on my hood. I tuck a stray hair behind my ear and straighten my trousers. The car ride has crumpled them slightly, which I feel a bit self-conscious over; in fact I should have ironed them. I can see that I'm coming apart; I just hope Ben can't see that I am. My breath quickens and my heart starts to hum. *Breathe it out, Marissa.*

My attention is drawn to the warm-looking shop window with its yellow lighting and my gaze settles on a collection of fancy baubles that hang on a spinning rack. The snowflake design reminding me of my earlier confusion and the haziness of my memory, then I see Simon in my mind; but this time he's dead. My mind is playing tricks on me, imagining what he would have looked like when the police found him. I feel so sick, the last thing I want to do is eat. What if that image in my mind is what I actually saw? *Act normal, be normal, Marissa.* The police will come to speak to me soon, that's a given and when they come to deliver the news of Simon's murder, I have to act like I didn't know. They can't find out that I was out wandering that night, let alone cutting my hand on one of the baubles that had to have come from Simon's home.

Hurrying, I focus on the pub next door and I see Ben sitting at a table in the window.

He holds what looks to be the wine list as he speaks to the aproned server. The young man nods and takes the menu away with him. I walk in, stamp the slush from my boots and hold a hand up in his direction before being approached by a young girl guarding the doorway.

'Welcome to the Drunken Duck. Do you have a reservation?'

I nod. 'It's under the name of Mr Forge. That's him, there.' I half wave. To think, before he came to my apartment, I found him attractive and a part of me really hoped that we might eventually date, but the things he says and the way he acts signals for me to be wary of him. Justine; she's not telling me something and we're meant to be friends. She thinks I can't tell but her warnings are running through my head, loud and clear. I know she lied too. I can tell that Ben is just the type of man Justine would sleep with.

'May I take your coat?' The girl smiles and holds out her hand.

'I'm okay, but thank you. I'll keep it on me.' I remember how precious everything I owned was when growing up, so I tend to keep my things close. I head straight over to Ben. 'Horrible day,' I say as I hold out my hand to shake his.

He ignores my hand and pulls out a chair at the table for me to sit on. 'It's really lovely to see you again, Marissa. I hope all the paperwork I emailed you was in order.' He kisses both of my cheeks but it feels uncomfortable. I'd rather sit and talk, eat lunch and go. I need to be at home, watching the news. Maybe the press have released more information. If they have it might help me trigger last night's memories. Playing the part of normal, today, is going to be harder than I thought but I have to give it my best.

'It was, thank you. Mr Duncan kept everything brilliantly and the handover notes are great too. I've started familiarising myself with all the clients and what stages they're at.' That was a lie. I'd opened the files and briefly glanced at them before coming. I'm not normally this unprofessional but given the events of the last day, I think I haven't done too badly. As soon I get home, I'll get to work on it all and continue late into the night after my dinner with Glen; I'll do all this while checking the news in the background.

'Good, good. I have some paperwork here for you too.' He holds up a bag and passes it over to me. 'First things first, I took the liberty of ordering a Chablis. I hope that's good for you.'

There's no way I'm sharing a bottle of wine with him. I got into a mess when I drank too much at Justine's and the gin and tonic I had last night seemed to make my sleepwalking worse. I can't risk anything else happening. 'I'll have to pass as I'm driving but you go ahead and enjoy. Just water will be fine, thank you.' I feel a warmth seeping up my neck. His gaze meets mine.

He nods at the waiter and orders me a sparkling water. 'I'm off for the rest of the day so it looks like I'll be the one getting merry while you remain ever the professional.'

'Well, I'm sure that wine is going to go down well.'

He passes me a large bag full of brown paper files. 'Here's the paper files I promised you. I mean, most of the things you need have been emailed but you have the notes that Mr Duncan took in there, some he didn't put on the computer files. Is there anything you need to ask me about what I sent over to you by email?'

This is when I feel awkward. The tables have turned in a matter of five seconds. I'm sure there would have been things I needed to ask him but not having looked, I have no questions. I pretend to recognise some of the client names as I flick through the files, nodding and smiling as I go but none of them are familiar. I have a sum total of nothing to ask him. 'No. They all seem straightforward. I'm sure there might be things as I go along if you're okay with me contacting you as I need to.' I hope he doesn't start talking specifics.

'Of course.' The wine is placed on the table. The waiter pours a little into Ben's glass and stands still as he sniffs the wine and swishes it in his mouth. 'That is so good, thank you.'

The waiter smiles. 'Are you ready to order?'

'Yes, sirloin, rare with chips for me.'

I try not to envisage Simon's stabbed body as I think of rare steak, instead I grab the menu. I'll chose the same thing I order every time I come here but I don't think I'll be able to eat it. I feel a jitter in my fingers as I grip the menu. An image flashes through my mind. I'm walking along a path, not too far from the cottage and the bauble crunches in my hand.

'Marissa.' I flinch and inhale swiftly. 'Are you going to order?' Ben stares at me like he's concerned.

'Sorry, I'm not feeling good today. I think I have a migraine coming on so excuse me if I look a little out of sorts. Could I please have the grilled salmon with a green salad and no dressing?' As I know I won't eat it, I'll be able to wrap it in a serviette and feed it to the cat.

Ben laughs and leans over, trying to look into my eyes but I look down. 'Ooh, you could live dangerously and have a side of buttery crushed potatoes.'

Live dangerously, I'm already teetering on the edge and I want to get down. I want all this uncertainty to be over. I want to know if Simon's killer is now coming for me. I want to know if the police are going to try to lay the blame on me, and all I really need is to remember. It's all in there; in my head.

'Is that everything?' The waiter remains poised to add to the order.

I realise I'm gripping my fork so I place it down as daintily as I can and smile at the waiter. 'Although I'm sure the buttery potatoes would be delicious, I'm good with just salad, thank you.'

'Couldn't tempt you?' Ben tilts his head slightly and I can tell he's not talking about the potatoes. He's definitely flirting with

me. Be careful of him – those words are all I can hear running
through my head. What does this man do if he's rejected? I'm
here to take work from him, I shouldn't have to think like this.

Another thought flashes through my head. The Christmas
bauble that I threw in the bin before I left. The blur of dream and
reality. Simon coming into my room as a child. I inhale sharply
and swig half of my water down. Ben is confusing me now and
all I want to do is leave.

'This wine is so good.' He holds it up and takes another sip.
'Sure you don't want a glass or a sip. Go on, try a bit.' He holds
his glass up to me and I shake my head. 'You can always walk
home or get a taxi. Live a little.'

I don't know whether the nerves in my stomach are because of
Ben's pushiness or because of Simon. A part of me is expecting a
police officer to march in now and drag me out for questioning.
'I'm really fine, thank you.'

'You know, you might enjoy this meeting more if you have a
little glass. That's what business lunches are about, Marissa. You
need to play the game.'

'Okay, maybe a small glass.' I don't like that he doesn't take
no for an answer but if I'm to get this over quickly, maybe I can
pretend to drink a small glass of wine. I'll leave it there, going
warm while I stick to my water. Anything to get him off my back.
He pours a large glass of the almost clear wine into my glass and
I take the tiniest of sips.

'It's good, isn't it?'

I nod and force a smile.

'You should loosen up a bit more. You look so tense, Marissa.
Life is about pleasure and wine is definitely one of life's pleasures.'
The side of his leg rubs against mine under the table so I pull
away. I'm hot and it's not helping; he's not helping. This has
to be why Justine told me to be careful. 'Anyway, let's get the
work stuff out of the way. I'll start off by saying that I'm glad

to have you on board. The files I sent you are just the tip of the iceberg. I have a large development on the go, a conversion of an old industrial building in the centre of Birmingham. It's set to be thirty luxury apartments and each one of those is coming up for sale, off plan, in the next couple of weeks. I hope you'll be handling all the mortgages and insurances. I'll certainly be sending everyone your way. I trust you implicitly. We're going to be great together.'

He reaches across the table and places his warm hand on mine. A loose strand of hair falls forward. I peer through it and pull my hand from under his. Removing my hair clip, I go to twist my hair back up but he's staring at me, no he's leering, and I'm not comfortable at all.

'Well, I'm looking forward to getting stuck into all this work.' I place my hair clip on the table and smile at the waiter as he places our mains down, introducing them as he does.

'You feel it, don't you? When I touched your hand. There's something between us. The moment I saw you, then again in your apartment, I knew I had to have you.'

'What?' I lean back and turn to see if anyone is watching, feeling exposed, like I'm naked for all the world to see. But, no one is looking.

'Is there something wrong?' The waiter sees that we haven't touched our meals. There is but it's not the food. I feel as though the walls are closing in on me and all I can focus on is Ben's grin. It's no longer a smile, it's leery and sickening, just like Simon's was. I don't want to have to sleep with him just to get work and I don't have to. My body is trembling away. I need to leave, now, before I knock something over or make a fool of myself.

'No, it's lovely here. Everything's fine. I'm sorry, I'm not feeling good at all. I have to go home now. Migraines, you know how it goes. I'll email you when I've been through the paperwork.' I stand and grab my coat from the back of the chair. 'So sorry.' I can't get out of the Drunken Duck quickly enough as I struggle to carry the huge bag of files. The cold air hits me like a wall.

My hair flaps in the damp breeze and I remember that I left my hair clip on the restaurant table. I don't care. There's no way I'm going back for it.

My mind flashes back to Simon holding his hand over his stab wound and I'm all jumbled up. Was I seeing the time I stabbed him at the farmhouse as a scared eighteen-year-old or is this a recent memory? Everything is closing in on me so I up the pace, almost jogging past the narrowboat owners selling food out of hatches.

Pulling my phone from my bag, I select Justine's number and call her.

'Hey, lovey. How did lunch go?' Her usual chirpy tone had been replaced with a more monotone sound.

'Not so good. The man's a right sleaze! I liked him when we first met but all he could do was leer and try to ply me with wine. Why did you say to be careful around him? There's something you're not telling me, isn't there?'

'I'm sorry he turned out like that but what I said, it was nothing. I'd just had a few. I can't believe he was like that with you. I have to get to the school. I know I said we could probably meet up for a coffee or a chat today but I remembered I have to watch Sam singing in the school Christmas choir today and I don't know what time I'll manage to get out. Got to go or I'll be late.' She hung up. That wasn't like Justine at all, she always wanted to talk and she hadn't mentioned any Christmas choir that her son was practising for when I visited the other week.

I run all the way back towards the river, glancing at the Royal Shakespeare Company as I pass, then I almost slip on a patch of pressed snow. Swallowing, I feel panic rising. Ben must have tried it on with her. It hurts to know she cut me off because I thought she could talk to me about things like this.

My fingers grip the heavy bag of work as I run over the bridge. Tourists are everywhere, full of the joys of Christmas to come and I find myself crashing into a few, apologising as I pass, then I stop and look back.

A figure in a dark hoodie stands out. It feels like there's only him and me and no one else exists. The people passing are merely a blur. I can't see his features or his face as he's too far away. Maybe it's just a lost tourist, but I'm not going to wait to find out. I turn and run as fast as I can, back to my car, where I pull off with a skid without looking back. Gasping, I feel like someone is sitting on my chest and I need to get home and shut myself away from the world.

My phone beeps, I glance at the passenger seat. Picking my phone up, I accidentally drop it into the footwell, then look up just before I almost crash into the bumper of a van as the traffic lights turn to red.

Slamming my hand into the wheel, I feel my loss of control spiralling. Someone is playing games with me and I have no idea who. The phone call. The horrible note. It has to be Dan. Everything was fine until he moved in. And as for Simon; everything was fine until he moved into the cottage.

My heart aches for my mother. I wish she was here. All I want is for her to hold me and to tell me that everything will be okay. I miss her more than ever. A tear slides down my cheek. Everything is falling apart.

CHAPTER EIGHTEEN

I'm still shaky from my encounter with Ben and seeing that figure on the bridge after has really creeped me out. A loud bang on my door almost makes me drop my coffee on the floor. I tie the belt of my dressing gown around my waist, concealing my baggy pyjamas. Beads of sweat begin to form at my brow as the person behind my door knocks again. I wonder if it's Dan coming to intimidate me or could it be Glen cancelling dinner tonight? No, it wouldn't be Glen, he'd text. Then, I hear the sound of more than one person shuffling behind my door and my stomach drops. I have no choice but to open up.

'I'm DS Brindle and this is DC Collins.' The woman who looks to be in her fifties holds up her identification and half smiles, revealing a set of slightly crooked teeth. The smell of cigarettes oozes from her clothing making me want to gag.

DC Collins is a shorter man with a bald head. He has rosy cheeks and a warm smile.

'May we come in?'

I nod and let DC Collins push the door open. The back of the door hits the picture and I tremble. Knowing my luck, the only time that knife behind it will fall to the floor will be the day the police turn up. I hear something drop to the floor. My heart begins to pound against my ribs as I glance down.

It's just DS Brindle's lighter and she's picking it up. 'Are you okay?'

The knife isn't there. It's still where I left it.

'Ma'am?' DS Brindle is getting impatient.

'Sorry, yes. Come in.'

They follow me through to my lounge area where DS Brindle stands in the kitchen area.

'Has something happened?' I know what's going on. Simon was murdered but I have to try and act surprised. They can't know that I know and they certainly can't have cause to go digging into my whereabouts in the early hours. Least of all, my neighbour saw me standing in the car park in my pyjamas. That in itself would look suspicious. My mouth is dry so I clear my throat and grab my coffee.

'It might be best if you sit down.' With every move DS Brindle wafts the smell of smoke around the room.

'Why?' I manage to ask in a quiet, squeaky voice.

'Are you Marissa Baxter?'

I nod once slowly and sit as she asked. 'What's happened?'

The two detectives sit on the couch. Brindle leans forward, elbows on knees, back hunched as she continues. 'I'm really sorry to have to deliver such bad news but we were called out to a crime scene in the early hours of this morning. Your uncle, Simon Ferris, has been murdered.' DC Collins looks down in sympathy as DS Brindle keeps talking. 'I don't know whether you've seen the news today of a stabbing in a house the other side of the river?'

I shake my head, so scared that if I speak I'll give myself away. A tremble starts in my hands.

'I know this is hard but I need to ask you a few questions.'

'That's fine. I want whoever did this caught.' And I do, the sooner the better, then I won't be implicated or under threat. At the same time, I don't want them to think it was me, just because I was outside in the car park following a sleepwalking episode at the time of his murder. I feel my heart fluttering away. I hated Simon and all he did to me. If the police knew that story too, I'd be prime suspect.

'Again, we're sorry to have to ask you these questions at such an upsetting time. Did he have any other family?'

'I don't really know. When I lived with him and Aunt Caroline we were quite isolated. A few people came to her funeral but I didn't really know any of his relatives. I wish I could help more but he was quite a loner in life.' That much was probably true. I never met any of his relatives.

'How about friends or work colleagues?'

'He used to own his own farm but I don't know who he knew.'

DS Brindle looks at her notes. 'Yes, we have an address in Herefordshire. A car that matches the same description as the one you drive has been reported as being parked up outside Simon Ferris's house on a few occasions. When we checked for any links, we discovered that he was your uncle and your adoptive parent.'

'That's right. I only visited him a couple of times but maybe my car was seen there on those occasions.' I wonder if there's anything about the time I stabbed him all those years ago on file. He obviously never reported me back then or I'd have been arrested. Maybe it wasn't as bad as I remember and he'd patched himself up and, of course, he wouldn't have wanted me telling everyone he was a child abuser. My underarms are getting sticky and I wonder if I'm giving off some kind of scent that tells the detectives that I'm guilty.

'During a search of the house, there was nothing to connect you to his murder but his old records and addresses brought up your name, which is why we're here today. We'll continue to try to contact any other relatives in the meantime. Can I ask if you and your uncle got on?'

I don't know why she's asking me this. She knows something. 'Yes, I mean we did at the farm. We didn't really talk much after his wife, Aunt Caroline, died about twelve years ago, I think. And when I left home we barely kept in touch. My mother was Aunt

Caroline's sister. I went to live with them when my mother was murdered twenty-three years ago.'

'I'm so sorry to hear that. I know this must be really hard for you.'

It is hard, the hardest thing ever. Now all I can think of is that day under the bed when my mother was taken from me. 'It is, I miss her every day.'

'Can you tell me when you last popped over to Mr Ferris's house?'

'A few days ago. I popped by but he wasn't in. I can't remember the day but it was dark so it must have been teatime or evening. One day last week.' I can't say I think I went there last night.

'We'll probably need to speak to you again at some point but in the meantime, if you think of anything that might help us, give me a call. I'll leave you with my card.' She passes one to me and the detectives stand. 'While we're here, can we call anyone to be with you? I know this must have been a shock.'

I shake my head and bite my lip. 'I'll call my friend in a minute but I really need to be alone.' I wipe the tear from my cheek. There's something in the way that DS Brindle looks at me. I know she thinks I'm holding something back, and I am. I can't tell her any more yet. I have to unlock those memories in my head, find out where I went in the early hours and work out who killed Simon. I have both motive and opportunity. If I say any more now, I'll be taken to the station and kept in a cell while they investigate. That can't happen.

CHAPTER NINETEEN

Simon is dead and I'm on the police's radar. DS Brindle doesn't trust a word I say, I could tell. Or maybe, I'm being paranoid. I can't stop thinking about Simon and what might have happened. I drop my bathrobe to the floor and step into the shower, enjoying the warm water as it washes away the dirt of the day. I think back to when I stabbed Simon to escape from that awful farmhouse. If he had reported me to the police, they'd have mentioned it while they were here. No, they'd have done more than that, they'd have taken me down to the station for further questioning and they didn't. I still have time to work out what happened before I woke in the car park. My mind wanders back to Simon and the farmhouse.

That first night when I left, I slept in my car and realised I had the world at my feet. I had worried that Simon would call the police but deep down, I knew he wouldn't want me telling my story too. I imagined that he got the first aid kit out and fixed himself up or maybe he lied about an accident he'd had to get treated at the hospital. I'd escaped Simon for good. I closed my eyes and prodded a map of the Midlands. That's how I chose my next step. For once I'd felt like I had a whole new life ahead of me where there was no looking back and I could be whoever I wanted to be. But, that was a long time ago and now I'm here, with a whole new set of problems.

I know that time is against me. Getting out of the shower, I pat myself dry and stare at my features in the mirror. My light brown skin has a purplish tinge under my eyes. I look like I need sleep or maybe I look sick. I turn to the side and my stomach is concave, making me look even sicker. I wonder if the police took note of how rough I looked when they were questioning me.

'Ouch!' Once again, the cut on my hand has just flapped open as I dried it with a towel. Opening up the medicine cabinet, I stand naked, pull out a bandage and wrap it around the wound.

Hurrying to my bedroom, I open the wardrobe and grab a pale pink jumper and a pair of grey skinny trousers. I look ridiculous, like a scrawny teenager who lacks confidence in dressing herself. Is that why everyone pushes me around? I'm fed up of being nervous little me. People can see it, which is why Ben treated me the way he did earlier. I know Dan can see it and that is why he's taunting me. That note still has my stomach turning. He must hate me more than anything to have posted that through my letter box. The more I think about it, he has to be my silent caller too. He wants to drive me mad so that I'll leave my apartment. I need to talk about this with Glen. At least dinner at his shouldn't be as uncomfortable as the one I almost shared with Ben and maybe I can forget the police for a while. They didn't take me in which means they have nothing on me. They will become suspicious if I stop acting normally though, which is why I have to carry on doing what a normal person would do; a normal bereaved person. I'm going to sit with a friend, there's nothing unusual about that at a time like this.

Throwing the trousers on the carpet, I tread on them until they're crumpled. No more safe work clothes, I've had enough. I need to look more like I'm not a pushover. There's a pair of jeans in a drawer somewhere. I begin to pull all my neatly folded clothes out until I find them. My room is in a mess and for once I don't feel the need to fuss over the items on the bed or the floor. I slip my skinny jeans on and a black jumper then I catch a glimpse of myself in the mirror. It's not me… yet. I want to be someone else. Someone who doesn't sleepwalk. Someone who probably didn't witness a murder and not remember a thing. Someone who isn't being harassed by my horrible neighbour. I finish the look with a pair of pumps that I've never worn. Casual but youthful.

A short while later, I'm ready to leave and as I do, Dan's music comes on – again. It sounds like there's a rave going on in his apartment. As I open my door, the woman who thought she was possessed at his house-warming party is going 'whoop, whoop' with her arms in the air as she dances with a bottle of cider from the communal hallway, past Dan, and into his flat. One of his teen boys loiters on the landing with an unlit cigarette dangling from his lips but he turns away from me as I lock my door. Several other people stomp up the stairs and nudge me out of the way. I roll my eyes and push past them, powerless to do anything.

'Oi,' Dan calls me. 'Just having a bit of fun. Do you care to join us… bitch?'

He called me a bitch, just like in the note he sent. I don't know whether I've just had enough or maybe it's the new clothes, but the word wanker slips out of my mouth. I've never called anyone that in my life but I can't deal with the torment he's putting me through. As I reach the top of the stairs, he thunders through the door and I swear under my breath, not at him, but me. I shouldn't have said that to him. Now things are going to get worse, much worse, and it will be my fault.

'What did you say?'

I shrug and look away, avoiding his piercing stare.

'You seriously are a fun-killing bitch but you know that already.'

I know this is my moment to try and diffuse the situation. Glen was right about not getting myself in too deep and simply sitting back and keeping a diary. This isn't worth getting hurt over and the note proves how angry he is. 'Look, Mr Pritchard, can we start again—'

'You think you know me, don't you?' I see the mottles on the sides of his cheeks, close up and I can smell stale cider each time he exhales. I shrug and go to say no as his fist narrowly misses my head and hits the wall behind me. 'You're lucky I'm in a good mood.'

I feel sick, and trapped. I need to get away from him but my whole body is numb and my muscles, they're not working. Perspiration beads at my brow and I want to cry. Just like all those years ago as a girl in my bedroom when Simon came in, I remained silently holding back my cries.

The sound of footsteps begin to fill the hallway. It's the man from number twenty-two and he's holding a bunch of flowers that are no doubt for his girlfriend and I couldn't be more relieved to see him. Dan brushes his shirt down and steps away from me.

Number twenty-two lowers his flowers. 'Are you okay?' He looks at me, then at Dan, then back to me. I can see the tension in his face as he sees Dan staring at me.

'Of course she's okay, aren't you, neighbour?' Dan kicks the door as he leaves.

'I'm fine.' It's only now that I feel the shakes reaching my fingers.

'Are you sure? It looked to me like he was upsetting you.' I don't answer so he continues. 'I don't know why I bought these flowers. No doubt we'll spend all night rowing about this racket.' He reaches the top step. 'He looked a bit vicious, didn't he?'

'He's a coward. He just gets off on intimidating people.' I force a smile as I pass. Now's my time to get someone else on board with reporting Dan. 'Oh, would you keep a noise diary? I'm thinking of going to the council with this. It might help if I have some backup. You know, power in numbers.' I sound like Glen now, but that's okay. I'm happy that a little bit of him is rubbing off on me.

He nods. 'Of course. It'll be my pleasure. The quicker we can get rid of him the better. I hope he drinks so much tonight that he falls down the stairs head first. Ooh, did I just say that?' He lets out a laugh.

I'm not the only one that wishes Dan would hurry up and go.

CHAPTER TWENTY

I rush across the road towards Glen's apartment block trying to force my encounter with Dan Pritchard out of my mind. Simon remains in my head but I have to carry on acting normal. A few flashbacks have come back to me today, now I need to work out what was dream and what was real before the police come back. The news programmes I watched earlier hadn't mentioned anything else about Simon's murder so I'm still as in the dark as I was. The police didn't give me any details either.

My hair swishes with the breeze and gets tangled across my eyes. This is new to me, wearing it down while out and it feels chaotic, a bit like my life at present. Taking a deep breath, I remind myself that I have to stick with everything I'm meant to do even though my instinct tells me to run home and go to bed. My stomach is turning, but this time I'm actually hungry. I haven't eaten all day and the constant pangs are making me feel worse.

Pressing the buzzer, I wait for Glen to answer and release the door. He does it almost immediately with a chirpy *hello* like he was waiting for me to arrive. I hurry up the stairs and notice how his block feels much calmer than mine. His walls aren't scuffed and the carpet looks and smells fresh. There is no loud noise and no drunken people taking over the stairs or landing. As I go to knock, he's already opening the door.

I'm instantly hit by the smell of his musky aftershave and I like it. He's wearing an untucked shirt covered in a light blue paisley pattern. His look is finished off with a pair of dark jeans and brown lace-up shoes. 'Shall I take my boots off?'

He ushers me in. 'No, please keep them on. As long as you haven't trodden in dog muck, we'll be fine.' He laughs and turns. I check the soles of my boots before stepping on the shiny walnut flooring and, in an instant, I'm scared my heels will scratch it but Glen doesn't seem at all concerned. The smell of his aftershave is then drowned by the savoury smells of onion and rosemary and my mouth waters. There's another smell; buttery apple. It reminds me of my mother's cooking. I swallow as I spare a thought for her and the image of the apple I was colouring for her on the day she was murdered comes back to me. I've never eaten an apple since.

'Marissa?' He looks concerned.

'Sorry.'

'I said, shall I take your coat?'

So consumed with my own thoughts, I hadn't heard him. I begin to shrug my way out of my thick coat and I pass it to him. 'Thank you.' He leads me into a room where the walnut flooring continues. The kitchen is at the top end facing out to a busy road and the other end is made up of a well-appointed living room that looks like it has come straight from a brochure. Totally not what I expected and a world away from my basic and poor home design. The television screen is filled with a roaring fire screen saver and Christmas tunes play in the background.

'It's definitely not too early for Christmas and I have company so it certainly feels like Christmas. It's not like I haven't tried to make friends around here, it's just everyone seems so busy. I asked the guy downstairs if he fancied a pint and he said yes, but he never got back to me. Oh well.'

'His loss.' I smile, trying to put him at ease. I can tell he's nervous as he keeps brushing his hair back with his fingers and looking back at me to make sure I'm okay. I glance at the effort that he's gone to. There are pans everywhere and bits of carrot on the floor by the sink. 'This is lovely. I didn't expect…'

'I couldn't help it. It's not often I get to show off my shepherd's pie so I thought I should celebrate it. Hail to the shepherd's pie. I'm famished. I hope you're hungry as I don't do small portions.'

'I'm famished.'

'Oh and there's something else.'

I glance up at him.

'Apple crumble for pudding. I confess. I didn't make it. I bought it in the frozen section of Sainsbury's but I'm sure it'll be great.'

Apples. I swallow and stare at the table for a moment, my gaze fixed on the snowman napkin that he's left folded under the knife and fork.

'Please, take a seat while I get you a drink.'

I sit at the small square table that sits against the wall between the kitchen and the living room. 'Thank you.' How can I get out of eating the apple crumble? I see my mother's body slump to the floor from under the bed. I'm back to being a child and my picture, the one she put in the drawer before the bad man killed her. Turning, I catch a flash of red in the corner of my eye and flinch. It's nothing, just Glen pouring a glass of red wine. Why did I flinch? I feel silly but grateful that his back is still turned. I'm now uneasy. Bitch – that note was also written in red ink.

'I have red, white, gin and tonic or coffee. I know you like a coffee.'

I feel comforted that he isn't trying to ply me with alcohol, not like Ben was, and I really think a drink may calm my nerves. 'I'll have a gin and tonic, but just a weak one. When we had the last one in the pub, I felt really drunk which is weird. I only had the one. I guess I'm a lightweight.' The last thing I want to do is start sleepwalking again. Maybe gin was a trigger. 'Actually, can I have a white wine, just a small one? Thanks.' Thoughts of Dan and Simon hang above me like a dark cloud that's about to burst. Glen looks awkward in the kitchen, almost comical. I turn my attention to the large picture on the wall, a red, blue and yellow abstract cityscape. Anything to stop me thinking about the police. I have to forget them for a while.

The bang of a knife slamming onto the chopping board makes me stand. 'Are you okay?'

I gasp and hold a hand to my banging chest as I see the slice of lemon swaying to a stop on the board. 'You just made me jump.' I smile and point to the knife.

'Gosh, I'm so sorry.' He picks up the lemon and drops it into his gin balloon glass, where it makes a plopping sound. 'I like lemon with my gin.'

I scramble to sit back at the table and he awkwardly joins me. My nervousness is obvious. 'No, I'm sorry. I don't know why I'm feeling so tense. I think it's because of everything that's going on with my neighbour. Every time I hear a noise, I'm on high alert.' It's more than Dan, it's Simon and what happened to him but I can't say that to Glen.

'I totally get it.' I know he doesn't, not in his lovely, quiet block. He also didn't come home last night in a state, not knowing what he did and he didn't get sexually harassed by one of his colleagues. He places a glass of wine in front of me. It's not the small glass I asked for. It's a large glass and it's almost full.

'Thanks, Glen. That's a mighty glass of wine.'

'What can I say, that's the way I normally drink it. Just leave what you don't want or say if you want something else.' He lets out a gentle titter. 'So, how's it been over there at party central?'

'Well, as I left, he was having yet another party where the masses seem to have been invited and it's only early. It never matters what day it is so I'm on edge all the time. I dread to think what I'm going back to so I'm feeling anxious.' I don't tell him about the other things in my life. I have no idea how he'd react if I told him about Simon's murder, my sleepwalking or the phone calls. That would involve me telling him too much of my personal story and I don't know if I'm ready to let him in yet. We haven't been friends for long and if I tell him everything, I'll probably scare him off. Thinking about scaring people off, my mind is still toiling over Justine and why she brushed me off earlier. Something's going on and I need to find out what. And then there was the man on the bridge in Stratford? I'm convinced it was Dan. That man hates me. My mind is awhirl and my stomach grumbles. 'I might have accidentally called him a wanker which didn't go down well. He challenged me on the stairs and, I must say, he scared me a bit.'

'Did he hurt you?'

'No, he just scared me, that's all. I shouldn't have antagonised him. He obviously has a short fuse.'

'Not good.' He pulls a baking tray from the oven. 'Definitely don't put yourself in any danger. He's not worth it and if you ever feel scared, you know you can call me. I'm less than a minute away.' Steam fills the tiny kitchen and he almost drops the tray on the trivet as he swears under his breath. 'Ouch, nearly burnt myself but whoa, dinner's looking good. Check out that crispy top. Yep, I'm pleased with that.'

He scoops the food up onto two plates, licks some spillage off the side of his hand and pulls some steamed greens from the microwave before pouring them into a serving bowl. 'Tuck in before it goes cold.' He passes a plate to me and pops the bowl of greens on the table. 'And help yourself to veg.'

'This looks delicious.' The huge mound on my plate splays to fill it. I politely take just one piece of broccoli, not wanting to take more than I can eat. Finally he joins me. His fresh-looking shirt has been splattered with gravy and a film of sweat coats his face showing up the open pores in his skin. He looks about as experienced as me when it comes to entertaining.

He turns off the main light leaving a couple of lamps on and the kitchen light. 'That's better. It feels a bit like Christmas. Shame I haven't got any crackers. We could be sitting here now wearing a silly paper hat too.'

'Maybe next time. Cheers.' I hold up my glass and he clinks his against mine.

'Now I know we're friends. You said next time. Maybe you can cook.'

I laugh as I place a forkful to my lips and realise how hungry I am. Before long, we've filled the evening with chit-chat while we eat and I'm happy to be distracted from all my problems. He tells me he has a child from a previous relationship and that he moved to this area for work. He sees his child as often as he can, which I like. There's no feeling in the world like aloneness. I tell him a little about how I came to live here, obviously missing a lot out. My mind wanders back to the day after I stood up to Simon and began my new life. I hadn't intended to come and live here, in Stratford-upon-Avon, and to begin with, I didn't, but the lure became too strong and I couldn't resist that urge to be near the cottage and my mother's memory any longer. It was like a calling, one in which if I ignored it, I'd never forgive myself. It was always meant to be; what my mother would have wanted. I came here with the intention of getting our cottage back, one day.

CHAPTER TWENTY-ONE

Ten years ago

Edgbaston in Birmingham, that's where my random point to the map had told me to go, right by a park called Cannon Hill. I was going to live somewhere by that park. This will be my new start without Uncle Simon. I will find a job and look for a room and in the meantime, I have my car and enough money for a bed and breakfast for a few days.

Several days pass and I've already looked at four rooms in shared houses and applied for eight jobs using the bed and breakfast's address. The murky-looking house on the main road wasn't exactly luxury accommodation but at thirty pounds per night it was expensive enough. Right now, with cash in my pocket, I feel rich but I know it won't last if I'm not careful and I don't find a way of making money. In another week, I need to be renting a room. I need a job, any job, or I'm going to spend my money quickly.

Every time I see a room that's up for permanent rent, I've been told because I don't have references I will have to pay three months upfront and a deposit and they're literally the pits. I remind myself that it's a start and I have the money I saved from strawberry picking, and the cash I took from Simon, to pay that. One day, I will have that sweet little cottage that my mother and I were going to live in. I'm going to Shakespeare Land, that's what she would call it. *One day when we can afford it, kiddo, we're going back there to live.*

As I enter the bed and breakfast, a little bell rings, reminding the old lady who owns it that I've arrived. The entrance is chintzy and warm with its floral prints and my heart melts at this. 'Hello, dear.' Her hair hangs like string in a ponytail on top of her head and she smells of biscuit. She always smells sugary.

'Hi, Mrs Mitchell. You okay? Lovely day today.' Although chilly, the sun shines and my thoughts are bursting with optimism.

'I'm all tickety-boo. I've left you some fresh towels. Oh…' She stood for a moment and scrunched her brow. 'Aha! I have a message for you. Wait here one moment.' Mrs Mitchell shuffles along the old burgundy carpet and through to her private living quarters on the ground floor. The smell of cinnamon escapes and makes my mouth water. I hope she left a cake in my room like she did the other day. Although it feels like I've entered a time warp and gone back to the past here, I feel safe and Mrs Mitchell is lovely. A moment later, the woman returns. 'Here it is. It's about one of those permanent rooms you were looking at. The man called me for a reference and said to ring him back. Here's his number. I told him you'd been here a month like we said, and how tidy and quiet you were.' I hated asking her to lie for me but it was the only way I'd get a look in and she didn't seem to mind. She could see I needed a little help in life and that started with me getting somewhere to live permanently.

I take the slip of paper from her and continue up to my room where, on arrival, I'm greeted with a sticky bun on a side plate.

Grabbing my temperamental mobile phone, I punch in the numbers and wait for Mr Perry, the landlord, to answer.

'Hello.'

'It's me, Marissa, I came about a room. Mrs Mitchell just gave me your number.' My voice is so meek, I want to tell myself off. I should sound confident and ready to embrace my new life.

'Yeah, like I said. Three months upfront and one hundred deposit and the room's yours. You can move in on Monday. Furniture included.'

I smile. That house is exactly where I wanted to live, a short walk from the park that I'd randomly chosen. It was all meant to be.

'Any breach of the conditions, any noise, mess or damage, you're out. I've given teenagers a chance before and I've been disappointed. You have one chance and if you blow it, it's goodbye.'

'I won't let you down, Mr Perry.'

'That's what they all say.' He tutted. 'I'll see you bright and early on Monday. Oh and one other thing?'

'What?'

'Get a job, quick. We don't take people on the dole.'

'I've applied for several and I have two interviews this week. I'm really hopeful.'

'Okay, that's all then. I'll run through everything else on Monday. Come with your three months' rent and deposit, all in cash, and I'll give you your key and tenancy agreement. It'll be for six months to begin with. See how you get on.'

'Thank you. Thank you so much.' I'm giddy with delight at the thought of having my own place. My first real grown-up home.

He ends the call and I stand on my flimsy bed and punch the air. I finally have a place of my own. It's far from special but I will have everything I need for a while. I grab the *Birmingham Mail* that Mrs Mitchell has kindly left on the bedside table. Flicking to the job pages, I begin ringing a few of the jobs with a marker pen. I'm not fussy, I'll take any job.

I take a bite into the deliciously buttery bun and I check out the vacancies. Cleaner – circle. Office trainee – circle. Care assistant – circle. Shelf stacker – circle. Bar person – circle. My eyes hover over all the jobs that I've picked out. All so different and I have experience in none of them. The only thing I've ever been is a farm helper and all I learned to do was to pick strawberries, but I want to experience new things. I want the office job. My GCSE and A level results were all top grade and I have intermediate IT skills but no experience in the workplace. I'll go for all of them and see where I end up.

My stomach flutters as I read about the bar person job and the expected earnings with tips make my eyes widen. This isn't just a normal pub, it's a strip bar. I can pull pints, easy-peasy, and it would be fun. I giggle and flick my hair before falling back on the bed. Staring at the whirls of water stain on the ceiling, I pop the last bit of cake into my mouth. The day was still young. I press the numbers into my phone and wait for an answer.

'House of Class.' I hear the sound of bustling and giggling in the background. Glasses chink and doors slam.

'Hi, I'm calling about the bar job.' This time I was far more assertive. I could feel my courage returning. This was me taking control of my life. Time for a fresh start. No more Simon and no more scared Marissa. I gulp as I remember what he put me through. I'll work through it and I'll come out of the other side stronger.

CHAPTER TWENTY-TWO

Now

I push the mound of mashed potatoes to one side of the plate to make it look like I've eaten more than I have. Hunger had come to me but once I'd started eating, those images of Simon kept flashing through my mind. I keep thinking I can smell DS Brindle's smoky clothes, like she's in the room. I know it's my imagination taunting me.

Glen's food was amazing but the thought of eating the apple crumble is making my head hurt. I glance up at the worktop where it sits, waiting to be dished up. Can he see the red prickles forming on my neck and reaching for my chin? That day in Mrs Mitchell's bed and breakfast when I applied for the bar job, I thought I had it all worked out. Little did I know then that I had so much more to learn – some good; some bad. I don't have any regrets. Everything that happened led me to be here, right now; ever nearer to getting everything I ever dreamed of. I frown. I never expected all this trouble to come my way and I'm missing my cottage, but Simon's murder has tarnished that. It was a part of my big plan, to find a way of getting the home back that my mother and I were always meant to live in. One day I'll have it back along with a peaceful life. I couldn't bear to think that I'll never live in the cottage again. Simon's murderer will be caught and the cottage will go up for sale again soon. I will get stuck into my extra work from Ben, keep out of his way, and all that extra money will go into the cottage pot.

'Let's put some more music on. I'm sick of random shuffle. Any preferences?' Glen shovels the last forkful of food into his mouth and starts messing with his phone.

'I'm not fussed.'

'You must like music.' He glances up at me.

I never really share my taste in music with anyone. Most days, I prefer the sound of silence but that makes me sound dull. Or, maybe I am dull. 'Simon and Garfunkel?' I remember my mother playing them now and again and they always gave me a warm fuzzy feeling when I heard them sing.

'What class. I just love the harmonies. Yes.' He presses a few buttons and 'Mrs Robinson' begins to play. He returns to the table. 'So, what else do you like?'

I shrug. This all feels a bit too intimate now. I know I like him as a friend, he seems decent, but do I want to let him into my world? I want to tell him that one of the only songs I detest is 'Mistletoe and Wine' because when I hear it, all I think of is Simon and how cruel he was to me. I swallow and almost choke on my own spit. That's not something I can talk about with anyone again.

Thoughts of Simon's hands on me and being in that cellar make the hairs on the back of my neck prickle. I'm sweating but cold. I came close to telling Justine once but the subject changed and she talked at me about something else for the next hour. A right time hadn't come up since.

'Marissa, what's the matter?'

I want to stand and run but it feels as though my bottom is glued to the seat of the chair. If I run, the apple crumble is no longer an issue and I don't have to talk about myself. I can go home and sleep this confusion and anxiety off. Then, I think of Dan with his party and I take a long swig of wine. A moment passes and I feel a warmth working through my body. 'It's nothing.'

'It's obviously something or else you wouldn't look this upset. Is it something I've done?' He places his dirty napkin on his plate.

I shake my head. 'No, it's just Christmas. It does this to me.'

'It can be a depressing time of the year for a lot of people. I'm so sorry. Do you want to talk about it?'

'No, I really need to let go of some things. What you've done is lovely. I'm an idiot. Take no notice.' I smile, hoping to put him at ease. I could do without any more questions.

'Is it your neighbour?'

I nod. It will help to change the thoughts that are running through my head. 'I guess I'm just anxious about going home.' This isn't me. I've never been scared of going home but right now, I'm quaking inside.

'I tell you what, I'm going to walk you home this evening. That way, I can see that you get in okay and I can also record what's happening over there in my diary. Strength in numbers. That's what we said and no confrontations.'

'Thank you.' It would help to have someone there who's on my side so for that, I'm grateful.

'Apple crumble?'

'Do you mind if I don't? I'm really full.'

'Of course not. You should take your pudding home. I'll put some in a takeaway box and you can have it tomorrow.' He gets up and begins scooping the crumbly dessert from the foil container into a plastic lunchbox and I stare at the art on the wall, allowing myself to breathe for a moment. 'Have you always worked in insurance?'

'Yes, it was my first job after school and that's all I've done.'

That was a lie.

CHAPTER TWENTY-THREE

No, I would never tell Glen or anyone about my first job as a bar worker in a gentleman's club. I'd rather forget some of the horrible memories and people judge. I couldn't bear for him to disapprove of me. The likes of Dan Pritchard would have a field day if he knew where I used to work. The notes he left me would say more than the word 'bitch' on them, I know it. And Ben, who knows what he'd think. Maybe he'd see it as a green light for him to pester me more. That part of my past is my secret, just like what Simon did to me. The less Glen knows, the less reason he'll have to hate me.

Carrying the plastic box of apple crumble that I have no intention of eating under my arm, I glance at Glen as we both hear the booming music coming from Dan's apartment. My stomach sinks knowing that I have to face this yet again. A loud roar of laughter echoes through the communal building. The man from number twenty-two is kicking one of the bins as he stares up at his window. My heart skips a beat as my friendly black cat darts off into the night. A stirring of guilt works through me as I'm aware that I haven't fed it today. The man shakes his head and glances at Glen and me.

'Are you okay?' I know he's not but it feels like asking is the right thing to do.

'Argh! No, I'm waiting for the missus. She said she wants us to check into a hotel for the night. It was either that or I confront him. I haven't decided which yet.'

'Wish us luck,' Glen says as he follows me through the main door.

The man puts his thumb up and lights a cigarette.

As I walk up the first few steps, I stop and take a deep breath in an attempt to quell my nervous nausea.

'You okay?'

I turn back to Glen and nod. 'No.' The two glasses of wine I eventually consumed are making the staircase slightly wavy. Gripping the handrail, I continue pulling my body up. Why was I so stupid? I'm not as sharp as I'd like to be but right now, I really want to confront Dan. Maybe it's the wine talking. Hell, I know it's the wine talking. I really thought I hadn't had that much but looks like I'm wrong on that front. Tonight is the final straw. 'It's time I put a stop to all this.'

'What are you going to say? Please leave it until tomorrow.' I feel Glen's hand on my shoulder.

I shrug it away. 'You'll see.' Pushing through the three men that almost block the fire door, I stomp over to Dan's and stare through the sea of people. 'Hey.' His curtain-haired son is leaning against the hall wall playing with his phone. He looks up and sneers at me. In the boy all I see is Dan and I shudder, wondering if I'm a product of such revulsion. I've always wondered if the bad man was my father and maybe, just maybe, I come across like he did. I wonder if it's true that the apple never falls too far from the tree. Never knowing him and him being dead will not give me the answers I need.

'Dad, the crazy bitch from next door is here.' His voice can barely be heard over the booming house music. That word bitch rings through my ears and I think for just a second, maybe the boy posted the note through my letter box or maybe he knew that his father had. The boy hurries into the lounge as a couple leave, almost falling over each other.

A man and woman begin kissing against the hall wall and Dan pushes through. 'You again! Here to ruin another party.

Why don't you and your boyfriend join us… wait, why would we want a party-killing cow like you here ruining the atmos?' His dark eyes are glazed over.

'Shut it off now. Shut it off before I smash it in.' Uncontrollable tears begin to run down my face. 'I can't cope with this, with you, any more!' The wine has given me all I need to say my piece. I slam past him and head straight to his music centre and yank all the leads out of the wall like some out of control, deranged person. The sound of people hissing a few choice words fills the living room and Dan is hot on my tail.

'Get the hell out of my apartment or I'm calling the police.'

I stare at him. Right now, I don't care if he threatens or hurts me. Glen politely nudges through, apologising to everyone he brushes against. He's all 'pleases, thank yous' with his not so scary diary entries. Everything Glen has asked me to do hasn't worked. I can't wait six months to present my diary to the council. I'm going to lose my mind if something isn't done now. The sea of people begin to chatter and I can't make out what they're whispering but their stares are all on me. Hushed voices behind hands spill into the ears of others. Words that are obviously being said about me, cursing me, laughing at me.

'Marissa, let's get out of here.' Glen places a hand on my arm, then he swallows.

'Go on, princess. You heard what the boyfriend said. Go home and be a good girl before you get hurt.' Dan's enjoying himself. I've done it this time. More tears are welling up and I can't let Dan see that I'm still upset. I shake Glen away, holding those tears back.

Dan is really pushing all of my buttons and I hate him more than anything. One of the partygoers has plugged the music system back in and the bass begins to thump. Dan turns it down a couple of notches as the other guests begin to dance and drink again. 'I said, get the fuck out of my apartment or, God help me, I'll drag you out by your hair.' I can see rage pasted across his face.

He's redder than before and the blood vessels on his nose look fit to burst. His eyes are now stark, like he's sobered up quickly.

Glen steps between me and him and holds both hands up in surrender. 'There's no need for this to get nasty.'

Dan's finger reaches towards Glen's shoulder and he points right at me. 'Tell that to her. She's the nastiest bitch I've ever met. She makes my ex seem like a walk in the park. Get her out of here, now, or I won't be responsible for what happens next.'

The boy flicks his long fringe away from his eyes. 'Dad, come on, she's not worth it.' He leads his father away and Glen pulls me out of the room and back out onto the landing.

With shaking hands, I pull my keys from my pocket. I can't get them in the door. My head is cloudy and I feel sick. Heart pounding, I just need to get out of this goldfish bowl of a landing. I want everyone's eyes off me. Dizziness is coming at me in waves and my legs feel heavy.

As Glen opens the door, he nudges me through and turns the hall light on. 'Marissa, what were you thinking? We could have both been hurt.'

Clenching my fists, I look up at him and roar. 'I just hate him.' I can't hold my tears back.

'I know, but going in like that… you could get yourself hurt. That could have escalated and we could have been in a whole heap of trouble. We need to do this properly. I'll write this up in my diary. I'm going to take a recording by your door in a minute. Rather than go in like a raging bull, we need evidence of ongoing incidents and it needs to be over a long enough period of time.'

'Properly! Do things properly.' I'm slurring. I shouldn't have had the wine. 'People like him aren't scared of the noise abatement officer, the management company, or the police. All they'll do is tell him to turn it down and as soon as they go, the music will go back up. This has to go on for years before something is done and in the meantime, I'll be driven to insanity. I can't live like this any more. Is doing it the right way really the best way?'

'What's the alternative?'

Shaking my head, I slump onto the couch and hug one of my cushions. I glance up at Glen and what I expect to see is fear and shock at the way I reacted tonight but what I really see is pity. 'I'm sorry. I couldn't help myself.'

'You must try. I promise that this won't last forever. Do you trust me?'

I shrug my shoulders. 'Yes. I'm just scared.' I fear that Dan will eventually drive me crazy. I fear the note that Dan posted in my letter box. His demeanour reminds me of Simon, so sure of himself and such a bully. The fact that I see Simon in him fuels my upset and that man took so much from me that all I have felt for such a long time is a void. An emptiness that I can't even begin to fill. Dan reminds me of that void.

My home phone goes so I reach out and grab the receiver. 'What?' Again, no answer. I slam the phone down.

'Who was that?'

Shrugging my shoulders, I stare at the phone. 'Another silent call.' Was it Dan? Was he intimidating me by making these phone calls? It's not like my business number is a secret. It's on the internet for all to find.

The phone calls. Dan. The horrible note in my letter box. Simon's murder and the police visit. I feel like my life is spiralling out of control and it all started with Dan moving in next door. The news flashes through my head again as if playing on a loop and all I can think about is what happened to Simon and me standing in the car park holding a crushed bauble. I let out a piercing screech and grip the cushion. I really need to remember what happened that night otherwise I'll go insane.

'Marissa, what's wrong? Is there something else? Do you know who's making these calls?' Glen sits next to me and pulls me close.

I place my head on his chest and feel his warmth as I sob. For so long, I've tried to push those memories of Simon away and not go over those nights I lay awake in bed, listening to his snores, hoping that he wouldn't wake up but now, they're all I can think about. His murder has opened a box I can't seem to put a lid on despite all the counselling I've had. 'I'm so broken, Glen.' By now, I'm wailing and dampening his shirt. I haven't cried like this for a long time, not since I told all my secrets to a close friend from my past. I wish that friend was here now. I'm crying for what could have been. I'm crying for the mother I lost and the childhood that was robbed from me. I'm crying for that little scared girl who is still trapped in her bedroom and can't see a way out and I'm scared the police will wrongly convict me for Simon's murder if I don't do something. But I don't know what to do. The room is starting to sway and my eyes are so heavy. Tears flood down my cheeks like never before – letting all my worries spill out.

'Do you want to talk about it?' He pats and rubs my shoulder. 'Come on. Let it all out.'

I do and I can't stop the sobbing. A few moments later, I pull away and wipe my heavy eyes. I'm exhausted and can barely keep them open.

'Shall I make you a coffee?' Glen stands and walks over to the kitchen area.

I shake my head. 'I shouldn't have had the wine. I'm sorry about this, about how I reacted with Dan and the mess I'm in. I bet you wish you'd never met me.'

'Don't be silly and don't be sorry. Everything will seem better in the morning once the hangover's over. I shouldn't pour such large glasses of wine.'

I let out a snorty laugh. 'Come on, I'm a grown-up woman. You didn't force me to drink them so it was my fault.' Yawning, I know I need to sleep this whole nightmare off. 'I think I need to go to bed.'

'Okay but call me in the morning. I want to know that you're okay. Promise?'

The bass is still pounding through the walls of the block but I can't contain my smile. For so long, I've lived a fairly solitary existence but Glen is here for me. I've let him into my home, my life and my problems – well, some of them. I'm grateful to have him in my life now and, well, he saved me from getting in way above my head tonight when I barged into Dan's apartment. 'I promise.' I'm going from bad to worse. My brain isn't sharp and my words are even fuzzier. It's like my tongue is too fat for my mouth. I need him to go before I embarrass myself or throw up. Maybe I'll call Justine in a minute. I shake my head. No, I won't. I'm clearly drunk; really drunk.

'Apple crumble's on the worktop. Who knows, it might make a good breakfast.' He does his coat up as I lift my legs onto the sofa. Dreams are calling me and I can't stop them. I try to get the image of the apple from my mind now that he's mentioned it. Too much food and too much drink are now causing havoc in my stomach and gullet. The acid in my throat burns and all I want to do is sleep and wake up tomorrow, leaving this whole night behind me.

I imagine I'm walking around Stratford along the river. *To be or not to be?* Right now, not to be. I don't want to be. Why am I thinking of Hamlet? I see Rosencrantz and Guildenstern shovelling earth onto Simon's coffin and the bizarreness of that thought brings me round slightly and I see Glen. He's still here, trying to comfort me.

'Here you go.' Glen's gentle voice is followed by the feeling of something soft being draped over my body. I'm warm and snug. The acid in my throat is calming a little as long as I stay in this position. Sleep is drawing me in. I think I hear my door close. I'm alone, all alone. Glen has finally gone home. Now it's just me, I feel the sobs begin to rise again. I feel dirty, I just want to wash the filth of my past away but there's some things that will never scrub up. I will always feel dirty. Simon stank and I can smell him all over me, even more so now he's dead. I repeat those words in my head. He's dead… no, he was murdered and I was there. I had to have been and it's only a matter of time before the police find out too.

CHAPTER TWENTY-FOUR

Ten years ago

I'd been working at the House of Class for only a short while and was taking everything in my stride. I'd learned to make all the cocktails and could pull the perfect pint but I'm not chatty enough with the customers; that's the feedback I got.

As the night grew later and the punters began to take their seats in the semi-circular booths, my heart began to pound. It was only a matter of time before they got all drunk and touchy feely and I didn't like that. They weren't meant to touch any of us, not the dancers or the bar staff, but that didn't stop any of them. The one security man on the door was always too busy texting his friends to notice anything.

As I serve several people in a row, another lot take their place at the front of the bar. I'm trying to keep up with the table service drinks and the ever-growing queue and my colleague, Max, isn't working all that fast. He said he was hung-over so that leaves most of the work to me. A suited woman wearing yellow tinted glasses stands at the bar. She's maybe in her early forties and looks tailored to the nth degree, sporting a smart waistcoat underneath her jacket. Her square face is crowned with a tidy short pixie cut that oozes style. She doesn't belong here. I watch as she waves to the three men in the booth and I wonder why she's here with them. The song 'Toxic' fills the room and flashing lights create an exciting red and blue feature of the main podium and Britney, the main dancer, struts across the stage in a black leather leotard that is sheer around the bust. All attention is now on her and the suited woman has left with her tray of drinks.

As Britney finishes dancing and leaves the stage, one man goes to touch her and she holds a firm hand up and winks. He sits back down. She takes a turn at several tables and several other women come to the podium, all dressed a little differently but still all eyes are on Britney. An announcement comes that Britney will be back soon and things simmer down a little.

I glance back at suited woman. She's totally ignoring the women on the podium while she converses with the people at her table. I find watching the customers interesting but none so much as this woman. You can tell when a person doesn't belong. She belongs here as much as I do. Someone shouts, 'Two mojitos,' at me so I grab a glass and begin preparing the drink. It slips out of my hand, splashing all over the floor.

Max takes over. 'Not on form tonight, Marissa. Grab a cloth and dustpan. I'll serve.' He's right, I'm totally distracted and although I've worked like mad tonight, I don't think working here is for me. I need to sort my life out.

My shift comes to an end and all I want to do is sleep. Kicking my low heels off, the ones management insists I wear, frees my toes. I slip my pumps on. Catching a glimpse of myself, I realise how scruffy I look compared to all the glamorous people that work at House of Class. All the make-up I'm wearing to try to blend in with them is causing me to get spotty, which then needs more make-up to cover up the blemishes. The weight is falling off me even though I've only been at it three weeks; I never stop. I guess I'm a size six now. My figure lacked curves before, but now I resemble a young boy. I need to start eating more in the day.

'You know, Marissa, I like you a lot but I don't think you're getting into this job as much as you need to. It's hard to begin with, working in a place like this, but you do get used to it,' my friend, Britney, says as she struts by, smacking her lips together to spread her lipstick further. She has one more appearance to make before her evening ends. 'Are you okay?' She reaches down and holds my hand as she gives me a sympathetic look.

'I don't know if I'll ever get used to this. I drop at least a couple of drinks at every shift. I'm fast but clumsy.'

'You'll get there. You're still quite new and the pace is unreal. I started off working the bar so I know how hard it is. Maybe you'll end up on the stage one day.'

I smile. 'I don't think so. I'm not cut out for that as I can't dance. I look like a baby giraffe trying to get into a teacup. Thanks for the vote of confidence though.' I've seen myself in the mirrored walls. I look okay but I'm clumsy. I can't do a sexy face or the pout. I can't wiggle and jiggle and I accidentally stare at some of the customers with a deep hatred, especially when they get really drunk and call me names. Some try to touch and it makes me cringe. It's not that I don't like to be touched, I just like to choose who touches me and how, like that time I slept with the Australian backpacker while I fruit picked on the farm. Even with all that was going on at home, I wanted him and I'd wanted to feel like a normal girl. But I don't like being touched by random strangers. It's sleazy, like what Simon used to do to me and I hate it. People can't be trusted and the punters at House of Class, they're the worst.

'I can't work you out at all. You sometimes look like you're on another planet.' Britney smiles and hugs me, like she does with everyone. Britney is the biggest hugger I know and it feels nice.

I give her a little squeeze back and laugh. 'Maybe I am on another planet.'

She laughs and glances up at the ticking clock. 'Damn it! I have to get my arse on that stage now. That's my music.'

'Maybe we could go out one night, dancing.' I'd like to get to know her outside work, maybe have a laugh with a friend.

'Oh, I don't think so. I have enough of nights out with this place.'

That's me told. Now I know I'm not friend material. Even she senses something in me, a part of me that's not worthy of love and friendship. The rejection stings a little.

'Right, time to rake the real money in.' She gives me a huge grin as she grabs her whip. 'I'll catch up with you tomorrow.'

At two in the morning, I know I need to get home and go to bed. Grabbing my bag, I hurry out of the back door, car keys in hand. Several other cars are parked up and a group of men hang around. I recognise them from earlier. They stand back and smoke as one steps away. I think I hear him calling a taxi.

I feel a swift kick to the back of my knee and I fall forwards onto the bonnet of my car.

'Hello, slag.' I recognise the tubby red-faced man. He was in there earlier. His beery breath hits my face as he yanks me round. 'The little girl serving at the bar, all flustered and butterfingers. You know, you're shit at your job and definitely don't have what it takes to dance on that stage but I tell you something you could be better at.' He reaches for my waistband and unzips my jeans. I glance back. The group of men are too far away. If I call them will they join in with him or help me? I can't speak. He grips my neck like I'm as light as a doll and begins to fumble with his jeans. 'You stand there all night, smiling from behind that bar, teasing me. You want it, don't you? How much? I'd say this is the going rate for a whore.' He pulls a twenty-pound note from his back pocket and throws it on the car bonnet.

'Get off me.' He's not listening. Once again, I'm back in my bedroom at the farm and I want to cry but I won't. I won't let this man read me. My throat hurts. I need to get him off me but he's so heavy. I had been trying to make eye contact with the customers and I had been awkwardly trying to smile and pout. That's what we're encouraged to do to earn our tips. Had everything been my fault? Is this what I'd asked for?

'You smell so good.' He tries to kiss me and as he slips his revolting cold tongue into my mouth I bite hard and he yells. I spit his blood onto his shoe. One of the men from across the way looks over and I hear shouting. They're coming for me. As he goes to grab me again, I kick him right in his groin and he falls to the ground. Adrenalin courses through my veins. I won't allow anyone else to treat me like Simon did.

'Stop, I didn't mean anything. I thought…'

'You thought what? That it would be okay to rape me.' His nose is bleeding. I manage to zip my jeans back up despite how my hands are shaking.

'Hey, I think you got him. Nice kick.' It's the woman in the tinted glasses. I don't answer. I can't. I stare at the man on the floor as I wipe the metallic taste of his blood from my tongue with my hand. His face is battered and bruised and there's a pool of blood under his nose. The woman also spits at the man I've just kicked. 'Piece of shit. I just caught what was happening, are you okay?'

Nodding, I fumble for my car keys in my bag. 'Yes. I just need to go home.'

'Shall I call the police?'

'No, no police.' If the police come, I may be linked back to when I stabbed Simon. I have to get away and quick, all while keeping a low profile. 'He tried to rape me and I hurt him; a lot. I guess we're even. Thank you, by the way.'

I get in my car and as I go to close the door, the woman grabs it. 'What's your name?'

'Please, let go of the door.' I'm shaking and I need to get away, now.

She holds both hands up. 'Sorry. Drive safely. I'm Regina, but if you see me again, you can call me Reggie.'

As I turn the ignition, that's when my whole body starts to uncontrollably tremble and tears spill down my cheeks. From now on I trust no one and my guard is up. I'm not good enough to be Britney's friend and men think I'm nothing more than a slab of meat. Everyone is out for something, you've just got to work out what it is. You don't even have to look too deeply. I do feel rotten for driving off so quickly without thanking the woman who helped me but I don't want her to see me like this.

I will only ever trust me from now on.

CHAPTER TWENTY-FIVE

Now

I jerk up as I hear a loud knocking on the door followed by the word police. Why am I asleep on the sofa? I gaze around. Maybe that's not a bad thing. With all that was going through my mind, it's good that I woke up where I went to sleep. There's another knock and the realisation hits me, the police are back. They've come for me. They know I was at the cottage on the night of Simon's murder. What do I do? My heart feels as though it's beating in my throat and I could be sick. Another knock; it's then I realise that it's not my door, it's the person below me. The relief is instant.

Scrunching my brow, I throw the tangled blanket onto the floor, releasing my wobbly limbs. My delicate head is another matter. I need some painkillers. Water, that's what I need. My throat is like sandpaper and it almost hurts when I swallow. Two drinks, that's all I had. I can't handle alcohol, which is why I should pack it up completely. Why was I so stupid last night especially when I need my wits about me? A memory flashes back to me and I shake my head. I remember barging into Dan Pritchard's apartment and wrenching the plugs out of his sockets to stop the music. We argued and I think Glen helped me into my apartment. Instantly, I reach for my underwear to make sure it's intact. No one touched me, that's good. I'm still wearing what I had on last night and I don't feel as though anything happened with Glen, I'd feel it if it had. I breathe a sigh of relief as I walk to the bathroom, desperate to pee.

Flinching, I catch sight of my reflection. That blood wasn't smeared over my face and neck before I went to bed. The bandage has come off my hand but I can see that the scratch has healed up quite well. The blood hasn't come from that. The white sink is sprayed with red spots and then I freeze, open-mouthed as I spot the bloodied knife in the bath. I have no idea how that got there.

My own door bangs and I hear those words I could do without. 'Police, open up.'

Heart banging, I feel bile rising at the back of my throat. They are coming for me. As I throw a towel on the knife, I run the tap, taking care of the blood specks and rubbing at my skin with my wet fingers. Quick wipe over with the black flannel under the sink and I'm as done as I can be. Then I run to the kitchen and glance along the worktops, in the sink and over the lounge area. Grabbing the blanket, I throw it in the washing machine.

'Police.' That banging again. It's not going away.

I want to scream and yell but more than ever, I need to keep my calm until I work out what has happened. Are the police here because of Simon? I shake my head. They wouldn't be knocking on everyone's door in this block if it was to do with Simon, so why are they here this time? I glance over my own body. I've changed my top since last night too, a half-hearted attempt to put my pyjama top on. I can't remember doing that. I wonder why I changed especially as I don't think I was capable of getting out of my clothes. I scoop my hair into a bobble, take a deep breath and hope with all I've got that the police don't go into my bathroom.

The knife, I should have moved it, not just covered it up. Stupid, stupid, stupid.

How did it get there? Who put it there?

The door is hammering like mad now. 'Police, open up.' My door is locked. No one else could have got in and I've never given anyone else a spare key. The silent phone call and the note in my letter box flash through my thoughts. This has to be down to Dan. Maybe something happened at his party and one of the guests got hurt.

I rub my eyes as if I've just been woken and open the door. 'Sorry.' I yawn. 'I was asleep.'

It's DS Brindle and DC Collins again. I've changed my mind, this has to be about Simon. I'm going to be taken away and there's nothing I can do about it. I've failed to unlock any more memories so I'm no help to anyone, least of all myself. 'Miss Baxter, sorry to call again so soon. May we come in?' DS Brindle asks, the smell of smoke clinging to her, just like the other day. My head is light and I'm so, so thirsty. I must smell of sweat and wine and who knows what? Blood! That gave me the short, sharp, shock that I needed.

'Of course, come through. What's happened?' I glance onto the landing and there are crime scene investigators entering Dan Pritchard's apartment. They are dressed like giant marshmallows, wearing masks and carrying toolkits. Then, I almost freeze as I see an investigator holding a clear evidence bag, in it is one of those blue snowflake baubles. My heart feels as though it's going to burst through my ribcage. I hear knocking at other doors and the same words repeated. 'Police, open up.'

Why are they carrying one of my mother's baubles out of Dan's apartment? I lead the detectives through.

'May we sit?' DS Brindle points to the sofa.

'What's this about? Is it about my uncle again?'

'No, well, we're not sure at this stage. An incident has occurred and we need to ask you a few questions.'

'What type of incident?'

DS Brindle clears her throat and DC Collins flicks through the pages of his notebook with his sausage fingers before finding a clean one. 'I'm sorry to tell you, but your neighbour, Dan

Pritchard, was found dead this morning. We believe he's been murdered so we're asking everyone if they saw or heard anything last night. We also have reason to believe that the murder of your uncle and the murder of Mr Pritchard are connected.'

'Murdered. That's awful!' I'm genuinely shocked. I know why they've been connected though; it has to be those baubles.

I shake my head and my eyes begin to water. Bringing my hand to my mouth, I don't know what to say next. I can't remember anything after falling asleep on my settee last night. I don't think I woke up… but how did blood get in my sink and there's still a knife in the bath. I place one hand on the other, hiding the darkness under one of my nails. It has to be a bit of dried blood. 'I can't recall anything except he was having a party when I got back home. There were a lot of people there.' Throw in some suspects, lots of them. I can't become a suspect. It had to be someone at the party. They had a row with Dan and jemmied my lock, using my bathroom to clean themselves up. One of them must have known Simon too. Simon was as unsavoury a character as Dan was. Maybe they knew each other from the pub. Simon and Dan both liked a drink. If I say anything about last night, they'll think it was me. It wasn't me. All I need to do is keep my mouth shut then when they've gone, I'll work out what's happened. I can tell Brindle suspects me and I can only guess that she doesn't have enough evidence to take me to the station. *Play it as cool as you can, Marissa.*

'What time did you notice this party?'

I shrug. 'I don't actually remember. It was after ten. I was really tired and went straight to bed.' It is now that I hope they don't want to look in my bedroom and see that my bed is still made. When I answered the door, I said I'd just got up, or did I? Everything is swimming around in my head. Is the door properly closed to the bedroom and my office?

DC Collins makes a note of the time.

'Let's go back a bit. Talk me through your arrival home. Tell me everything you saw or heard.' DS Brindle coughs like she smokes eighty a day, a real rattling chesty cough.

I sit. 'I was with my friend, Glen, last night and he walked me home after dinner. As we approached the block, I could hear music so I knew there was a party going on. When I came up the stairs, there were people spilling out everywhere.' I stare at the coffee table. Should I mention going in and arguing with Dan? I know someone will say something. Too many people were at that party for that to go unnoticed.

'Miss Baxter. Go on.'

'Oh, sorry. I was just trying to think back. The music was really loud and I went into his apartment and asked him to turn it down a bit. I wasn't too happy as I was tired and wanted to sleep when I came home. He wasn't too happy with me asking him either. My friend, Glen, told me to leave it as Dan was drunk so I did, and then I left. I eventually managed to fall asleep even with the music on, but that's all I remember of last night.'

'Can you identify or describe anyone you saw at the party?'

I shake my head. 'I wish I could but there were so many people, the lights were low and I didn't know any of them.' I pause. 'Wait… one of them was Mr Pritchard's son. He has two but it was the boy with the curtained haircut, not the other one. He was there.'

'Such a shame. It was the same boy who found his father's body. He came back this morning with a bacon sandwich for his dad.' DS Brindle swallowed and glanced at DC Collins's notes.

'How awful for him.' I don't like his son but I know how it feels to see the corpse of a murdered parent and even given the boy's faults, I wouldn't wish that on anyone.

'Are you sure you can't describe anyone else? Male or female.'

'I really wish I could. I'd had a couple of drinks myself and I was so tired. There were mostly men at the party, I can recall that much, but I didn't take any notice of anyone in particular.'

'When you walked home, did you see anyone suspicious hanging around?'

I press my lips together and shake my head again. The only suspicious person in all this is me.

'Okay, did you hear anything? Maybe you heard someone shouting or arguing?'

'As I said, I fell asleep and that was it. Next thing I know, you knocked on my door just now.'

DS Brindle edges forward on the sofa, then stands. 'If you remember anything, however seemingly insignificant, please call me straight away. You already have my card.'

DC Collins glances at me. 'May I use your toilet while I'm here?'

I feel as though my throat is closing up. If he moves that towel, he will see the knife. If he sees that and looks further under the sink unit, he'll find the flannel that I wiped the blood from my face with. Saying no to the police isn't an option, it will instantly make me look suspicious. There's a fleck of blood on the edge of my pyjama top, so I hug a cushion to cover it up. My hands are clammy and the nausea has returned. Parched, I can't swallow. In a croaky voice, I reply with a smile. 'Of course. It's the first door on the right.' I point towards the hallway. He leaves the lounge and pulls the door closed behind him.

Brindle smiles at me. I smile back. 'Do you want coffee?'

'I best not. So many houses to get through today.'

What do I say? What do I do? Any minute now DC Collins might come out and haul me into the back of a police car.

'What did you say your friend's name was? Maybe he saw something when he walked you home or when he left?'

'Glen. I don't know his surname but he runs the residents' association of which I'm a member.' I remember all the sixes. 'He lives at number sixty-six. It's the block closest to the entrance of the street.' The neighbour's dogs begin to bark so I know the police have just knocked there.

'That's great.'

Collins is taking his time but I hear the toilet flush followed by the tap running.

'Do you think I'm in danger, living here, after what happened to Dan?' It would seem odd if I didn't ask that question.

'We hope not but you can't be too safe. Don't answer the door or buzz anyone into the block that you're not expecting. There is evidence to suggest it's a more personal attack though so please don't over worry about your safety. Just be vigilant. We will be checking on the area and working his apartment for a while so at least there will be a presence around here. If you feel worried in any way, call us, and if it's an emergency, don't hesitate to call nine-nine-nine.'

I nod and smile a little as DC Collins walks back in from the bathroom with a stern look on his round face. 'We have a problem.'

CHAPTER TWENTY-SIX

Heat rises up my neck and I'm prickling. I want to scratch until I bleed.

'You ran out of toilet roll.'

My heart bangs and I'm sure they can hear it but DS Brindle gives a little laugh. 'Right, on to the next.'

DC Collins places the toilet roll tube on the worktop next to the apple crumble and I'm trying with all I've got to control the urge to tremble like a dog on Bonfire Night.

They leave as quickly as they came and before long, I hear them heading out towards the stairs. I dash to the bathroom and kneel over the toilet bowl, emptying my stomach. Leaning back against the wall trying to cool down, I close my eyes as sweat drips down my forehead. I feel as though I'm spinning. Simon and Dan are dead. My memory is blank on the nights both of them were murdered and how did that bauble get into Dan's apartment? No more drinking. Not one drink, ever again. I need to clear my head if I'm to work out what's going on around here.

My phone buzzes with an email. It's Forge.

> I've sent some more files over to you. Let me know when you've been through them all. The individual client contact details are on the header sheets. I'll call you in a day or two, see how you're getting on with them. As always, everyone wants an answer now so I trust you'll get on with them. Forge.

He doesn't mention me running off looking ill the last time we met. In fact, his email is straight to business. I drop the loo seat down and flush before using the sink to half pull my body up. The towel is still in the bath where I left it, no sign of blood seeping through at all. I wonder if he's a little fed up that I didn't message or call him yesterday but why should I? I don't need to be made to feel uncomfortable. Ben isn't important right now. Before I message him back, I really need to know what Justine has to say about him. I'm determined to press her a little harder on why she said I should be careful and why she's not telling me the whole story.

Lifting the towel, I stare at the knife. It's definitely the one I keep behind the picture. It has to go. I grab some bleach and begin spraying it on every surface and the tiled floor, then I leave it for a few minutes so that it kills everything. Someone is setting me up, that's the only explanation.

I press Glen's number and call him but he doesn't answer. The police must be with him now. I wonder if he'll go into detail of the argument I had with Dan or if he'll just skirt over it, like I did. That tremor in my hands has come back. I hurry to the kitchen sink and pour a large glass of water then guzzle the whole lot down trying to get the sour taste in my mouth to go away.

Staring out of the window, I watch the activity below. A forensics van and three police cars. Another officer talks on the phone and some of the neighbours from the houses huddle around the edge of the car park, watching and trying to get the attention of the police. The sound of barking dogs and crying babies ring in my ears. I want everyone to shut up and I want my quiet life back as it was before Dan moved in.

My life as I know it is over. Maybe I should definitely move if I manage to survive this without being convicted of two murders that I didn't commit. I shake my head. Who's going to want to buy an apartment across from where a murder has recently taken place? I know I wouldn't. A message pings from Glen.

Police here. I'll call you later.

I run to my bedroom and climb into bed, dragging my quilt over my head, hoping all this will go away. There's talking on the landing. I hold my breath and hear the words, 'stabbed in the chest.'

I call Justine but her phone rings out. It's not like her to ignore a call so I leave a message. 'Hi, call me back when you can. I really need to talk to you.'

There's a stirring within me. I don't know if it's nausea, hunger or adrenalin, but it's grey – that much I can tell. It's a swirling cloud that's gathering momentum and I fear where it's going to take me next. I know there's a storm coming. Question is, how long have I got. Will the police take me first or will the person who killed Simon and Dan come for me? I pine for Reggie, she wouldn't have ignored my desperate call.

CHAPTER TWENTY-SEVEN

Ten years ago

I glance at the window of the third recruitment agency that day. I'm already registered with them but haven't had a single sniff of a job. Being a bar person hasn't really helped me and neither have my top A levels results in accountancy, business, IT and maths. Kicking a can, I begin to walk along the streets of Birmingham, a takeaway sandwich in one hand and my satchel full of CVs in the other. I don't want to go back to my room in Edgbaston and stare at the walls all day. Pretty soon, I'll even get thrown out from there if I don't get another job. Everything is conspiring against me. I should have known I wouldn't pass the one-month test at House of Class and since the attack, I couldn't face going back to finish the week off.

As I go to step onto the road, I'm yanked back just as a tram trundles past. The tall buildings above send me slightly giddy as I regain my composure.

'That was close. You should watch where you're going.' Glancing back, I scrunch my brow as I try to recall where I've seen this woman before. House of Class.

'Tinted glasses.' That's all I can think of to say. I know she told me her name as I drove off but I can't remember it.

'I barely recognised you like this. Nice business suit. You look very professional.' She stands back and looks me up and down.

'The bar career didn't work out so I'm pursuing other options.'

She put her hands in her pockets and shrugged. 'Hey, I know I scared you that night, around the back of the club—'

I shook my head and smiled. 'It wasn't you. It was the man who attacked me. I'm sorry I just drove off without thanking you. I think I was in shock. When I got home I realised how rude I must have seemed.'

She shrugged. 'I tell you something, you fought your corner well. You should forget bar work and take up street fighting.'

I let out a small laugh. 'Anyway, thank you for saving me from stepping into a tram. I suppose you're busy and I have a job to search for.'

She looked at her watch. I could see the shiny green watch with the Rolex branding, around her wrist. Whatever she did, I wanted to do the same. Maybe not the wealth, but the freedom to not have to worry like I am now. I want enough money to live on. To buy my own place, to buy a new car.

'It's lunchtime, can I buy you a coffee?'

People nudge past me as they cross, one swearing under their breath as their shoulder hits mine. 'Erm, I don't know.' Sometimes people can seem all nice too and when they get you alone, that's when they pounce. People always thought Simon was nice. Good old Simon and Caroline – taking on her murdered sister's poor little kid.

'It's just coffee.' She paused. 'Well, it isn't but it's not what you think. I'm not a sleaze and I'm definitely not trying it on with you, I promise. You're definitely not my type.' She lets out a little laugh and runs her fingers through her short hair. 'When you saw me at the club, I was entertaining clients. It was their choice of venue. I don't normally hang around dance bars. I personally hate them.'

She seems pleasant and friendly. Maybe I should let my guard down a little and one coffee can't hurt.

She points to a coffee shop across the road, a little independent with naked bulb lights and wooden benches. 'They do an amazing mocha there. My shout.'

In the cold light of day, I can see that she has a slight reddish tinge to her blonde hair and her eyes are a deep brown. She has a sense of humour from the look of her Road Runner tie. She's definitely a larger than life character. 'Okay.' We hurry across the road with a crowd of people. A part of me is dazzled by the big city with its museums and theatres, but another part of me hates the noise; the constant hum of chatter and traffic.

Reggie pushes the door open and a little bell rings above the light jazz music. There is one table left by a large shelf full of local history books that are all for sale. I spot one called *Birmingham Murder and Crime* and I shiver slightly as I think of what I did to Simon when I left.

'Do you want to grab that seat before it goes?' she says.

I nod as she joins the queue.

'What would you like?'

'As you recommend the mocha, I'll have one of those, thank you.'

She is soon distracted by the barista. I watch her like a hawk. She might spike my drink. I still don't know why she wants to buy me a drink. I trust people even less since my attack.

The barista places the drinks on the tray. Reggie thanks the woman and turns around without hesitating. She had no time in which to drug me, maybe I can relax a little now. Placing the tray on the table, she hands me the frothiest drink ever. I take a sip and enjoy the creamy chocolate and coffee flavours. 'You're right, this is lovely.'

'Don't you just love the city?'

I shrug. 'I'm not sure that I do. It stinks of pollution, there's rubbish everywhere and there are far too many people all ready to attack you when they get the chance.' This is me trying to push her away. I still don't know what she wants or why I'm here. I'm grateful that she came to help me the other night outside the club, but that's it.

She leans back and sips her drink. 'You have a dark view of the human race but I totally get what you say after what happened the other night.'

'I suppose that comes from my experience of life.' I can't believe how easy she is to talk to.

She pauses and looks into my eyes as if weighing me up. 'Look, I don't even know your name.' She holds out a hand to shake mine. 'Let's start again. I'm Reggie Broughton.'

I now remember her shouting out her name as I drove off that night. 'You don't look like a Reggie.'

'I guess I don't. Regina was my grandmother's name. I got picked on at school for my name but, hey, I grew up and I showed all those little bullies what I was made of.'

I'm fascinated by her. 'Did you get revenge?'

'No, I became successful. Those losers hate to see that you're happy and living your best life. You say your cynicism comes from your life experiences?'

'I'm not a cynic, I'm a realist. I prefer the truth over something that makes me happy. I suppose I'm a bit of a depressive realist.'

She shakes her head and sips her drink. 'How old are you?'

'Eighteen.'

'Wow.'

I'm confused. Does she mean wow, I think you're an idiot, or wow, she's interested in me as a person? I read the news. I think about what's going on in the world and I realise it's the first time I've actually had this kind of conversation with a real person and not just in my head.

'Okay, so you know my name. What's yours?'

'Marissa. Marissa Baxter.'

'So what are you looking for in life, Marissa?'

I shrug. 'I know I've had enough of full-time study for now, especially after doing my A levels. I want to get a job and work my way up. Maybe even continue studying through work. I just need the job first.'

'Today might just be your lucky day.' Reggie bites her bottom lip and smiles.

I want to smile back but I can't help thinking she's hooking me in for a reason and there will be a catch. No one offers just anyone a job on a plate. 'Really?' My smile is gone and I place my drink on the table. I feel as though I should leave before something gets said that ruins the whole day for me.

'Why do you look worried?'

'I'm nervous about what you might say or ask.'

'Why?'

'People always let me down and they're never as they seem.'

'Which is why you have no faith in them at all.' Her tone is serious but she still has a comforting smile on her face, which puts me at ease a little. 'Let me change that.'

I want her to hurry up and spill out what she has to say but she's taking her time. She controls this time well. I need to learn a lesson from her. 'I own several businesses. I buy them when they're down and I build them up. That's what I was doing at the club when I saw you, buying a business. Sometimes these things happen in the unlikeliest of places. I don't like to brag but I will because it's the truth. Some people just seem to have the Midas touch and I'm one of them. Do you know what that means?'

'Of course I do. I've read the story. Everything Midas touched turned to gold.'

'Great. I suppose I've been a combination of lucky and hard working. Don't underestimate the latter. You can be what you want if you work hard. One of my businesses is an insurance company. It's my newest acquisition.'

'Not protection rackets and extortion?'

She sniggered. 'You make me laugh… in a nice way. I'm not mocking you. To answer your question, no, life and mortgage insurance.'

'Sorry. I should learn not to say everything that comes into my head.'

'I love your honesty. I could see on the first night I saw you that you weren't cut out to work a bar.' She paused and sat a little forward as she talked, while waving her hands about. Her enthusiasm spilling over. 'So, I have this company and I need someone to train as a financial adviser. I'd normally only recruit someone with a couple of years' experience, even though the role involves training, but something tells me you will grasp the job quickly and with ease. I'm going to put my neck out here. I don't know you. I only have your word when it comes to your qualifications but something tells me you won't let me down. I'd like you to consider taking the role on a one-month trial and if it doesn't work out, we can simply part ways. If you remain in the job, it will then involve a full study package where you would study a Diploma in Financial Advice in the evenings. I was about to advertise this role today but I'm willing to give you a break because I can see you need one. I've been very fortunate in life and I want to pay that good fortune forward.'

I go to open my mouth but I can't speak. For once in my life, someone is giving me a real opportunity and I know I need to grasp it. Before I get too excited, I have to make sure it's real. My voice croaks as I speak. 'Will I get a contract?'

'Yes, first for the month, then permanent after that. I was lucky, my father has built up a lot of businesses and capital and he helped me to get started. Not just with money but with knowledge. I feel as though I should give others a chance to succeed, which is where you come into it.'

Allowing myself to be happy, I bite my lip and smile. 'Yes, I'd love the job. You won't want to get rid of me. I'm hard working, meticulous, a stickler for detail and make good conversation about how the world is going to end.'

She looks at her watch. 'However much I'd love to stay and talk all day I have to get back to the office as I have a meeting with a client.' She pulls an embossed card from her inside pocket that says Regina Broughton on the front with her email address and phone number underneath. There is no business name on it but she did say she owns a few businesses. After putting her yellow tinted glasses on, she grabs a napkin and begins drawing lines and names on it. It's a map. 'Right.' She pushes it closer to me. 'We're here. Follow my arrows to this road and keep going until you see the six-storey building on your right. Tell the security staff who you are and that you have a meeting with Reggie of RB Financial Services Limited at ten. Be on time.' She stands and begins to brush down her suit. 'Right, see you tomorrow. Ten in the morning.'

Before I can say, I'll be there, the little bell on the door rings as she leaves. She glances back and waves through the window before disappearing. I do a silly little chair dance and the barista gives me a funny look. I don't care what she thinks. I don't care what anyone thinks. I've got a job with prospects and I'm so happy I want to tell the world.

I pause for a moment. There are so many things I didn't ask that I should have. I don't even know how much I'll be paid or what the hours will be. I shrug as I finish my mocha. I don't care. It will be at least minimum wage. That will pay for my room. I feel as though I've just won the lottery and my life is just about to begin after a false start. I have the world at my feet.

CHAPTER TWENTY-EIGHT

Now

Reggie isn't here, Marissa. You need to think for yourself now. The loss I feel when it comes to her is as raw as ever. For so long, I've managed to bury my sadness over how it ended but an image of her forms in my mind. Her signature tinted glasses, her shiny watch and her tailored suits. Those funny ties and cravats she used to wear. She made me what I am today – well, as far as my career is concerned. We could talk freely for hours. I thought Glen and I could be friends, like Reggie and I were. I swallow. That term 'friends' is bittersweet and for the first time in ages I feel this deep sense of sadness, especially as he too isn't picking up his phone and Justine is ignoring me. All my friends are abandoning me in my hour of need. I need to know what the police said to Glen. He didn't call me back like he said he would. No one is calling me back. I check my phone again to see if Justine has messaged and she hasn't.

I message Glen. The not knowing is killing me.

Glen, please call me. You have to call me. X

Against my better judgement, I pop a kiss at the end of my message. That's what friends do so I should do it. He needs to know that we are friends and that I'm desperate to hear from him. I imagine him sitting in his flat either worrying that he's betrayed me after speaking to the police or wracked with guilt that he's lied for me by not mentioning my outburst at Dan's party. I hear a bang and I flinch thinking the police are coming back for me, but it's nothing, just another slamming door in the building.

Pacing around my apartment, I'm fully aware of the pile of work that's building up. Ben will be on my back soon if I don't get it sorted. Maybe I should get dressed, it might make me feel more human. I thought a shower might help but my head is still fuzzy. Why can't I remember anything that will help me?

Focus, Marissa.

Closing my eyes, I try to retrace my steps the night before. My head had been swimming after the wine and I remember the acid in my throat. Glen placed a blanket over me and I heard the door bang when he left. The party was still going on. After that, I recall waking up to the sound of people doing karaoke… maybe. That's it. I do remember something after Glen covered me up and left. Karaoke. What happened after? Did I see or hear anyone else turn up? An image of me staggering through my hallway flashes back. I did sleepwalk but the rest is blurred.

Running to the door, I hold my breath as I glance through the spyhole. A police officer stands guard and a crime scene investigator comes out with a box of what looks to be more exhibits. Trying to see what's in the box is impossible. Before I know it they've passed and all I saw was the shine of the communal light on plastic.

Keep calm. Get dressed and do your work. It's time to act normal and see what I can find out. The race against time is on. Either I get to the truth or the police blame me for these murders. There's nothing more I can do right now and any suspicious behaviour on my part could have me arrested, after all, there was a knife in my bathtub… my knife. I didn't do it though. Someone is framing me and I have to find out who. The silent caller… what do they want? I can't go to prison and be branded a killer. My head is swimming again. What I think I need is to stay away from people until I find out who's messing with my head. Getting to know Glen was a mistake. I should never have attended that neighbourhood meeting, I should have stayed out of Dan's way and simply bought some earplugs, then maybe none of this would have happened. I sigh. Dan hated me from the start. Staying away would have done me no good whatsoever. *Think; think.*

Hurrying to the bedroom, I pick up my jeans and begin to pull them up one leg, then I stop. Sweat drips down my forehead but I'm cold. I haven't put the heating on this morning and there's a frost outside. I snatch open my wardrobe and pull out several jumpers until I settle on a fine knit white jumper. I throw the rest of my clothes that need rehanging into a corner for now, amongst the newly found chaos that is my life. After I've dressed, I will go to the kitchen, make a black coffee, then I'll have a bowl of porridge while I think about my work. I will start the washing machine, cleaning my blanket, top, the towel and the flannel, before working out what to do with the knife. It has to go today. The police cannot come back and find that bloody knife in my apartment.

I slip the jumper over my head and that's me dressed.

Shuffling sounds come from outside. A woman is talking to the police. I peer through the spyhole but I can't make out who she is. Her hood is up and her coat is so big it makes her almost look misshapen. 'I need to get in there, my son needs his phone.'

The curtain-haired boy joins the woman. She must be his mother.

The police officer shakes his head. I can see him clearly enough. 'Sorry, ma'am, but you can't go in there. It's a crime scene. You'll need to contact the station.'

'Damn it.' The woman's hands come down, slapping her waist in frustration. 'Come on, son.' Her voice is muffled, like she's talking through a scarf but it's familiar. I can't think back to where I've heard that voice before.

I catch sight of the boy and his eyes look puffy. It must have been a shock for him. There's a lump in my throat. This boy no longer has a father and I know exactly how that feels. At least he actually met his.

Glancing in the mirror, I now see calm, collected Marissa; albeit with a sullen undertone. I will stay this way until Glen messages me back or I can talk to Justine. The police haven't come back so they can't have garnered that much from Glen.

My phone rings and I run back to the bedroom. Glen's name flashes up. I swallow my sob away wondering if I'm ready to hear about his conversation with the police and then I wonder if I should even trust Glen. I keep coming back to the fact that I barely know him… no… he's been nothing but kind to me. I should open my heart a little, just like I did with Reggie. I find myself choking on a sob.

CHAPTER TWENTY-NINE

Seven years ago

Reggie swans in flashing a wide smile towards Bethany and Christine, the former a qualified and experienced financial adviser and the latter, a reception and administrative whizz. Often we all go to lunch together but Bethany and Christine have been friends for longer so I'm left out sometimes, even though I've worked here for three years now. Reggie sees this and she works hard to make sure she includes me, like a regular mother hen, and that warms my heart.

The two women are so colourful with their bright printed tops and summer dresses. Bethany literally walks past looking like and smelling of roses. In fact, she's beautiful and stands out far more than I ever would. My uniform has developed into grey trousers and white shirts. I also wear only the smallest of chunky heels and a plain unisex watch. My hair is always tied back and my make-up just follows the natural look.

Reggie breaks my thoughts. 'Baxter, lunch, fifteen minutes. There's some files I want to discuss with you.' She's taken to calling me Baxter all the time and I don't mind. It's funny really.

I finish typing the email I was working on and hit send. 'Be with you in five.'

A few minutes later, I've grabbed my phone and I'm following her past my favourite feature in Birmingham centre. The Floozie in the Jacuzzi. The statue lies in her bath looking as free and bubbly as ever. A couple of children sit on the wall while their father tells them off for fighting over a purple pig toy. They're quite cute and funny. Reggie walks really fast, like she's on a mission. 'Wait up.' I know my heels aren't high but my legs are shorter than hers. I'm almost running to keep up.

'Sorry, Baxter.'

'That's okay, Reg.' She sniggers at my shortening of her name. I don't call her this when we're in the office. 'So is this a work meeting?'

She shrugs. 'Partly. I need someone to discuss the meaning of life with and however much I like the other two, I can't imagine that the convo will be scintillating.'

I laugh. Our discussions were something I looked forward to, a safe space to agree and disagree, but the meaning of life? That was a new one. We'd already exhausted communism and fascism. Nature versus nurture. Who profits from war? The climate crisis – no topic was off-limits. Today, she seemed different like she was deeply absorbed in her thoughts. She'd looked a little distracted lately. Some days she'd even ignored my calls. Other days, like today, her eyes were shiny. I wondered if she was on drugs but then I pushed that thought away. Her stance on drugs was always no, not ever. She felt that life was a drug to be embraced. 'Where are we going?'

'To try something new.'

I scrunch my brow. She never ceased to amaze me with her spontaneity and surprises. A few months ago, between Christmas and New Year, there had been a hunting demonstration where pro and against people screamed at each other over fox hunting. 'Which side are you on, Baxter?'

'Do I really need to say? I think you know.'

'Okay, get on that wall and shout? Allow yourself to feel something. You'll love it.'

'What?' I'd been stunned. I'd never attended this kind of thing in my life. The moment I stood on the wall and began to chant, I felt empowered. I was chanting not only against the cruelty but against what Simon believed and that made me high. Simon loathed foxes. 'Blood on your hands, blood on your hands.' A torrent of abuse came back from the other side. Reggie laughed as she chanted, her hair wet from drizzle and a stare that seemed as wide as a saucer.

'Go louder, Baxter. I bet you've never felt so alive.' I smiled as I put that memory to bed. Just another one of Reggie's surprises. She was right though. I'd felt the adrenalin coursing through my veins. I don't know what she believes to this day, as when we speak on this topic she tends to play devil's advocate a lot of the time. She does this a lot too. I know she's trying to make me a better and more thoughtful speaker and thinker.

Another time she grabbed a holy book from a preacher, not even knowing which holy book it was and she shouted, 'Praise the Lord,' over and over again. Even the preacher had looked confused, but Reggie had just thrived on the exhilaration after.

'Here it is. Your surprise.' Reggie stopped outside the door. 'In this pop-up restaurant, today's delight is stir-fried crickets.'

I let out a puff of breath and shook my head. 'Seriously? I don't think I can do this.'

'You have to try. It's what will save the world. I mean all that steak we're eating is killing the environment. Insects, they're aplenty. Come on, Baxter, live a little.'

I love her so much. She's become my best friend, my confidante and, I'd go as far as saying, she protects and looks out for me, like my mother would have. She hugged me and shrieked with joy and pride when I fully qualified, then we went out for beers. Well, she had the beers, I had my trusty coffees as I'm not a good drinker and letting my guard down while out scares me. 'Okay.'

She can see that I'm wary. I guess I'm scared I'll throw up when I'm chewing a cricket between my teeth. My cheeks burn with the thought of how embarrassing that would be.

Reggie pushes the door open, then a young woman greets us and shows us to the table Reggie has booked. She orders for both of us. 'Two of the stir-fry cricket dishes, please.' The orange plastic benches lack comfort. 'I wouldn't normally take away your freedom of choice like that, Baxter, but this is a good dish for a newbie. Sit.'

It might sound like she's commanding but she's not. She's fun to be around and I don't know what I'd do without her in my life. 'So, why the meaning of life?'

She sighs. 'Why not? I was thinking about it all night, which is why I barely slept. The thought of universe upon universe, the ever expansion and what's beyond. I watched this space documentary and it blew my mind. I mean what the hell are we? Without consciousness we wouldn't care. We are like this cruel trick of nature. We get to think about our death and we get to dwell on the past. Do you think a rabbit does that?'

'I've seen a lot of rabbits growing up on the farm and I'm certain they don't contemplate their past or their future. Life is about eating and breeding, then they mostly get eaten by something or end up as roadkill.'

'Why? Why don't they think and why do we? I can't fathom it. Mind blown.' She pauses. 'It got me thinking.'

'About...'

'The lack of achievement in my life. I don't have a wife or a husband – either would be fine, you know me. A person is a person and we are free to love and connect with anyone we choose. I don't have kids and I prefer to talk bollocks with you than trying to get these things. Besides, you're the daughter I never had.' She looks at me in a serious way.

'And you know I love you, Reggie. You're always there for me and you've helped me so much.'

'We've helped each other. Besides, I don't want kids. The last thing I'd do is bring another human into this world knowing how cruel it can be.'

She sniggers. 'Yes, little snot and puke machines. Yuck.' She jokingly pulls a face that makes her look like she's sucking on

Carla Kovach

a lemon. The way she speaks, I'd never have guessed she was approaching her mid-forties. Her occasional lack of maturity sometimes makes me feel like I'm older than her.

The server places the dishes on the table. Little bits of insect fried in soy sauce with vegetables and beansprouts are neatly arranged on the plate. I push the food around with my cutlery.

'Woohoo, tuck in.' Reggie grabs her fork, stabs a fried cricket and pops it into her mouth. 'Delicious. Go on then, Baxter. Your turn. We can carry on talking about my existential crises later. For now, we eat.'

I stick my fork into a carrot and chew. 'Mmm, lovely.'

'Oh, come on. We all know what carrots taste like.'

This time I get a cricket on the end of my fork. My mouth waters with nausea as I place it to my lips, first taking in the smell but all I get is soy sauce. I cautiously bite as if it may explode in my mouth, my frown telling Reggie that I'm uncomfortable.

'Well?'

I chew. It's not bad. 'I judged it harshly without giving it a chance. It's a bit nutty.'

'In a good way.'

I nod. 'Actually, yes.' My grimace turns to a smile. I feel like I've conquered something massive. That's what Reggie does for me, she shows me that I can take on the world and I hope she'll always be in my life. I'd go as far as saying my life would crumble if she was taken from me. I couldn't bear to lose her as well as my mother.

Soon we have finished our meal and we head back to the office. Something stops me, a reflection in a window. The woman turns and glances across the road as she stops to cross.

I never thought I'd see her again. When I needed her more than anything, she'd abandoned me. I wonder if she'll recognise me. She frowns as she stares, then her gaze meets mine and I can't stop staring at her.

CHAPTER THIRTY

Now

I'm daydreaming when my phone rings. It bounces across the table, threatening to fall. I snatch it up. 'Glen, I'm so glad you called.'

There is a pause. As he goes to speak, the signal cracks and all I hear is the odd half a word. I run to the kitchen window where it's often at its best. 'Are you still there?'

'Yes, sorry about that. I'm on a building site and the signal is dire. I would have called earlier but the police already made me late for work so I needed to get a move on. Are you okay?'

'I just wondered how it went with them.'

He paused. 'You're wondering if I said anything about the argument you had with Dan.'

He seemed to be able to read my thoughts. 'Sorry to ask. It's just I told the police about the party and that I asked him to turn the music down. I didn't tell them how angry I was and that I literally lost my temper.'

'It's okay, I kept it brief and basically said what you did. There was nothing to tell anyway. It's not like you murdered him and the less time they waste talking to you, the more time they'll spend catching the killer.'

My legs weaken and I steady myself against the worktop. He hadn't said anything. My friendship with Glen hasn't been compromised at all; at least I don't feel like it has. Maybe now that

Dan has gone too, there won't be any more horrible notes and I won't be scared to come and go. Not that I wished him dead, but my life will be easier. I think of the knife and feel dampness spreading across my palms. I still don't know what happened or how it got there. It can't have been my doing. I was out of my head and could barely move once I'd lain down on the settee. 'Thank you.' I pause, wondering what to say next. I need to know more but I don't know how I should phrase my next question so I blurt it out, 'Glen, how did I seem last night? I can't remember much as I'm obviously a total lightweight when it comes to drinking. The wine obviously floored me.'

'Oh, you seemed exhausted, especially after the confrontation with Dan. I suppose you were a bit wobbly. I offered you a coffee but you just flumped out on the settee and kept dozing. I threw a blanket over you and left.'

'I'm really sorry you had to see me like that.'

'What are friends for? It was nothing, honest.' He shouted something about cabling to someone who had just entered the room he was working in. 'Sorry about that. I suppose now that your nuisance neighbour is sorted we won't be seeing each other as much and I must say, I'll miss your company.'

I run my tongue over my cracked dried lips. 'Nonsense. We're friends now. You've seen me drunk.' Maybe it was a mistake to say that. I should tell him to get as far away as possible from me and all my problems. Whoever killed Simon and Dan might target him next. I can't push him aside though. It takes me ages to make friends and once I do, I don't want to lose them. I know that Glen or Justine will never replace Reggie but I have to find a way of moving on, otherwise I'll go crazy. I let out a small laugh. 'And not many people have seen me drunk so we really are friends.'

'Good to hear. Besides, there are plenty of problems to tackle on the estate but hopefully those ones won't be people related and will be more to do with the management company and what they're doing for our money. We will stand up for our rights and demand transparency. Together, as friends, we'll go to battle.'

I laugh remembering how empowered Reggie made me feel. Maybe I do need a cause in my life, something to start believing in; take my mind off everything. 'Don't expect me to knock on doors getting people to sign petitions. I've got better things to do with my time.'

'Should have known. Fix your own problem, then abandon the cause. It's all about you, Marissa.' He laughs so I can tell he's joking.

My heart rate has calmed now. Order has been restored. There will be no more horrible notes, no more silent phone calls and once that knife is disposed of, I'm going to move on from all this. There's the police but I'm hoping that I'll find something out that will take the heat off me. Everything will come back to me at some point, I know it will. Maybe I need a night out. When Justine eventually calls me back, we can talk about whatever is on her mind, she'll clear up my concerns about her and Ben, and we'll finish the conversation off with plans for a big night out. Who am I kidding? This is nowhere near over.

'Oh, I have a call coming through which I have to take. I'll message you later.' Glen hangs up on me and I finally let my tense shoulders relax. I haven't been incriminated but maybe it is only a matter of time before Dan's son or some of the other partygoers tell the police what happened between me and Dan. The police will be back, I know they will; but I know they have nothing on me because I didn't do anything. I think about the knife. I know what happened, it's the only explanation. I sleepwalked. I went into Dan's open apartment, took the knife and threw it in my bath. That's what happened. No one jemmied the lock, no one came into my apartment and I know I should give the knife to the police… but it's my knife. My mind's all over the place. Is this the end of it or just the start? Maybe I have all that wrong and someone's trying to set me up. I'm so confused.

I glance through the spyhole again wondering if I left any DNA behind. But I was in his apartment that night anyway; that will be my explanation. If they find my hair, a fingerprint or a nail, I can cover it. But first things first, I have to smuggle the knife past the police officer who has been lumbered with sentry duty. Gulping, I know I have a lot of nerve but this will take some, and more.

After bleaching the knife and cleaning it down for prints, with gloved hands, I wrap it in a tea towel and pop it into the bottom of my satchel before grabbing my coat. It's now or never. When the police return, at least the knife will be gone. I just have to get past the police officer stood outside of my door first.

CHAPTER THIRTY-ONE

A blast of arctic air rattles the window and sends a chill around my ears. The police officer who guards Dan's door seems unaffected.

'Sorry about the window. It was getting hot out here.' He smiles.

'It does after a while. People keep leaving the heaters on.' Glancing down, I see the heater is turned up to full. I feel a warmth that is quickly turning into a burn on my cheeks. Regardless of the cold landing, my body is betraying me. Just knowing there is a knife in my bag is too much. I need to get out.

He leans down as if he's read my mind and he turns the heater off. 'I'll shut the window now. Should have done that earlier. Are you okay?'

I realise I'm flushing and staring at him. 'Yes.'

'I suppose it's the shock.'

'Yes. Makes a person scared to be in their own home when something like this happens. I'm in the residents' association. We'll send something around to make people think more about security.' Glen will be proud that I'm immersing myself into helping the estate. It's the least I can commit to doing.

'I'm sure everyone will appreciate that. It's good that your estate has someone like you, who cares. Gosh, is it that time already?' He pulls a sandwich from his pocket and begins to unwrap the cling film.

A waft of tuna hits my nostrils and I feel a little dizzy with nerves. I need to leave before I pass out. 'Well, I best get on. Work to do. If you're still here later, I'll do you a nice hot drink.' I'm being a little over the top now. This knife has to go and I need to work out who murdered Dan and Simon before it's pinned on me. There's a connection: the bauble. I had one in my hand on the night of Simon's murder and I saw the police taking one out of Dan's apartment in an evidence bag. The police know that there is a connection between the victims and I can only guess that there was another bauble at Simon's when they examined the scene. A little flush of nerves makes me weak at the knees. The only connection between the two of them is still me.

'Might take you up on that. A hot drink is always welcome.' He smiles as I leave. When I reach the bottom of the stairs, I see that I have post. I unlock my box and on the top of the thin pile I see another note written in red pen. This must have been posted after the postie had been otherwise the note would be underneath. My heart rate thrums and the sound of my racing pulse fills my ears. I'm hot and I can't breathe. I grab the note and push the main door open where I run straight to my car.

The paper is rough on my fingertips. I want to read it now but someone might be watching. I know what this means. Dan did not send the first note, it was someone else. My mind flits over the residents in the block. Maybe I've upset someone but I can't think who. I've only confronted Dan. Maybe it was someone else at the party… the murderer; the person who is trying to set me up.

Pulling away, I drive out of the car park. I don't know where to go. I don't have a plan but I know where I'll end up. That's the thing, I'm so drawn to this place, I can't help myself. I need to be there so that I can be alone with my thoughts and this note and I dread to think what it will say.

CHAPTER THIRTY-TWO

Before I reach my destination, I drive towards Justine's office. She still hasn't messaged me and I need her. I need my friend. I pull up in a short stay parking space about a five-minute walk from her office and I step out into the cold. Greyness blankets the sky and there's a mist in the air as I hurry past the terraced houses towards the crossing in the road. I see her office in the distance and I spot the café where we always go to have our meetings about new clients, then I stop as I see her storming out of the café.

I go to call her as the lights change and I cross but she's still too far away to hear me. Then I see him. Quickly, I lean against the window of a bakery that closed down a few weeks ago, dipping into the recess that is the entrance. Justine isn't looking in my direction, she's looking directly at him as she hits him with her bag. She didn't mention that she was seeing anyone. I can tell she's upset.

As he turns around and I see his face in full, I stare, open-mouthed. Ben. Did she tell me to be careful of him so that she can have him to herself? Or has Ben let her down. Did he try to get me to sleep with him when he was already seeing Justine and why didn't she tell me? I wonder if they're arguing over me. I hope not.

He goes to touch her face and she bats his arm away. Words are said, arms go up and he walks away. She stands there staring into a shop window, fixing her hair before striding back to her office in her killer heels and going in.

I've changed my mind about seeing if Justine wants a coffee. This is something I need to digest before I confront her. In the meantime, I now know for definite that I need to stay away from Ben. I won't message him, I won't meet him. I'll stick to doing the work that he's sent me.

Hurrying back to my car, I drive straight to the cottage. I'm going to sit there and try to calm down before doing the deed with the knife. All I want is to feel the warmth of home and the cottage is the only place that gives me that feeling. It will clear my head, I'm sure of it. I need to think. Not about Justine and Ben, but about the woman I saw outside Dan's flat. The woman I know as Petula. My childhood social worker.

CHAPTER THIRTY-THREE

Seven years ago

Reggie is completely out of view now that she's turned a corner back towards our office block. I'm now alone with the woman from my past, tears damp on my cheeks as she pauses, thinking of what to say. Of course, she has no idea that she abandoned me and what I went through.

'Marissa, my lovely. I'd recognise you anywhere. It's been so long.' Petula's lipstick is a shade lighter than she used to wear and her clothes, they're not quite as bright as they used to be but I'd recognise her anywhere too. Her hair is now a shade of burnt orange, which suits her complexion and her jewellery is still as bold as ever. She releases me from her embrace and wipes the tears from my eyes.

'Petula.' I become that child again. Scared as I contemplate telling her about what's been happening. Why I cut myself as a child. Why I had no friends and why I couldn't leave that farmhouse.

'You look really well. What are you doing with yourself these days?'

I let out a little squeak as I go to answer. It's no good, I need to compose myself. The tremor in my hands threatens to expose my nerves so I pop them into my trouser pockets. 'I... err... work as a financial adviser.'

'I'm so proud of you, that's amazing. Why are you so upset, my lovely?'

'I'm just really happy to see you again.'

She checks her pink watch. 'Do you want to join me for a coffee? I'd love to hear about it all. I've thought about you a lot over the years.'

Nodding, I send Reggie a message, telling her that I'll work over and explain everything when I get back. I put in loads of overtime so I know she won't be upset with me.

'There's a Costa just over here, shall we go there?'

'Actually, I know an independent that does the best mochas ever.'

Petula smiles and follows me across the road, the exact same place where I first met Reggie when she stopped me being decapitated by a tram.

'We have so much catching up to do.'

'We do.' As I push the door open, I spot a table in the window that is set a little back from the main counter. I can tell this conversation might get personal and I don't want the staff who know me to overhear us talking. With the jazzy French music and the general chatter, I feel safe on that front. 'I'll get these. Do you want to save the seats?'

'Oh thank you, lovely. I'll try one of those mochas you speak so highly of.'

Soon I'm back with the drinks and I get comfy in the purple velvet bucket chair and she does the same. She pops her shopping bag full of folders down next to her oversized handbag and leans back. 'Well this is lovely. I'm so happy to see you again and it's brilliant to see how well you're doing. The last I remember was you being so quiet at that kitchen table back at the farm. You were such a shy little girl.'

'You don't work out of Birmingham, do you?' This is me trying to avoid talking of the past. Part of me wants to, part of me is scared. If I face it, it feels real. She sees me as one of her successes whereas, really, I was failed by the system. Or was I? I don't know. I didn't speak up. I'd decided it wasn't Petula's fault a long time ago. I chose to stay with my cat Riffy rather than face any alternative option.

'No, I'm on a course. I've just finished the last day after being here all week. It's nice to see you. I'm dying to know more about you? Do you have a partner or a cat, anything?'

I shake my head. 'No, it's just me. I'm doing fine though. I have my job, which I love, and I work for my friend.'

'Oh, Marissa. I'm just glad things have worked out so well.'

Looking at my feet, I wonder if I should speak my mind. 'Can I ask you something?'

'Of course, sweetheart, go ahead.'

'Why did you never come back after that day at the farm?'

Her gaze meets mine and I know she can tell what I'm thinking. She's reading me with accuracy. 'I thought all seemed fine. I knew you'd had troubles at school but I checked with your teacher regularly after that and everything improved. You were seeing the school psychologist too and she didn't express any further concerns. Your aunt and uncle said that you were much happier after that period.' The woman swallows and glances into her linked hands before looking back up. 'Did I miss something?'

I nod and feel my throat choking a little. 'There's something I've never told anyone before but I trust you, so I'd like to tell you.'

'Okay.' Petula leans in a little with a look of concern on her face.

'Simon abused me, sexually, and Caroline used to lock me in the cellar. She was always so nasty and cruel. I never said anything that day because when you were talking to them, Simon stood behind you with our cat, Riffy, in his arms, and he had his hand gripped around his throat.' I clench my fingers in front of her, just like Simon did that day. 'If I'd have spoken out, he would have killed Riffy.'

'So you stayed in that house all these years pretending that you were fine?'

I nod and feel the slither of a tear slipping down my cheek. Saying it has now made the abuse real and I want to curl up into a ball and cry.

The barista glances over as she tidies a table opposite. 'Is the mocha good?'

Neither of us have touched our drinks but I smile. 'It's the best, as usual.'

As the barista continues, Petula places a hand over mine. 'Oh, Marissa, I am so sorry. You poor child.' She pinches my cheek and strokes my hair tenderly. 'I should have known.' She leans back and wipes a tear from her cheek.

'It's not your fault, Petula. It was Simon and Caroline's fault. They were horrible people and you couldn't have known. You couldn't have saved me either. I'd have denied everything to save Riffy. They knew exactly how to control me.'

'It's my job to see the signs.'

This time, I comfort her. 'Petula, I didn't give you the signs to see. After that, I made sure that everyone knew I was okay.'

'You cut yourself, you were struggling with other kids at school. All that pain you were carrying and being such a young child. Do you need to speak to someone? I can still arrange that. Just because you're not on my caseload any more and you're all grown up, I won't abandon you if you need my help.'

Shaking my head, I smile to lighten the mood a little. I've had a long time to accept my past, Petula has had approximately twenty minutes to accept what she will see as her failing. Maybe I shouldn't have said anything to her. Was I selfish to unburden myself and burden her? Am I unburdened? I'm not sure. I don't feel any better, or relieved, and I'll never stop thinking about what Simon and Caroline took from me. I laugh a little. 'You know, Riffy was my best friend. I told him everything. How stupid is that?'

She sips her drink, which must be getting cold. 'I could have helped you if you'd said something.'

'I know that now but then, not only did I fear for Riffy's life, Simon told me about how I'd get hurt and abused if I got taken into a children's home, so I guess I resigned myself to staying at the farm. I make it sound like nothing now, but at the time it was everything. He'd painted this dark picture of how I'd never survive in a home. How the other kids would pulverise a scrawny, ugly kid like me. I believed everything he said.' I pause. 'Can I ask you something, about my mum?'

'Of course. Ask me anything.'

'I know she was killed but that's all I know. Do you know who my dad was? I know he's dead but I've never even been given a name.'

'Do you remember anything at all?'

I shrug. 'Snippets. I remember being in a really cold flat and I still have a woollen scarecrow that I used to take everywhere with me.'

'Do you remember the night your mother was murdered?' Petula's head was tilted to one side as she gently spoke.

'Some of it. I remember lying under the bed, the killer's boots and my mother's glassy eyes looking back at me with blood surrounding her. I can't remember what was said. It's like I was screaming inside my head. Just before, I'd coloured in this picture of an apple with a happy-looking worm poking from it and I'd gone over the lines. My mum put it in a drawer moments before her attacker came in.' I pause and feel my throat closing a little. 'I never got to tell her that I loved her, before it happened.'

'Oh, sweetie, you were her little girl and she loved you so, so, much. She loved you and she knew you loved her. She only moved around all the time to protect you, I know that much from the files. She'd never say who she was running from but I always suspected it was your father. She was such a closed book and embarrassed to speak of her problems. You were everything to her.'

I can't stop the tears from spilling. Knowing that my mother loved me so much meant everything. 'And my father?'

'Your mother wouldn't talk to us about him. She said the further away from him you were, the better. His name wasn't on your birth certificate either. I wish I knew more.'

'The man who killed my mother, he's never been caught. If it was my father, he died a free man.'

'How would you know he had died? We had no idea who he was.' Petula's brow furrows.

'Caroline seemed to know but she couldn't tell me. She said he'd died.'

'I can't remember her saying anything to us at the time. Going back to the night of your mother's murder, no one in the block of flats saw anything and your mum wouldn't talk about the man who was harassing her. She wouldn't say if he was your father or a previous boyfriend. She just wanted to run.'

I think back to before that when I only have a few vague memories. 'I remember living in a cottage before moving to that flat.'

'Yes, I don't know where that was offhand. It was such a long time ago.'

I know exactly where the cottage was as Simon and Caroline had the address crossed out in their diary, and, for some reason, I had dreamt about it lately. I know one day soon I'll drive there for a look. Maybe seeing it with my own eyes will trigger further memories. Maybe I'll remember something about my mother's stalker or my father. I'm sure they're one and the same. Who knows? I also have to resign myself to the fact that I may never find all the answers.

Petula passes me a card. 'Here's my number if you want to give me a call again. We could always meet for another coffee.' She checks her watch. 'I have to pick my kids up from school soon and then take one to football practise and one to swimming – oh the joys. I hate leaving our conversation where it is.'

'Do you know anything else about my past?' I need to get my questions in quickly before she leaves.

'I'm sorry but what I've already said is all I know. It's a case I remember well because of your tragic circumstances. What happened to you and your mother isn't something we come across every day, which is why it sticks here.' She points to her head.

'Thank you.' I stand and walk out with her as I take a deep breath and try to clear my head a little, ready for an afternoon of work.

'Please do give me a call and keep working hard. I'm so proud of the lovely young woman you've become and what you've achieved.' Petula hugs me again and I want it to last forever. She's warm and lovely and I feel safe. The fact that someone feels proud of me means a lot.

As we part, I continue to wave at her until she turns a corner. She's gone and I feel hollow. I'm glad I spoke to her. It's like a dark part of my life has been acknowledged. Maybe I can find a way of moving on from my past.

I glance back and see a figure, someone watching from afar. He quickly turns and in a flash, he's gone. Shrugging thoughts of that person away, I think of my mother and the day of her murder. There are so many blanks still.

Tonight, I'm driving over to Stratford-upon-Avon to see the cottage. It's been a long time coming and I can't hide from what I need to do any longer. I need to do something to trigger all those locked childhood memories in my head.

CHAPTER THIRTY-FOUR

Now

Snow begins to pelt the windscreen and I can barely see the road ahead. Red tail lights glimmer as the cars in front of me navigate the speed bumps in the road. Two hours I've been out and I'm no further forward. I glance at the note on my passenger seat and slam on my brakes as I realise I'm about to mount a kerb.

My phone buzzes so I pull over for a second. It's Ben messaging me, requesting an update on a file marked Gibbons. At least he's not asking me to meet him for lunch or dinner again. I've decided that if he does, I won't be going. There's something going on between him and Justine and I don't need complications like him in my life.

I haven't even looked at the Gibbons's file. I haven't looked at anything. Another message pings through. It's him again.

Meet me for dinner again. I know you want to. X

What's he playing at? I know I said I'd message him then I didn't. He should have got the hint but he's making things awkward now. So much has happened over the last few days and my head's all over the place and now he's once again trying to complicate things. I have to speak to Justine sooner rather than later. She owes me the truth. Then it hits me. All my real problems started around the time that Ben came into my life. I grab my phone and try to call Justine. If there's something she knows about Ben that puts me in some sort of danger, I need her to tell me. It's time I had it out with her. She cuts me off immediately. I'm being ghosted by my best friend and it isn't on. I send a message.

You didn't tell me why I should be careful of Forge. In fact, you've been avoiding me and it isn't fair. I saw you arguing with him today, by your office. Is there something I need to know? Please call me, Jus! I'm going out of my mind and I need someone to talk to. I thought we were friends. X

I continue driving and moments later I park up outside the cottage. This time, it's covered in police tape and the garden is covered in a blanket of snow. All the things I love about it seem to have gone. The warmth has been replaced by a coldness and it looks smaller and more unkempt than I remember. How could this have happened in such a short amount of time? Death, that's how. Murder. It changes a place. It changes a street, a neighbourhood, and this one was no exception. It's the reason there are no kids outside making snow people. Parents are probably telling their little ones that there is a dangerous person on the loose.

The letter isn't going away. I feel as though it's staring right at me and I can't avoid reading it any longer.

Open me, Marissa. Have a good look.

'But I don't want to.' The same handwriting and the same shade of red states my name on the front of the folded sheet of A4. I was so convinced that Dan had sent the last one; that he was totally out to get me but now, this changes things. He still wasn't a good person but he didn't send the note calling me a 'bitch'. Someone else did this and I have no idea who.

With shaking fingers, I open the note.

Marissa, Marissa! What have you done now?

The sender is accusing me of killing Dan, they have to be. It's the person who's setting me up. I was right. Someone is out to ruin me and they know a lot about me and about my past. I think back to my neighbours. Maybe it was someone at Dan's party. His son always gave me strange looks while he lurked around but this note seems too sinister to be written by a teenager. His mother is Petula; she knows about my past. Maybe she said something to her son if he mentioned me. She'd have known who I was by my name and the boy could have seen my name on my post box.

Is someone else watching me? I think back to how my mother was stalked. This sense of panic must have been exactly how she felt. I glance out of the windscreen and then out the back of the car, checking to see if I'm being followed. I can't see anything or anyone out of place.

At Stratford, when I'd met up with Ben, I was convinced a man in a hoodie had been following me. My phone rings. 'Justine.'

'I'm so sorry, lovey. So, so sorry. I've been an awful friend but I had to work things out in my own head and when you said you were meeting Ben for lunch, I panicked. I didn't know how to tell you.' She sounds out of breath.

'Tell me what?'

'He's a friggin' weirdo, that's what, and I meant what I said when I said be careful. I thought you'd just take some work off him and that would be it.'

'What about him?'

'I've been sleeping with him. Well, I had been until the other day. After your meeting at the Drunken Duck, he called me and I met him at one of the apartments he's selling. I don't know why I met him again as he was so rough before. I was stupid, so stupid.' She pauses.

This time I pause. I hate Forge for playing us like this. 'Why didn't you tell me you were sleeping with him?'

I hear her swallow. 'I knew I had to end it, which is why I met up with him after you met him for lunch. I went out with him a few times previously and he was really nice but I made it clear that I didn't want a relationship. You know Sam is my life and I don't like to complicate things. The reason I knew I had to end it was the last time we had sex, he gripped me around the neck and I thought he was going to strangle me. He's got two sides to him and I think he's dangerous. I recommended you to him when I first started seeing him and he was okay then.' She paused. 'I bet you think I'm a horrible person but I got lonely and he was there.'

'No, I don't. I'd never think you were a horrible person, Justine. I just wish you'd told me. He sounds like he's dangerous. He came to my apartment and I was alone with him. Anything could have happened by the sound of it. What a creep.'

'He is that and a dangerous one too. Anyway, I argued with him earlier today because I saw him loitering around by my house last night, looking through my windows from the street; then he had the nerve to turn up at my office this morning. I had to get him out of there so I took him to the café where we go. Anyway, I was telling him to stay away and to not hurt you. If he hurts you, I swear I'll kill him. The worst of it is, I keep getting these phone calls where someone hangs up all the time. I'm sure it's him, trying to scare me. He denied it, of course, but I know it's him.'

'I have a silent caller too.'

'It has to be him. I'm going to stay with my mother for a few days with Sam and hope that he gets the message to leave me alone. If not, I'll be calling the police. I can't have him hanging around my street stalking me. I'd recommend that you keep it professional and stay out of his way on a personal level. I'm really sorry I ever gave him your details. I had no idea what he was like until these past few days. I'll call you later but I have to go. My other phone is flashing away and I have to pack.'

I feel as though I have my answer. Ben obviously enjoys instilling terror into the women who come into his life and I'm one of his targets. I need more proof though before I go to the police with what I think I know. I can't work out how or why he got to Simon or Dan or why he's chosen to gaslight me, but I am going to get to the bottom of it all for myself and for Justine.

A message pings up on my phone.

I open a photo from Ben and it's of my hair clip laid out on his bed. I never want that thing back.

'Go away!' I throw my phone down. Is that all a part of his game? If he's been watching me closely, he may have seen me at the cottage or he may have seen me arguing with Dan through one of the windows. Now I imagine him stalking me in the same way my mother was stalked. I have no proof of anything and that bothers me. All I have is what Justine has told me.

The cottage windows are concealed by a film of snow so I get out of the car. I need to look at the cottage properly not through a screen and then I'll get rid of the knife. Stepping out into the cold, I stand there, staring at the cottage, disappointed that the warm feeling it always gave me is no longer there. Simon has tainted it.

I hear a snuffle and a little Shih Tzu dog nudges past me, its owner holding the lead. 'Sad, what happened in that cottage.'

'Yes, just awful.' I recognise the old lady who I had hoped would one day be my neighbour. Glancing down at the hunched up woman, her stare pierces through me. I smile wondering why she's eyeing me up.

'I see you around here a lot.' Her mouth breaks into a smile.

My heart begins to jump around in my chest. 'I, err…'

'Did you know him, dear?'

I shake my head. Think, Marissa, think. 'No, it's so tragic, what happened.'

'It is. I know you didn't come to see him, the man who was murdered. You've been visiting this cottage for years and he'd barely been here a couple of weeks. I've seen you looking up at it and smiling.'

The dog snuffles at my feet.

'She likes you and Trixie is a good judge of character. So, why do you come here?'

'I used to live here many years ago, which is why I visit sometimes. I love this cottage.'

'That's lovely to hear. I love mine too. You know, we must have met before. I've lived here all my adult life, that's fifty years, but don't tell anyone else.' She winks and points a gloved finger at her nose.

'I was little more than a toddler when I lived here.'

She scrunches her brow. 'What was your mother's name?'

Maybe she could tell me more about my mother. 'Laura, she would have been in her early twenties when we lived here.'

The woman smiles. 'You were the cute little girl in those frilly dresses that I think she used to make herself. I actually remember that summer and you used to toddle around on your chubby little legs. You'd play with her in the back garden, such a happy little girl, then you both just left one day, not telling anyone you were going. I wondered where you'd both gone so suddenly after only living here a few months. Your mother seemed so happy and she loved you so much.'

My heart feels as though it might burst and I want to cry. 'I barely remember my mother.'

'You poor thing. Did something happen to her?'

'She died when I was young and I moved in with my aunt, her sister.'

'The one with the long, dark hair? She looked a lot like your mother. I didn't like her.'

'Oh.'

'Just the way she used to scowl. I heard them arguing once and there are some things a person never forgets.' The woman paused. 'Look, I live just here and it's cold. Do you want a cuppa?'

I glance at the time and wonder if I care about what I should be doing any more. Nothing could be more important than learning more about myself and my mother. Maybe that might be the key to unlocking what's going on with me now. I can't live with this confusion for much longer. 'Yes, please. That would be nice.'

Locking my car, I follow her and her little Shih Tzu into the warm. Coming into her house might be my biggest downfall. It only takes one person to have seen me around on the night of Simon's murder but I need to know more. I won't rest until I do.

CHAPTER THIRTY-FIVE

As the old lady makes the tea, I sit at the kitchen table. The layout is familiar, like a reflection of next door. My past in that cottage is becoming a little clearer as I take a tour in my head around the ground floor, until she brings me out of my trance by shifting the dog from under her feet.

There are doilies everywhere and teapots. So many teapots, mostly in the shape of animals. The little dog nudges my hand and yaps to be stroked. I pet its head. Dogs versus humans. I'd have loved this talk with Reggie. Maybe I should move, cut all humans out of my life; become a total hermit and get a dog. I run my finger through its fur and I feel the urge to lift it onto my lap and cuddle it.

'She'll stay there all day if you keep fussing her. Come on, Trixie.' The woman places a bowl of food on the floor and the dog runs over, its face soon snuffling away in the food.

'You were saying you heard my mother and my aunt arguing.'

'Yes, she was so mean. She'd go on at your mum, saying that she'd ruined her life by getting pregnant and telling her that she was now stuck with no hope and a life of poverty. I don't really like telling you all this.'

'Please do. My aunt wasn't the nicest of people so it's not a surprise.'

'Your mother was young and single and bringing you up at the time was hard. She had a couple of little jobs and I knew she struggled. I used to make her some cupcakes now and again, or give her a box of veg from my garden. I used to grow my own.'

A memory flashed back, one of me sitting on the living room floor with Scarecrow and a couple of other teddies. My toy teapot in one hand and a cupcake in the other. I'd pour the pretend tea while my mother cried in the kitchen. I remember her slamming the phone down and running in, her hands shaking and tears streaming down her face. She ran to the window, stared up and down the road before closing all the curtains in the house. That's how we spent the next couple of weeks. I think we left after that. 'I remember you now, well I remember the cakes with the pink icing and the glace cherries on the top.'

'That's them. My cherry cakes.'

'About my aunt.'

'Ah her. She'd just wear your mother down. After her visits, your mum would cry. I remember hearing when she left her windows open. I wanted so much to go round and see her but your mother was a private woman. She'd thank me for the cakes but never let me in for a drink. I would have helped her if she was in any sort of trouble. Anyway, your aunt used to visit and I'd hear her shout at your mother. It was the same things over and over. You've ruined your life. Don't expect me to help you with your snotty baby and she'd say she told her so, and that getting involved with him was a mistake.'

It breaks my heart to know that Caroline was so cruel to my lovely mother too. 'Do you know who the "he" was that she referred to?'

The dog licked its lips and clipped along the floor to the old woman. She lifted it onto her lap and stroked it. 'I never saw the *he* she was referring to. I assumed he was your father but I don't know for sure.'

'I never knew my dad, and my aunt told me that he'd died. I don't even have a name for him.'

'I wish I could help you. Wait…'

'What is it?'

'Actually, I saw a man go there one evening, it was just as I was about to go out so I have no idea if he stayed, or he may have been a boyfriend. All I saw was the back of him going into the house. When I returned, I heard shouting and thudding. Something had happened and I wasn't there to see or hear. I nearly called the police but it ended quite quickly and I saw him leave so I thought that was the end of it.'

I took a sip of tea. The cup rattled in the saucer as I placed it down.

'You're shaking, dear.'

'It's just so much to take in. Can you remember what were they shouting about?'

'He was calling her all the names under the sun. I heard shouting, then laughing and things being thrown about. Your mother screamed a couple of times, then cried. I had my hands on the phone ready to call the police but he left saying he'd be back and that wherever she went, he'd find her. I ran over there when he was out of sight and knocked but your mother wouldn't answer. In fact, she told me to go away and mind my own business through the letter box. The next day you were both gone and I never saw either of you again. If I think about it now, she was running from place to place to protect you and herself. Whoever that man was, he was dangerous.'

'Did you see what he looked like?'

Her brow scrunched up. 'Average height, dark boots. I remember the boots as they were quite heavy looking, like work boots, and he stomped in them loudly. But, it was quite dark and it was also a long time ago.'

'Did anyone else on this street know us?'

'No. The neighbours did always pass comment as your mother was always closing the curtains and peering out, even in the daytime. It was as if she knew someone was coming for her. One of the neighbours saw someone lurking around the back of her garden sometimes, and speculated that she was being watched. It was probably just gossip though.'

I nearly choked on the tea. My mum was being watched and now I am. The links between Ben and my past aren't readily coming to me. I'm going to have to dig harder and deeper until I have answers.

'Do you want another tea?'

I shake my head. I still had a knife to dispose of. There's no way that thing was coming back to my apartment with me.

'That house has seen so much tragedy, I feel as though it's cursed. Of course, I don't really believe that but it's had its accidental deaths, its disease-related deaths, your mother and her problems, and that man who got killed. Let's hope it will be a luckier place for the next person.' She let out a titter. 'Don't worry, I'm not senile. I don't really believe it's cursed.'

'Did you know him? The man who was killed.'

'Simon something. Didn't care for him much even though he'd only lived there a few weeks. In that time, he managed to drink too much nearly every day and he'd be peeing and spewing on the front step or in the garden. I also think he was taking something, some drugs maybe. He was probably in some sort of trouble with a drug dealer; seemed an unsavoury type. He fell asleep on his doorstep one night too after shouting abuse at no one for about an hour. I know he probably had problems and I should be more sympathetic but I just didn't like him. Sometimes a person can spot a rotten apple and he certainly was that.'

I know he was.

'There's one other thing. On the night he was killed…' The old woman paused in thought and stared into thin air as she thought. 'I thought I caught a glimpse of a figure standing outside. I stupidly thought it might be you as I've seen you here before but it can't have been because when I looked again, the figure was gone. I think I'd just been half asleep.'

'How strange.' I don't know what else to say.

I smile, knowing I have to get out. My smile is pasted on though. The last thing I feel like doing is pretending that I'm happy and everything is okay. 'Thank you for the tea and chat.' I bend and stroke the dog one more time.

'You're welcome. It was lovely to have some company. If you come to look at the cottage again, you know you can always pop in for a drink. Trixie and I would love to see you again. Can you see yourself out? My knees are playing up.'

'Of course.'

'Will you come back soon?'

The woman's creased green eyes look like they're pleading with me and I like her and her dog. 'Yes, I'd love to. It was lovely to chat. Bye, and thank you again.'

'The name's Alice, by the way.'

'Bye, Alice.'

As I step out into the snow, I have so much information running through my head but I'm no nearer to finding any answers. I remember being in bed the night the bad man came and then we left the cottage in the middle of the night, never to return, but he found us and he killed my mother. All I remember is his dark boots and that's all I have to go on. I glance at the cottage one last time before getting in the car. What if Alice did see me on the night of Simon's murder? I glance up at all the houses and wonder if anyone else did? Was I the figure at the back of the house, stalking Simon before he was murdered? Was Forge there too? I hate my mind. I wish it would give me the answers I'm looking for. I was there on the night of Simon's murder. I saw it happen. I came home with one of those baubles in my hand and then I woke up. What happened before?

CHAPTER THIRTY-SIX

My idea to throw the knife in the river wasn't very original but that's what I did and now I've come home to a quiet building. I pass the police officer on the landing and he smiles. The window is thankfully closed and I feel a lot calmer. I am calmer. My tremor has gone. My heart rate isn't erratic and I'm actually hungry. What I need to do is eat, rest and then think; think back to those nights. Something is in that brain of mine and I need it out. I know it links to Ben too. He's in my life and Justine's. She's that worried about his behaviour that she's going to her mother's. I can't sit by and do nothing. Finally, I find my door keys at the bottom of my bag.

No one saw me at the cottage on the night of Simon's murder; the neighbour, Alice, confirmed that fact. The knife has gone and I'm as clean as I can be which is what I need for now. When I have more information I will tell the police, but I'm not letting them pin these murders on me. 'Would you like a hot drink?'

The policeman undoes his jacket button as I unlock my door. 'Yes, please. Anything as long as it has two sugars.'

As I enter, the warmth hits me. I've left the heating full on. This afternoon, I'm going to at least catch up on the most urgent jobs; that will at least keep all the customers happy. I will work through the night if I have to. Acting normal is the only way through this so that's what I'll do. It's my only option with the police outside twenty-four seven.

I listen.

No noise, no music; even the neighbour's dogs aren't barking because there's no disturbance to start them off. I pull the note from my bag. Everything would feel totally fine if it wasn't for the author of this note. *What have you done now?* They're accusing me of being a murderer, just like the man who killed my mother. Someone knows and that someone isn't even making any demands. What is this going to end up as? Blackmail? Not knowing what they want from me is worse than anything. I have to just sit here and wait and work until the next note appears or my memory decides it's going to give me a break.

First, I need to make a coffee. Moments later, I take a drink out to the police officer and he thanks me. To him, I'm the considerate person who looks after the residents' interests, which works for me as I need time.

'Ooh, good coffee.' He slurps as I smile.

Closing the door, I head to the kitchen to get my own drink. Thoughts of my mother living in constant fear for her life with all the curtains shut, checking the streets for her stalker fill my head. I should do the same. I bet Ben comes by watching, and he'll be here more now that Justine has gone to stay with her mother for a while. It had to be him on the bridge and I can safely say he's our silent caller. Heading past the sofa to the lounge window, I gaze out at the snowy path. Again, no snow people. No children at all. This is now an area of danger where people will stay safely in until the killer is found. I catch a glimpse of dark clothing on a person loitering at the end of the path that feeds into the back of the road. It's quite far away from me and there's a mist in the air. All I can see is an outline that is shaded in a dull black and grey. I press my nose against the glass for a better look, but he turns away. I'm sure it's a he and I'm sure it's Ben. He was watching my apartment. It has to be him leaving the notes, phoning and hanging up and generally playing with my mind. I have to know why?

Leaving, I force a smile at the police officer and hurry down the stairs. A piece of paper sticks out of my post box. Another note. I knew it.

Running out without my coat, I hurry to the path, almost slipping on a pile of compressed snow. Shaking, I reach the path. Spiny bushes line either side then I hear the clip of a shoe and see a shadow getting smaller. I'm losing him.

My top gets caught in the spines that have overgrown. They tear a gash in my sleeve. Something else I'll have to hide when I pass the police officer to go back into my apartment. I can't lose this man now. As I reach the end of the path and look up the road that it feeds onto, all I see is a fine mist of snow floating down in front of the orange glow of the street lamp. Then I see something else and I want to scream. The picture stuck to the lamp post takes my breath away. Gasping, my chest tightens even more.

Can't breathe.

Can't see.

Prickles fill my eyes and night is looming fast. It is as if the white grey mist had turned charcoal within seconds, like the clouds were falling from the sky so that they can suffocate me.

Only the person who killed my mother would have this picture. Only a father would have taken it. Aunt Caroline said my father had died. He's dead. This is Ben's doing and I badly want to know how he's managed to find out so much about me. How did he get this picture?

I snatch the weathered colouring I did of the apple and the friendly worm and I clutch it to my chest. 'Who are you really?' I yell. There's not a soul in sight. I run up the hill and onto the main road but I can't see my stalker any more. My teeth chatter and the path ahead is swaying because of my anxiety-addled vision. I know he'll be back and I'm so scared. I'm everything I'd set out to never be. All that counselling was for nothing. Feeling a sickness churning in my stomach, I know I have to go home and read that note so that's what I do.

I feel a sense of déjà-vu. I've been here before. How many years has he been in my life, lurking in the distance?

As I enter my apartment and sink into the settee, a certain night comes back to me. I'm back at the office in Birmingham and I remember it as if it was yesterday.

CHAPTER THIRTY-SEVEN

Seven years ago

It's late and I'm hungry. Everyone has left the office for home but me. I message Reggie one more time but she's not answering. This is the third time she's let me down in as many weeks and I'm worried about her. She's not been herself. The conversations we used to have no longer fill our lunch hours and evenings. I thought I'd try to entice her here with the offer of a meal at her favourite restaurant, but still she doesn't answer me.

I turn my computer off and grab my bag. I'm going to pop by her apartment, check up on her. Without her presence over the past few days, my life has felt hollow. I want my best friend back. Seeing her withdrawing like this is killing me but it's not the first time. She's so up and down that I can't keep up with her. I head to Reggie's office and check her desk. Maybe something in there will help me fathom out what's causing her weird behaviour. Nothing.

The corner of a piece of paper sticks out from behind the filing cabinet. Bending, I place my finger over it and slide it out. It's an A4 sheet of paper and it's completely coloured in red. I try to shift the cabinet and a few more sheets begin to slip out. More sheets of paper, some coloured in red, others in black. Then there are those with messages on them.

Loser!

I know what you've done.

Keep one eye open all the time.

A few days ago, she looked like she was frantically scribbling. This is what she was working on. I fear she's losing her mind. Grouping up the pile of paper, I drop it in my satchel. Grabbing my bag, I hurry to get the lift down, then I say goodnight to the security guard. He barely looks up but I can tell he's not the usual man who works the front desk. He's hunched over and about a foot shorter. He also has his coat on like he's ready to leave. 'Goodnight,' I call, but he doesn't answer.

I run through the streets, panic rising within me as I race towards the canal area where Reggie's penthouse is. I buzz and buzz for her to let me in but there is no answer. Fairy lights from a passing narrowboat reflect in the canal.

Stepping back, I look straight up to the top of the block and see that there's light flooding onto her glass and stainless steel balcony. She's in. She wouldn't leave her lights on and go out. She always went on about wasting energy and the impact of it on our planet.

I should have been more insistent with her, checked up on her more. Maybe taken some food around to make sure she was looking after herself. She's been depressed before but never for this long. This time feels different. She's been waffling under her breath and the tick on her eye has been twitching away. My heart thuds in my chest.

Looking up again, I can see that she's now outside and she's leaning back on her balcony. She sits on the ledge and puts her arms in the air. 'Reggie, let me in. Don't do anything silly.' I can see her wobbling and my stomach drops. Tears spill down my face as I stare, feeling helpless. 'Reggie.' She slips and my stomach lurches. I close my eyes as I can't bear to look but when I prise one open, I see she's gripping the ledge. My heart is racing like a rickety train. She looks down and sees me, then waves.

'Let me in.' I shout so loud, a couple of people come to their windows. A few drops of rain land on my nose. Out of the corner of my eye, I catch a glimpse of someone watching me. As I turn, they disappear behind the building. All I saw was a figure clad in darkness.

A moment later, I hear the buzzer humming. Darting through, I get straight in the lift and press the button for the tenth floor where she's already waiting to welcome me in. She sways and bumps into the door frame. Bottle of wine in one hand and an empty glass in the other. 'Baxter. It's you.'

'Of course it's me. I thought we were going out tonight. I was worried, and what were you doing leaning back on the ledge like that?'

'I just wanted to feel like I could fly. Don't come here and play the fun police with me.' She waggles the glass at me.

'Well, you can't fly, do you hear me?' I snatch the wine and grip the sleeves of her crumpled T-shirt. 'You scared me.'

'Oh, Baxter. Don't be silly. Grab a glass and you can be pissed like me.' She sits on the back of the large corner settee in the huge open plan kitchen-cum-lounge, with its floor-to-ceiling windows. I stare at the shiny white baby grand piano where crystals from the chandelier reflect a rainbow across the top; another one of Reggie's impulse buys. The huge balcony goes all the way around the top floor and has views of the canal and city but this doesn't make Reggie any happier. 'We can forget all our problems.'

'What problems? You can talk to me you know. And what are these?' I pull the weird notes out of my bag and drop them onto the coffee table.

'That's me; loser.' She laughs manically as she falls backwards onto the settee cushions where she remains for a moment as she stares at the ceiling light. 'The room's spinning like a merry-go-round. Isn't that cool?'

I push her legs around and head to the other side, where I pull her up to a sitting position. 'Reggie, look at me.'

She doesn't do as I ask. She stares right through me. 'Have you ever done something so terrible that you can't see a way back?'

'You know I have.' She knows that I stabbed Simon to escape that house and she knows of the abuse I suffered. After telling Petula, I felt I couldn't keep my past from my best friend but I wondered now why she was keeping something from me. I thought we told each other everything. She would never betray me by revealing my secrets, I know that much. I wouldn't betray her either. 'There is always a way back.' I think of the knife I plunged into Simon. At that moment, I thought my life as I knew it would be over but it wasn't. Simon left me alone after that. Never once came looking for me. I will save Reggie from any of those kind of thoughts too.

'But what if there isn't?'

'Reggie, tell me what's going on? You're my friend, my best friend in the whole world. You gave me a chance in life when I was literally in the gutter and I love you so much with all my heart. You're like my second mother and it hurts me to see you like this. I need the other Reggie back, please.' It's taken me a long time to trust someone like I trust Reggie and if I lose her, I won't be the same person ever again.

Tears spill down her cheeks and she sobs. 'Will you ever forgive me for what I put you through?'

'I'll forgive you for anything.' Reggie doesn't know how to hurt people. I can't understand what she's done that's so bad. I hug her and she sobs loudly, letting it all out.

'Can we go and eat now? I'm hungry. I need something to soak up the vino.' She wipes her face with her arm.

'Of course we can. Get out of those lounge pants and we'll go. A bit of food and a chat might make you feel more human.'

She wobbles a little as she stands. 'Thanks, Baxter.'

Several minutes later she comes from her room looking a little more like the Reggie I know. She's flattened her kinky hair with water and found her glasses. 'That's better, I can even see properly now. Right, I'm not totally steady but I'm ready.'

'You forgot your watch.' Reggie never leaves home without that Rolex she loves so much.

'I'm not keen on it any more.'

I scrunch up my brows.

'What? Don't look at me like that. It doesn't suit you. You'll get wrinkles on your forehead.' She pauses. 'People change.' Her smile warms me a little. That's more like the Reggie I know but in the absence of her watch, I think there's more to the story than she's telling me. She forgets how well I know her. 'You know, Marissa, whatever happens I love you so much and I'm incredibly proud of all that you've achieved and become. Don't you ever forget, okay?'

I feel a little tear slip down my cheek as I hug her. 'Love you too, Reggie, now come on, let's go and get some food in you.' As we head out, I catch sight of the dark figure again. Leaving Reggie standing there, I run over but the figure runs away too. I can't leave Reggie in the state that she's in so I quit trying to catch up with this person.

CHAPTER THIRTY-EIGHT

Now

A couple of days have passed and I realise I've started to wallow. Whoever has been watching me has been in my life a long time. They've always been there, in the background, waiting and watching. For what?

Ben; the notes; the dark figure; Ben. It keeps coming back to Ben and I can't work out why. I can't work out how his presence in my life relates to my past and the murders.

All I can think about is how much I miss Reggie. When I said to her that there was always a way out of a bad mindset or situation, I now wonder why I spurted such rubbish. Sometimes life closes in on a person, like it's doing with me now. I've called Justine but she cut our conversation short, saying she can't talk much with her mother around.

I haven't left my apartment for what feels like forever and my curtains are still closed. The police officer has now gone from next door so I'm assuming that forensics have all they want. Firing off the last work email of the day to Ben, I feel a sense of accomplishment as I play the game of not letting on that I know about him and Justine, while I try to work things out. Not only have I got back on top of all my work, I've done it under the most worrying of circumstances and I've even done it before everyone breaks up for Christmas, which now feels as though it's fast looming.

Every time I hear a noise, I fear it's Brindle and Collins coming back to interrogate me. I head out of my office and glance down by the front door where I've begun scattering marbles on the floor. That way, if I sleepwalk out of the apartment, I'll tread on them, feel the pain and wake up. I can't wander about any more and not know what I've seen or done. Whoever is trying to set me up won't win.

I started off sleeping in my bed last night, but I woke at five under my desk. I know I'm still active while asleep but the control is coming back. I will leave the marbles there every night for the foreseeable. They're obviously acting as a deterrent, even on a subconscious level. Over the past couple of days, I've been checking outside for the presence of my stalker but I haven't seen anyone around. It's snowier than ever and too cold for anyone to be lurking for too long. There haven't been any more notes or phone calls. My mobile lights up. That's the fifth message today from Glen asking if I'm okay. It feels nice to have someone show that they care.

Thinking back to the dark times with Reggie, I'd probably felt like Glen is feeling now. I'm shutting him out and he's started seeing me as fragile.

I glance at the notes on the table and I'm taken back to the evening I found those notes behind Reggie's filing cabinet. Shaking my head, I kneel next to the coffee table. No, this can't be happening. I'm being paranoid but then again, they are too similar. It's like something has clicked and it makes total sense.

A4 sheet of paper, a brief note in red. But… I thought Reggie had written those notes herself. My hair falls over my shoulder and I scratch my neck until it's sore. Why didn't I see this sooner?

I run to my bedside drawer and search for the letter. Underneath everything, I find it. Reggie wrote it to me and the pain of reading it again is too great to fathom. I throw it back in the drawer. I can't read it now. There are more pressing things to do like work out who sent Reggie those horrible notes all those years ago and who is sending them to me now. To think I blamed Dan. *Who are you, Ben?*

Turning on my computer, I do a Google search of Ben Forge's name and all I get is his business life. I head to page two of the search, then page three, but there's nothing. Continuing, I scan page five and stop on a link that makes my stomach churn. It's the tiny 'in court' section of a newspaper article in Staffordshire and it dates back nearly twenty years. Ben was convicted of actual bodily harm on his then wife. He did two years in prison. Justine was right to warn me about him. She had sensed she was in danger and now he was after me. A sick feeling rolls through me. Maybe he knew the man who killed my mother. Maybe he was my mother's killer. Has he come back to kill me and finish the job? But he's not trying to kill me, he's trying to drive me insane. It might explain how he knows so much about me. Setting me up, what's all that about and how? Everything is a blur. I want to go to the police and tell them everything but what I have to say is all a jumbled mess that doesn't entirely make sense. No, I have to be patient. One of us will slip up and it has to be Ben.

I have to get out of here or I'm going to lose my mind. Darting to the bedroom, I grab my coat and then I glance at the woman in the mirror. She has bags under her eyes and her lips are sore. I touch my reflection and know that I no longer know myself. The cut to my hand has faded to a silvery shiny line.

My phone touches my ear and I wait for an answer. 'Glen, are you home?'

'Hi, Marissa. Yes, I've just got in. I'm getting dinner on, you want some? It's just microwave moussaka but you're welcome to share it with me.' His voice, so calm and reassuring. If there is someone out there watching me, they're waiting for a chance to send me further out of my mind, but I can't stay in alone for another night. Before all this, solitude was my friend but now

I need to get rid of the constant inner dialogue that won't leave me alone. It's like the hum of an insect that's slowly driving me insane. I'm going crazy.

'Yes…'

'Are you okay? You sound a bit weird.'

I'm feeling weird. A thought flashes through me. Maybe by seeing Glen, I'm putting him in danger. Would Ben harm Glen? If there's any way it was him who killed Dan and Simon, he's capable. It's no good. I need to talk to someone. In the absence of Justine, Glen will have to be the one. 'Yes, I'm okay. It's just been a long couple of days. I've been working flat out.'

'See you soon, then. Got to go, the peas are bubbling over.' He ends the call, leaving me standing in front of my reflection with the phone pressed against my ear. I jolt and inhale swiftly. My inner self is telling me I should leave Glen well alone but I need a friend. I can't deal with this alone but if Glen gets hurt, I'll never forgive myself.

CHAPTER THIRTY-NINE

'Come in, shall I take your coat?' I allow the thick woollen coat to slip off my shoulders.

'Thanks, Glen.'

'New jumper? It suits you. It looks really smart. Have you had meetings today?'

I nod and smile. That sounds like a normal thing a person like me would have done today. I can't tell him that I've barely been out over this past couple of days; that I've been stuck in my apartment like a petrified little hermit. My plan to talk to him and unburden myself wasn't going to work, I can tell. Looking at him now, I don't want to talk. Talking involves letting people in, properly, and if I do, I'll put him in danger like I did with Reggie. Everyone around me is being destroyed, whether they're friends of mine or whether they've hurt me. I don't want Glen to be the latest victim.

'Anyway, come through. I'm famished. It's been a long day and I ate my lunch at eleven like an idiot.'

I don't know what else to say. Knowing I should push him away now is the hardest thing ever as I like being around him. I walk to the back of his lounge and glance out of the window, wondering if I've been followed. There's no one suspicious around unless you include the group of teens that are hiding a bottle of something in a bag as they pass it along the line.

'Here you go. Microwave moussaka and tinned peas. Living the high life.' He places two plates on the table.

'Thanks, Glen.' I sit and join him, picking at the food as he eats.

'Have you heard any more from the police?'

I shake my head and struggle to swallow what's in my mouth. 'Have you?'

'No.' He pauses as he gobbles a few more mouthfuls down. 'Are you glad he's gone?'

'You mean Dan?' He knows something. Why would he ask that question?

He shrugs. 'It just worked out so well. He's dead and now all the problems go away.'

He suspects me. I'm sure that's what he's hinting at here. I didn't do anything. Someone is trying to send me crazy and set me up.

'This is a safe space. I know you didn't do anything but you can tell me how you're feeling.'

A line of sweat is forming at my brow.

'I mean, he was a prize prick. A part of you must be glad that the problem has gone away.'

'I guess.' I don't know what he's getting at.

'Do you have any suspicions as to who might have killed him?' Glen has soon finished his food.

My plate is still quite full. It's hot. I'm hot and I feel sick as thoughts of Ben fill my head. 'I need a bit of fresh air.' Standing, the chair crashes onto his walnut flooring behind me. I stride out of his apartment allowing his front door to slam, then I'm running down the stairs before inhaling sharply as I step out into the cold night air. If that didn't make me look suspicious I don't know what else would.

He pushes his kitchen window open and calls out. 'Marissa, what happened?'

'I'm okay,' I shout. 'I'll be back up in a moment.'

The window closes. I glance up and down the road, watching cars pass then I glance back at my own block of flats and I see a car outside that I recognise. It belongs to Ben. As he gets out, I duck behind a bush and watch as he walks up to the door, then around the side. I can't see him for a minute or two, then he reappears and gets back into his car. Light comes from his phone through the windscreen and I check my own. He's not calling me. Maybe he's calling my home number, withholding his number to scare me again. His headlamps flash on and he begins to drive towards me. I stoop further behind the bush and watch as he leaves.

'Marissa, what are you doing?' Glen's standing behind me. 'Should I rephrase that, why are you hiding?'

'I'm not. It's nothing. I just saw someone pull up at my apartment block, someone I know and I didn't want him to see me.'

'Is this person worrying you?'

'No, it's nothing like that.'

He places an arm around me and guides me back towards the communal door. My teeth are chattering as a real harsh frost lingers in the air. He removes his coat and throws it over my shoulders. 'Let's get you a hot drink and you can tell me everything.'

Shaking my head, I step back and throw his coat into a pile of snow. How can I tell him that everyone around me is in danger and I'm losing my mind with all that's happening? Wide-eyed, I step back into the road and a turning car beeps, sending me falling against the kerb. He runs over to help me but I put a hand up, turn and run as fast as I can. The further he is away from me, the better for him. 'I'm not safe to be around any more.' I don't know if he heard me say that but I mean every word.

CHAPTER FORTY

As I reach my own apartment block passing the meowing cat, I fumble to get the key in the lock and burst through the door. My letter box looks untouched but I need to open it to see if Ben left me anything. I'm wondering if I'll find another note. The figure I see following me all the time fits his size. It's him, I know for certain, now.

The man and his girlfriend from number twenty-two enter a few seconds later and he nudges past me. She is wearing a reindeer antler headband and looks a bit tipsy. For once they're not arguing, in fact, their hands are linked and they're laughing. 'Looks like someone else couldn't stand our lovely neighbour either. Whatever, I'm glad he's gone.' He leans past me and opens his post box.

'Hmm.'

'Well, I can't say that I miss him. I'm glad all our problems are now over.' He bends to kiss the blonde-haired woman and gives me a wink that comes across as disturbing. Does he know something? 'Have a good evening.' I now officially suspect every one of doing bad things.

They hurry up the stairs and they're gone.

The straight line of the letter box looks like an expressionless mouth. If it was a mouth, I wonder if it was about to laugh at me right now as I stand and stare. I push my key into the dinky keyhole then step back as the hair clip I left at the Drunken Duck falls out. The woman from number twenty-four is being quickly led downstairs by her three dogs. I hold my hair clip, then I smile and coo at her dogs in an attempt to appear as normal as I possibly can.

'Oh, hi. You made me jump.' She gently tugs the overexcited dogs away from me before glancing out of the glass in the main door. 'Such a shame about that cat.'

'What?' I could do with this conversation being over now but silly as it sounds, I care about the cat I've been feeding.

'Owners moved about a month ago and left it behind. Poor thing. I know you feed it. I think he likes you. They say that cats choose their owners.' Her dogs begin to bark and drag her to the door. 'Catch you later.'

I scoot past her and run up the stairs. Owning a cat isn't on my list of priorities right now. I can't even look after myself. The poor creature would be doomed. Once inside, I throw the hair clip onto the red-penned notes that I left on the coffee table. The man following me has to be Ben. His number flashes up on my phone. He's trying to call me now. I want to talk to him, to have everything out with him, but my throat feels as though it's closing up. I can't do this. I grab my hair in my hands and sob.

I wonder now if this was his plan all along. To destabilise me. Something isn't adding up. The more I think about it, the more I know my so-called dead father has a lot to do with this. My apple picture stuck to the lamp post was a clue. I only had Simon and Caroline's word that he was dead. Back at the farm, I used to see a figure in the darkness, outside. I thought it was my imagination or Simon trying to scare me.

A message flashes through.

I saw you. Boo!

The ghost emoji at the end of the message sends a shiver across my shoulders. Ben knows he has me scared. He's not only playing me, he's enjoying the game. My mind darts back to my mother's murder and the nights where Simon would come to my room. I run to the bathroom suddenly feeling sick and dirty, then I turn the shower to hot and step under it fully clothed. *I'm disgusting, dirty, and I put everyone around me in danger. Those I hate and those I love. It doesn't seem to matter.*

My stomach is turning and I cry, my tears mingling with the water. I hate life. I hate everything and I hate myself.

As I step out, I hear banging on my front door so I look through the spyhole. Relieved, I exhale. It's Glen.

'Please let me in, Marissa. I need to know that you're okay.'

I can't do to him what Reggie did to me when she shut me out so I open the door. In my dripping state, I force a smile but he can see right through me. Why? Because he's my friend and he wants to help. All I have to do is let him in.

'Marissa, come here.' He hugs me and I don't know what to do. I can't hold him back. I can't ruin this and I can't tell him why I feel so disgusting. He'd never look at me in the same way. He'd see filth before his eyes and I don't want that. I can see why Reggie did what she did and to think I've never been able to forgive her until now. She couldn't face what was next, just like I can't. It's all too much. *I forgive you, Reggie.*

CHAPTER FORTY-ONE

Seven years ago

I woke up this morning with Reggie on my mind and I sense something is off. People scoff at these feelings but it's like the air had changed. Maybe it was the churning unease in my gut because Reggie has been shutting me out. One day she'd be full of joy, walking with a bounce and other days, that dark cloud followed her around everywhere. Her mood swings were draining both of us. I'm going to persuade her to get help, maybe speak to her doctor, or get her a therapist. I can tell her how counselling has helped me through my problems. She needs it and I'll be with her all the way. My stomach churns.

Okay, my sense of unease isn't entirely unfounded. I'm looking at my bank account online as it's payday and I normally get around two thousand pounds per calendar month, that's with my commission. I have received a second payment of over ten thousand pounds, Reggie has gone weird and now she's paid me the wrong amount. However much I'd love to put this payment down to a Christmas bonus and keep all that money for my savings pot, I know that wouldn't be right. Three times I've tried to call Reggie but her answerphone keeps kicking in.

As I drive to work, I enjoy the twinkly Christmas trees that fill people's front windows and I know it's going to be a long day. It's our annual Christmas bash in town tonight which Christine, Bethany and I have been excited about all week.

As I pull into my parking space under the building, I consider the extra ten thousand pounds again, wondering if it's a bonus of some description. Shaking my head, I conclude that although Reggie likes me and even considers me family, she still wouldn't give me that much of a bonus without saying something. My stomach feels a bit sickly. I've never known her to make a mistake with wages before. In fact, she doesn't even do our wages. She employs a payroll/HR person to handle the wages for all her businesses. Surely they would have questioned the extra ten thousand pounds.

A churning sensation starts irritating my stomach. Something really isn't right and I know Reggie won't be at the office. She won't answer her phone this early so I'm going to do the only thing I can think of, which is drive to her apartment and check on her. Maybe she went on a huge bender last night and has been taken ill or had a fall.

After battling through the ever-increasing morning traffic, I finally reach Reggie's apartment block by the canal. I park in a no parking zone at the front and hurry to the door and buzz. There is no answer. I look up but I can't see a thing. My heart is pounding against my chest after I've convinced myself that she's hurt and in pain. A few seconds later, I see a resident exiting the lift so I step back and turn away as if I'm waiting for someone. As he opens the door and hurries away, I grab it just before it locks, and I run into the building.

As I step into the lift, 'Last Christmas' plays gently in the background. I nervously pull at my braid as I wait for the slow moving lift to reach the penthouse, then I see Reggie's door. I go to knock as loud as I can but the door pushes open. My first suspicion is a burglary gone wrong. Reggie has a lot of expensive items and jewellery. I hurry through, taking in the piano and the room. There's nothing to suggest that a burglary has taken place.

It's a little messy and there are empty wine bottles everywhere but that's not unusual. Reggie has been drinking a lot more than usual lately. I just wished she'd open up to me.

It's so dull, I turn the lights on and swallow as I glance at the door to the hallway. Written in pen on the door is a message – 'Do not enter'. There's a smell, the closer I get; like something has gone off in a fridge. I ignore the note and go through. There is another note stuck to her bedroom door. Cautiously stepping closer, I reach for the letter and it's addressed to me in Reggie's beautiful cursive writing.

As soon as I have it open, it's like the air has been sucked out of the room and I fall to the floor, sobbing. 'No,' I yell as I clutch the note.

I don't care that Reggie doesn't want me in her bedroom right now but it might be my only chance to save her. It's a cry for help, just like the night on her balcony but when I open the door, the smell hits me first, then the sight of my very dear friend looking lifeless and pale, tucked up in bed. An empty whisky bottle has fallen to the floor and there are empty packets of paracetamol everywhere. I run towards her and feel for a pulse but there isn't one. Reggie has gone. I place my arms under hers as I cry and hold her until I feel as though my lungs are burning from all the sobbing. I've lost her after promising myself that I'd do all I could to help her. I should have called her more.

The signs were there all along. Her extreme behaviour, one minute manic, the next in the dark grip of depression. Reggie chose me from the start to be her friend. From the moment she checked on me outside House of Class when that man tried to assault me, she'd been there. She was the only person in the world who knew the real me and I feel so lonely now. Kissing her hair, I lay her back while I read the letter properly. This time I imagine it in Reggie's voice.

Dear, darling Marissa,

First things first. Do not show anyone else this note. All the answers that everyone will need are in my top drawer. Point everyone to that.

I'll fill you in first. Before you question my sanity, my mind has never been clearer. I'm in so much debt and the sheriffs will be at the office for ten in the morning to clear the place out. Your monthly salary should set you up! If you haven't checked yet, have a look. You really need to go it alone, Baxter. You don't need a person like me taking a cut of all your hard work for doing sod all. Work for yourself. Become the creator of your own destiny. Don't be someone's underling, you're too good for that. About my watch. Hmm, right, I'm guessing that only the truth will do. I sold it to set you up. I had already chosen this path, planned it all perfectly. The rest of the company money now belongs to my creditors and the taxman.

Don't be angry with me, please. Oh God, now I'm crying. It wasn't meant to be like this.

Sometimes there is no other way. I know you said there is always a way out, but not this time. Don't be sad for me, I've chosen to take control of my situation. Life is just life. We're born, we live, we often breed, and then we die. Today is the day I've chosen to die. Does it really matter if we go now or later? Death is the only thing in life that is inevitable. I get to be scattered across the earth where my atoms will be reassembled. Did you know that all matter in the universe came from the Big Bang? We're all stardust, that's all. How exciting is that? I know you're now thinking, why isn't she taking this more seriously instead of leaving me with useless facts? The answer to that is, I always did take this seriously, which is why I've chosen this path. I've been stupid, really stupid. Always seeking thrill upon thrill that led me to the casino and I just went too large. If only I could have mastered your poker face. The Baxter look that I've so often joked about.

Now on to the part where I hope you don't hate me. Please forgive me and remember all the good times we had. You really are the daughter I never had. I know now that you're beating yourself up. You promised you'd always be there when you could see I was suffering, and you were. Only, this time, I didn't want you there. I came into this world and my mother died as a result and now I'm choosing to go out alone. After all, someone can be there to hold your hand at the end but it's not them who takes that last breath. The bridge to death is a journey we take alone, I don't care what anyone says.

I realise I've said so much. I didn't think it, I just wrote it so I'm sorry if I haven't covered everything. Anyway, the sheriffs will be with you soon. Leave all this behind and make me proud. If you opened that door, you are now seeing my angry face.

All my love,
Reggie. XXX

My tears blot the writing on the page. This writing sounds like the Reggie I used to know before she got so depressed. She was philosophical, eccentric and full of energy. I want to smile as I feel as though I've heard her voice again, albeit in my head as I read the letter. Then, I glance back and my legs buckle. Her glasses lie smashed on the wooden floor. My lovely friend, Reggie – forever gone, taking the most important piece of me with her. I feel like a stone, cold and detached.

I know what I need to do next, I need to call the police. I reach up and gently close her eyes so that I feel she's resting.

I pull my leather gloves on then I open Reggie's bedside cabinet. I see bank statements, all in the red with huge chunks of money being withdrawn. Then debt letter upon debt letter fills the drawer. Court letters, betting slips, not just for a few pounds on the horses but for thousands in one go. Closing the drawer, I leave Reggie's room and call the police.

Storming out onto the landing, I scream so hard, I feel as though my eyes will pop out. I can't stop and it's that intense, my chest and throat burn. I love her but I hate her. I hate her so much. How could she do this to me? It's at this point that I realise, I'm back to square one in life. Not one person in this whole world truly knows me, and Reggie was special. No one else could understand me like she did and no one can ever replace her. She's gone, just like my mother. They all leave me.

As the police officers step out of the lift, I stuff the folded-up letter in my pocket. I will respect Reggie's wish that no one else sees it but I don't respect what she did. She abandoned me!

CHAPTER FORTY-TWO

Now

I wake to the smell of burning. 'Reggie?' Glen looks confused and continues to spread jam over a couple of slices of toast. My head feels as though it's bound in cotton wool and I wonder if even my words will come out coherently. 'You stayed.' My lips feel fat and cold.

'Look, Marissa. I don't know what you're going through at the moment but I wasn't leaving you last night. At one point I thought about calling an ambulance.'

My brows furrow as I push the snuggle blanket off my body. 'What?'

'Don't you remember?'

However much I try to think, I can't remember. My brain hurts and the throbbing in my forehead is making me nauseous. I remember Glen turning up and I was soaking wet. Maybe I made him a drink after that. Did I drink something alcoholic? Shaking that thought away, I try to focus but my head feels woozy. There's no alcohol in my apartment. I think he kept asking me what the matter was and… blank. 'What's happening to me, Glen? I can't remember anything. I remember getting out of the shower and I was wearing my clothes.' I glance down and I've changed into pyjamas. I wonder how I ended up in them. 'Did we…'

'No, of course not. I'd never take advantage of you. You were soaking wet and upset. I got some nightwear from your drawers and you changed in the bathroom. I made you a coffee and we sat on the settee where you kept crying and mumbling incoherently about someone called Reggie before you eventually fell asleep. I covered you up, then I grabbed a blanket from your cupboard. I hope you don't mind that I did that. You were in a worrying state so I didn't want to leave you. I thought that maybe you'd had a drink before coming to mine or maybe you'd taken something.'

I glance at the chair and see a scrunched up blanket. It looks like that's where Glen slept, sitting up in an armchair. 'Thank you for what you did. I'm so sorry I put you out. Should you be at work?'

'I called in sick. There was no way I could leave you in the state you were in. I know you don't want to talk to me, but I'm here to listen. Last night scared me. I've never seen anyone breakdown like that in my entire life. Was it the man who was parked up outside your apartment block last night? And, what are these?' He places a cup of coffee and the toast on the table and picks up one of my notes.

I shrug.

'If someone is sending you letters like this, you need to call the police.'

'I'm okay.' He can't know that I could put myself in the frame for the murders if I call them. I know I'm close to finding out what's going on, then I will go to the police with everything.

'You are not okay.' He sits on the chair and sips the drink he's made himself in my kitchen.

It's time to say something. He's not about to stop asking, not now he's seen me in such a state. 'I'm being followed. I thought the first note was from Dan but then I received another after he'd died. It can't have been him. Someone was watching my apartment a few nights ago so I ran after them but by the time I'd got down there, they'd gone.'

'You should have called me. I could have confronted them with you. It's dangerous for you to be running around chasing a madman. No wonder you're not yourself. Was it the same man that came to your apartment last night?'

As I shrug my shoulders, I bite my dry lip. 'Maybe. I've only seen this person from afar and he's always dressed in a dark hoodie with the hood up. I think it's him but I have no proof.'

'Okay, so who's the man from last night?'

'Look, it doesn't matter.'

'It does. I saw the way you were looking at his car. You were freaking out when I caught you hiding. Who is he?'

'Why does it matter? What are you going to do?'

'Nothing. I thought we could start keeping a diary, like we did with Dan. I will help you gather evidence for the police and you can look at things like restraining orders.'

I let out a small laugh and I want to say, is that all. I'm relieved Glen is who he is but I don't think Ben would be worried about a piece of paper and Glen doesn't realise how close I am to being implicated in these murders. I'm literally stuck. 'Okay, we'll keep a diary. I'll start writing it tonight, catching up on all I have so far.' I pause. 'I really need to be alone now. I have to get up properly and do my work. Bills to pay and all that. Maybe we can talk more later and I'll bring my diary along.' I need to be alone while I work out what to do next. I can't think with him here.

The frown on his face sharpens. 'Okay, come to mine and this time, can you stay and eat the food? If you get an urge to run or you get panicky, we can talk through those feelings. I will help you through this and you are going to come out of it stronger. I promise.'

He's a good person and I'm tainting him with my situation but if I say no, I fear he'll be here all day fussing. I like him being in my life but I have no option but to sort myself out. After, we can then work on having a normal friendship. How I get to that stage, I have no idea, but I will; I need to. Then I swallow. How can I carry on the way I am? 'I have a lot of things to catch up on but I promise I'll come over later.'

'Good.' He smiles and stands, leaving his cup on the side. 'Going back to that man, is he a friend or someone you work with?'

He's not going to drop this line of questioning, I can tell. 'He's definitely not a friend but I do get work from him. He's a recent client and I know I have to deal with him, set some boundaries – that's all. I'll tell you more later. Promise.'

'Okay. Any sense that you're in danger, being watched, or any more silent phone calls, write it all down and if you're in any immediate danger, call me. I'll come straight away.'

'Thanks, Glen.' Finally, I'm seeing him out. He stares at the line of marbles against the skirting board but he says nothing. I can't tell him that when I'm alone I have to leave them scattered so that I don't sleepwalk myself into any more trouble. As soon as I close the door behind him, I place them back where they belong. If I was awake last night and I don't remember things, I'm definitely getting worse. I've gone from sleepwalking to full-on bouts of amnesia; that's what the stress of everything is doing to me.

As much as I fight for a memory, one that will unravel everything, I can't remember last night. I check my bed – not slept in. I check the bathroom – my toothbrush is bone dry and the sink is clean. The bath is still a little damp from where I had a shower and my wet clothes are heaped in a corner giving off a damp smell. I'm not making sense to myself and that is the scariest thing I've ever had to face. Running to the window, I look out. There is definitely no one there. I stare at the home phone and for some reason I think that will make it ring. It remains silent. My mobile isn't even flashing which tells me that I don't have any messages or missed calls. The silence is both welcoming and scary, then I flinch as the home phone rings and, with shaking hands, I pick up the receiver. This time the caller speaks and I feel a shiver running across the back of my clammy neck.

CHAPTER FORTY-THREE

'How did you get my number?' I'm immediately on the defensive.

'Online. You run your own business. Your number was easy to find.' Her voice is gentle and she speaks clearly.

'Who are you?' I'm woozy with nerves so I sit.

'My name's Elizabeth Worrell, was Forge.'

'Ben's ex-wife.'

She pauses for a moment. 'That's right.'

'Why are you calling me?'

'It's for your own safety. I keep a track on him and what he's doing, then I call every woman he ever has any involvement with and he hates it. It's my way of taking back control. He nearly killed me, did you know that?'

I exhale slowly and pull a blanket over my knee. It's cold and I'm sure she can hear the tremor in my voice. 'My friend had concerns so I looked him up. I read about what he did to you. Have you called me before?'

'I have to apologise for that. What I'm doing isn't easy and sometimes, I can't find the words. I'm sorry if I scared you but it's hard for me to talk about what happened too. I just needed you to know what kind of a man he is and you can then decide if you want to get involved. If I didn't try to warn you, I couldn't live with myself. That man can charm the pants off any woman. He has this way about him that makes you feel special and it works fast too. I married him after only seeing him for two months but I should have known better. The violence started just before, just small things that could be explained away as being in the height of passion. As soon as I had that ring on my finger, he badgered me to pack up work and we moved away from friends and family. I realise this was a perfectly honed strategy for him. Then that was it. Two years I put up with him hurting me but then he nearly killed me. I had to stop him so I called the police and he was sent down. I vowed then that every woman he got involved with, I'd warn them. I keep a close eye on him so that I can tell everyone that will listen.'

I lean back and lay my head on the soft chair.

'Do you think he's capable of stalking? Someone has been watching me and not just recently.'

'Oh yes. I still have to keep moving now as he finds me. I fear that this is my life forever. My advice would be to keep as far away from him as possible. He's no good.'

'Thank you.' I'm now relieved I didn't meet him again for lunch or even call him. But, he's not going to let me go. 'How do I stop him harassing me?'

'I wish I had the answer. Just stay safe, okay?' She hung up. I press 1471, needing to know more but as before she's withheld her number. Instead, I call Justine and she answers.

'Hi, lovey. I can't stop, just heading into a meeting. I was going to call you this evening.'

'About Elizabeth?'

She pauses for a second. 'Yes. She spoke to you too?'

'Yes. And I read an old article about Ben's conviction. He almost killed her and the bastard got out after two years.'

'I know. And look at us. Can we talk tonight, preferably late as I have a lot on?'

'Yes, course. Are you still staying with your mum?'

'I am, for now. I'm really sorry but I've got to go. Talk later.' She hangs up.

I realise that my heart is pounding and I can't breathe. I dash to the kitchen sink and turn on the cold tap, then splash my face until I feel a little calmer. Tugging a piece of cotton on my pyjamas, I realise that I'm unravelling at the seams, just like this top. I have to talk and I have to trust someone. I wish Reggie was here, but she's not and I will forever miss her. Or, I wish I still had my mum, then I could run to her just like Justine has done. I wish I hadn't pushed Glen out the door so quickly. I swallow, tonight I'm going to tell Glen everything.

I can't go on like this any more. Facing my problems is the only way to keep my mind. Right now, that's more important than anything and if all this comes to a head with the police then so be it. The truth will find its own way out, even if the police temporarily arrest me until they find out what really happened to Simon and Dan. But first, I'm telling Glen everything. As soon as I have I'm calling the police.

I hear the fire door slam and then someone shuffles in the corridor. Peering through the keyhole, I gasp as Dan Pritchard's wife turns around. Petula. Kicking the marbles away, I open the door and croak out a few words not knowing how she will react to me.

CHAPTER FORTY-FOUR

'Marissa.' Petula hugs me like she did the last time we spoke, back at that coffee shop in Birmingham.

Her coat rustles in my ear and I'm embarrassed that I'm still wearing my pyjamas. 'Petula, what are you doing here?' I already know the answer to that but I can't quite believe she was married to someone like Dan Pritchard.

She leans back and looks me over. 'You look poorly, are you okay?'

'I should be asking if you're okay.' I nod at what was Dan's door, acknowledging her loss. She always did seem to put others before herself.

'As his next of kin, I have to clear out his apartment and sort through his things.' A slither of a tear started to roll down her chubby pink cheek. I remember her wearing bold make-up but today she was pale and blotchy, like she was carrying a heavy burden. She puts the key in the door and stops. 'I can't face it yet. Can I talk to you, about him? I mean, he was your neighbour and we know each other well.' She pauses and places her stray hairs behind her ears while removing her bobble hat.

Petula is one of the only people who has ever liked or been kind to me and I have disappointed her, she just doesn't know it yet. I mean, I sleepwalked and took the knife, which means I saw something. Problem is, nothing is coming back to me. For a second, I see water, like I'm staring at my reflection in a bath full of it. Was that a clue?

Scrunching her nose, she stares out of the landing window at the car park. 'Actually, that was silly of me to ask. How could you know him and why would you want to? I'm imposing on you and I'm sorry.' She turns away and I can hear her choking back a sob.

'Petula, please, come in. I'll put the kettle on.' I leave her to amble behind me as I run ahead, removing the letters from the lounge. I throw them into the plate cupboard just as she enters and they land on my picture of the apple and worm. 'Take a seat. Sorry about the mess. It's my day off which is why I'm not dressed. I was going to have a duvet day.'

'Until I came along and ruined it.' She removes her huge handbag from her shoulders.

'Honestly, you haven't.' I grab my pillow and blanket and throw them into a corner and she sits. 'It's lovely to see you again, really it is.' What else can I say? It would be wrong of me to tell her that I didn't like Dan at all and that he scared me. I look at her and I wonder what went wrong in their marriage, maybe he scared her too. Dan was certainly touchy when I mentioned his marriage so I guess a lot went on that he wasn't happy about. Maybe it was his drinking. I imagine him being violent and cruel, but he was also intimidating in the cold light of day. Flicking on the kettle, I prepare two drinks. 'Milk and sugar?'

'Just milk, please.'

I pass her a drink and sit on the chair that Glen slept in, then silence. Should I say something or should I wait for her to speak? Do I reassure her or give her another hug? Maybe she'd like some food. I'm sure she can sense my awkwardness. As I go to speak she beats me to it.

'You know, he wasn't always a good person. He was an awful husband towards the end of our marriage, but it's still hard knowing someone killed him.'

I swallow and I'm sure she heard me do it. Petula is a people person and I know she's sensing something. Maybe she already suspects my involvement but even I don't know what I know. Her boys had to have told her about the 'horrible neighbour' that their dad didn't like. 'Have the police found anything out?'

She bites her lip and shakes her head. 'No. They haven't even managed to identify everyone at the party on the night before his murder. I think he went a bit mad, inviting a load of people over that he barely knew. My younger son said he didn't recognise anyone, not enough to name them anyway. He did say you came in to ask Dan to turn the noise down. I'm sorry he wasn't a good neighbour.'

That wasn't what I expected her to say. 'Well, I'm sorry about what happened to him and I hope you and your boys can get through this.' I'm sure I heard this phrase in a film once. It sounds silly now. Of course they'll get through it. What else are they likely to do? I wish I could be more helpful. I'm trying and soon, I'll be speaking to the police where everything I know will come out, but it's not much. Everything leads to me but I didn't kill him. I will prove that Ben is behind all this, somehow.

'What was he like recently?'

She must know what he was like. My neck and jaw tense so much, I feel a pain starting at the back of my head as I clench my teeth. 'He was a tough neighbour to live next to.'

She lets out a huff of a laugh. 'He was a tough husband too.'

'I gather you were divorced or divorcing?'

'I hoped to divorce him but he wouldn't sign the papers. He was so, so angry.'

'Did he hurt you?' I shouldn't have said that. 'That was nosy of me. Please excuse that question.' I drink a bit of my coffee and hope my cheeks aren't flushing too much. I'm itchy now. I want to scratch. My gums itch too so I clench my jaw again then I realise I'm grinding my teeth.

'Oh good God, no. I hurt him.'

Now I'm confused. My mouth opens a little as my brows scrunch.

'Not like that. I didn't hit him. I found someone else and fell in love. Dan had spent so many years going out on his own and he began drinking so much, I felt like I no longer had a life and he could be really mean when he was drunk. Anyway, life with him was one long cycle of arguments and me nursing his hangovers. Truth is, he didn't really want me until I told him we were over. Suddenly, I was his everything and he needed and loved me.' She paused. 'It was too late. I'd already met someone and he's everything Dan wasn't. Attentive, loving, intoxicating, in a good way. I fell for him instantly and I knew that me and Dan had to end.' She paused. 'I'd put so much of my life on hold for Dan and the boys and now it was my time. I often felt that Dan had become the way he was just to hold me back for longer. He resented me having a life, a better career than he did and he hated me going out on my own. I sound like such a bitch now because of what's happened.' Her jaw began to shake as she waved away her tears.

'You definitely don't. You deserve to be happy and it sounds like he was really selfish.'

She shrugs. 'But, when I heard he'd died, I was relieved. I'd spent so long asking for that divorce and now it means the fights were finally over. You see, this man I met, I want to move in with him and marry him someday. He's really opened my eyes to what living really is. Then I think of Dan. He was murdered. It must have been terrifying.'

'I'm so sorry, Petula.' I'm sorry for a lot. I'm sorry I can't tell her exactly what happened.

'No one deserves to die like that. He worked hard and he did a lot for our boys but he'd become bitter and selfish towards the end of our relationship and he couldn't accept we were over. I made sure he knew that my new man was more attentive, I even said it to his face. I think I wanted to hurt him, revenge for all the neglect and lack of affection in our marriage; for the anger and intimidation that he'd scared me with near the end.'

'Petula, I'm sure the police will get to the bottom of this and you'll probably find that there was a reason. I know Dan came across as intimidating and aggressive so whether he was into something you didn't know about or he'd done something to really upset someone…' I don't know where I'm going with this so I stop talking.

'My boys have to live with what happened. The youngest found his father dead. That image will stay with him forever and that thought is killing me.'

I swallow. 'Poor kid. I know how he feels.'

'Oh, I'm sorry. This must be bringing up so many bad memories for you.'

What do I say? 'You love your boys and they love you. You're their mother and you have to be strong for them.' However horrible Dan was, he was their father.

'I'm taking up your time. I suppose I can't delay the inevitable.' She stands, grabs her bag and brushes her coat down.

'Well, I'm here if you want to pop back, for a drink or a chat.' She ignores me and carries on into the hall.

'You always were such a lovely girl, Marissa.' She stops and looks like she wants to say something, then she smiles at me like she did back at Simon and Caroline's farmhouse. A twinge of guilt churns in my stomach. 'I know he was an awful husband but he loved our boys more than anything. They now have to grow up without a father and that hurts me to the core. Whoever killed him needs to be locked up!'

CHAPTER FORTY-FIVE

It's only two in the afternoon but darkness has already fallen given that it's so gloomy out. I turn off the main light and open the living room curtains. After Petula left, I felt like the world was closing in on me and that every waving tree or shadow was my stalker. Curtains shut, lights off and staring at the walls stark-eyed had been the only thing I'd done for the past hour. I glance down, there is no one there. The phone call from Elizabeth has shaken me too.

As I sit back, I try to think of the night Simon was murdered. I saw water earlier. What did that mean? My brain hurts from thinking and my thoughts drift to what happened after Reggie died; back to when I moved into this apartment.

Like now, I'd never felt so alone. Reggie's death had been formally classed as a suicide and the enormity of her debt finally came out. She'd been on a slow descent for a couple of years. As soon as the post-mortem had delivered the results and the police had finished up, her assets were all taken in readiness to pay her creditors. The sheriffs came without regard for the tragedy of a life lost.

Christine and Bethany both found other jobs, as did I, taking insurance calls in a call centre all day long. Soon, I gave my notice in and took Reggie's advice to work for myself.

At first I was angry at Reggie for killing herself, but that anger turned into bouts of hurt and guilt because I could have helped her. It brought back so many memories of my mother and the way she died. There had been no bounce in my voice, no warmth in my heart. That went on the day Reggie took her friendship away from me. She knew how much I needed her too but she left me and now my existence feels pointless.

Anyway, I did the only thing I felt could help me. I moved back to Stratford-upon-Avon so that I could be near the cottage that was one day going to be mine; the only place where I could feel close to my mother. I bought my very first property, my apartment. Reggie gave me a chance with that money and she gave me my profession too. After living frugally in that crummy shared house in Edgbaston for so long, I'd saved a huge deposit and I still had the ten thousand pounds from Reggie to start up my own financial advice business.

My mother left me, not that that was her fault. Reggie chose to leave me. Caroline and Simon abused me. I was lost for ages. The aim was to save up and as soon as that cottage came up for sale, I wanted it. It's the place my mother promised we'd go back to and one day I will honour that memory and make it mine. Soon after, Justine came into my life and I got so much work. Things were starting to work out and I will always thank Reggie for that.

I shake my past away. It's not helping me think about the things that matter now. It's a distraction I don't need. There's a few things I need to do. As I don't know how the conversation with Glen will end this evening, I really need to sort my affairs out. If the police take me in for questioning, or even decide to arrest me based on what I tell them, I don't want to be the reason people don't get their mortgages or insurances in place. I'm up to date with Justine but I have some open jobs with Ben. Besides, I want to have things out with him and now is the time. I'm going to confront him with everything I know before I see Glen tonight. I need to get to the bottom of all that is going on. Ben has to be the missing link and I'm sick of getting nowhere fast, especially as the police will be back. I can ask him if he's stalking me and even tell him to leave Justine alone. She shouldn't be afraid to live in her own house. I don't even care about the work any more. He can have it back. No work is worth this much sacrifice.

The plan: I'll drop all the files and documents back to Forge's office so I get to speak to him in a place I feel safe. He won't intimidate me while there are other people around. I can tell him I know about his ex-wife and that I know about his treatment of Justine. I can tell him I know that he watches my apartment, that I've seen him following me and I want to know how he knows my father? He knows too much. Then, I'm going to tell Glen everything before I go to the police. Tonight is the night when all this will be over.

I hurry to my office and begin boxing up the files that he gave me, gently placing them in alphabetical order, attaching handover notes to each for the next person. I leave the box by the door then get dressed in my smartest white blouse with a scalloped neckline. I grab my favourite trousers, the one with the seam down the front and my shiniest shoes. My hair is slicked into a bun and I apply my make-up.

Remembering my picture of the apple and the worm in the plate cupboard, I hurry through my apartment turning on all the lights and I grab it. I can now return it to its rightful place with Scarecrow. He lives in my bed drawer with the couple of photos I have of my mother and me. All I have that matters is in that drawer. The little connections to my past. I kneel down with the folded picture in my hand and I slide the drawer open, then I stare open-mouthed. Scarecrow has gone and so has one of the photos of me and my mother. I begin to empty my drawers and fling everything from my wardrobe. I must have moved it last night in my weird state. But where? I push through everything in every cupboard or drawer but I can't see it. I haven't got time to keep looking, maybe that's a job for later. My unravelled Scarecrow is lost.

Several minutes later, I'm standing amongst the chaos of my search and I still haven't found the toy. I'm losing the plot. Seriously, I don't know who I am or what I'm doing any more. This can't go on otherwise I'm going to lose my mind and there will be no way back.

Suddenly, I feel exposed, like I'm living in a glasshouse that everyone can see through. I dash to the window then I catch sight of the figure at the end of the street and he's disappearing into the darkness. Do I run after him or do I take Glen's advice and give him a call to back me up? Grabbing my notebook, I write down the time and date, mentioning again that he is wearing a dark hoodie under a coat and that he has the hood up. The hood covers most of his face and it's too dark to make out any features, especially as I'm looking down on him. I look again to see if I can see more. A photo might help and that'll prove it is Ben. Maybe I can lighten it with my editing app. I snatch my mobile off the table and go to point it in his direction but he's gone. Throwing my phone to the sofa, I raise my arms and let out a roar. My hands tremble and my face reddens. The knock at the door silences me. Maybe Petula is back again. I can't let her see that I've turned over most of my apartment. She can't come in. I'm dressed for work so my excuse is I'm about to go out. I need to get to Ben's office before he closes for the evening and I'm already wasting time. Also, if I get there quickly and he's not there, I'll know for definite that the figure watching my apartment is him.

There is a louder knock, then another. I hurry to the door and peer through the spyhole and my heart sinks. No way? Why are the police back? I'm not even going to be able to sort out my affairs before they take me away. It suddenly clicks; the person watching me could be from the police. Maybe I've been under suspicion all along. DS Brindle knocks again so I answer. 'Hello. Is everything okay? I was just about to leave as I have to meet a client.' I'm holding my cardboard box. My white blouse and grey trousers look like suitable attire. I feel a string of sweat forming at the nape of my neck.

'May we come in? I have a couple of questions and this won't take long.'

'I've told you all I know. I didn't really know my neighbour that well.' Someone has told them about me arguing with him that night, I know they have. That's why they're here. I think of the mess all over my apartment. It makes me look unhinged. They can't see it.

'It's not about Daniel Pritchard. It's about another matter. We're just doing another follow up on the murder of Simon Ferris.'

I can't swallow. My throat is closing up. Dropping the box, I step back and gasp. The communal landing looks like it's swaying behind them as the prickles appear across my eyes. I'm going to faint, I'm sure I am.

CHAPTER FORTY-SIX

After a couple of deep breaths I bend over and put all my paperwork back in the box. 'Sorry about that. All this is just really upsetting.'

DC Collins scratches his red nose. 'We'd rather not discuss it on the doorstep. May we come in?'

I have no choice but to let them in. I've missed my chance to catch Ben out but I have bigger problems. I'm not ready to tell all to the police yet. They follow me through to the lounge where all my doors are open and there is mess strewn everywhere. 'Excuse the mess. I lost an important work document so I had to go through everything to find it.' I tap the box that I've now placed on the coffee table. 'Found it in the end though.'

Brindle and Collins gaze around, taking everything in. I'm glad the notes are still in the plate cupboard and not on the table. Their presence would have thrown a few more questions up. They don't sit this time. They stand in the living room. Brindle clears her throat a couple of times, then coughs. 'We wanted to update you. What we have is two murders, both stabbings, and you knew both people. There was also something left at each scene that links the two. I can't discuss that though but all I can tell you is the same person murdered both victims.'

I know it was the snowflake baubles; after all, I was holding one the night Simon was murdered and I saw one come out of Dan's apartment in an evidence bag. 'Please sit down. I didn't know my neighbour. He'd barely moved in.' I'm sweating badly and I can't help it. DS Brindle stares deep within me and all I want her to do is blink. I look into my lap. 'This is so awful. I can't believe what's happening.' And I can't. I want to find out what has happened as much as they do and as soon as they leave, I can have things out with Ben, and we'll all get to the bottom of this sooner.

'You are the only link we can find to the two victims and we have to consider that whoever committed these crimes could target you next. There have been reports of someone loitering around the estate. A man in a hoodie and he's been seen outside your apartment block. We are concerned for your safety. A man of the same description had been seen loitering on Mr Ferris's road too. Have you seen anyone suspicious hanging around?'

'I can't think of anything or anyone. I don't know who Simon would have been spending his time with and, as I said, I didn't know Mr Pritchard.' My stalker is on their radar but I'm not saying anything about Ben until I've been to his office. I need to totally clear my name and all I need is a few more hours. It's not looking good for me, especially as there's a small knife right underneath the sofa where Brindle is now sitting. I try not to look in that direction.

'We're asking that in the meantime you take extra care. If you see this person, you need to call us straight away. Don't hesitate. Whoever committed these murders is highly dangerous so under any circumstances, do not approach them. We'll also arrange for uniform to drive by regularly.' Her gaze meets mine again and I fear she can see through me. 'Are you sure there's nothing you want to tell us?' She's now staring.

A tremor begins to form at my fingertips and then it reaches my knuckles and wrists.

'Miss Baxter. Are you okay?'

I nod. 'Just a little scared, I suppose.'

'Can you tell me a bit more about your uncle, Simon Ferris?'

I shake my head. 'Whenever I saw him, which wasn't often, he didn't say much. I'd just check that he was okay. He'd tell me he was fine but I know he'd been drinking a lot.' I remember what his neighbour, Alice, had told me and I relay a bit of that information. I can't tell them the full truth until I know what happened myself. 'I'd seen him in a stupor the once, on his doorstep. He never got over Aunt Caroline's death even though it was many years ago, I guess he was lost without her.'

'Did he have any friends or acquaintances that you knew of?'

I shake my head. 'He never told me about any. He was quite a loner after she died.'

'Do you know of any enemies he might have had?' Brindle coughs a little and as she shuffles back in the seat, a waft of cigarette smoke fills the air and dust motes dance in front of my eyes.

'No. I mean, maybe he did have enemies but he never told me about any of them. He never said someone was watching him or upsetting him.' I need them to go. I am not a suspect at the moment and I want to get to Ben's office. I'm not ready to tell them any more yet. I glance at my watch. 'I have a work appointment. Could I speak to you another time?'

DS Brindle and DC Collins stand. 'We have all we need for now. Is there anything else you'd like to tell us or ask us?'

She knows I'm holding something back. I keep my mouth closed and shake my head before heading to the door in the hope that they follow. 'As I said, if I think of anything, I'll call you and if I see anyone loitering, I'll report it straight away.'

'Thank you. We'll be in touch.' As they leave, I close the door. Leaning on the wall, I gasp for breath. It's only a matter of time before this comes back to me so it's never been more important for me to work everything out first and to find out more, I need to speak to Ben. As my heart rate returns to normal, I grab the box full of files and hurry out. As I do, I overhear DS Brindle talking to Petula behind the door of Dan's apartment.

'Have you found the murderer?' Petula's voice is shaky.

I stall on the landing and place the box on the carpet where I pretend to be looking through it as I listen.

'Not as yet. We've gathered all the prints and DNA from the scene but there is so much to go through as you can appreciate. It always takes longer than these TV dramas make out. We do have a link. Another man was murdered in exactly the same way. His name is Simon Ferris.'

There is a pause. 'Simon Ferris. Can't think that I know that name. Wait… no, it's not one I recognise. I meet so many people in my line of work…'

It's only a matter of time before Petula makes that link so I hurry down the stairs and out into the bitter cold afternoon. I'm in such big trouble. The police aren't stupid and my DNA may well be amongst Dan and Simon's things. They'll find it. I mean, I definitely ended up near them even though I don't remember. The last thing I would have done is cleaned up evidence while sleepwalking.

I run to my car. How long do I have? An hour. A few minutes; seconds. Before pulling off, I glance up and down the road, searching for the dark figure but I don't see him. I'm now disappointed. If the man watching me was Ben, he'd have had plenty of time to get back to his office. The police are exiting as I turn onto the main road out of my street. They look to be in a rush. Maybe Petula has remembered who Simon is and has filled them in on my abusive past and they're coming for me right now. That would give me a motive and the fact that I lied and said that Simon and I were on good terms would make me look guilty. I'm prepared for the worst, but not right this minute. My heart pounds. This is what it must feel like to be running from the law. They're coming for me.

CHAPTER FORTY-SEVEN

I've already run through a temporary red traffic light and been honked at by three cars. I need to calm down otherwise I'll crash and then it'll be game over. Pulling up at the kerb, I park right outside Ben's office and get out with his box of files. I grip them like my life depends on it. Relaxing even slightly could result in me dropping them again and I haven't got time to mess around. I'm so hot but there's frost on the ground; it's the nerves getting the better of me. I'm finally going to have everything out with him. I'll ask him about his wife, about Justine and about what he's putting me through. If he lies about not stalking me, I think I'll be able to tell. It has to be him who was creeping me out on the bridge at Stratford and it has to be him who has been watching my apartment and sending those awful notes. He has to have pinned my apple picture to the lamp post. His history of abuse also gives me another reason to believe he's capable of doing this to me. How does he know about my past and my father? I can only find out by asking him. His staff will be there which means he's going to have to keep calm. I shiver; at worst I'm about to confront a double murderer. Then, there's Reggie and her notes. This has been going on a long time and my mind is awhirl. This has to stop. I can't live like this any more.

I almost drop my phone as I select the recording app and start it. Whatever he says will be there for all to hear. I place it in my pocket and hope that anything said won't be too muffled.

My shoes are slippy on the soles and I nearly fall through the door, just recovering my balance at the last second. My neatly tied up hair has come loose, falling like rats' tails over my face. I look like I've been at battle and I guess I have. It's now me against time; against the world; against everyone.

A man and a woman glance my way and another woman, who I guess is in her mid-sixties, steps forward. 'Hello, how can I help you?' Her white blonde bob looks stiff and her jaw angular.

'I'm here to see Mr Forge.'

'And you are?' Her enquiring look is annoying.

'Marissa Baxter.'

'Mr Forge is a busy man. He doesn't take any visitors unless they have an appointment.'

I feel as though I'm chewing on gum as I try to get my words out, but they come out in a squeak. 'Could you please just tell him that I'm here to see him?'

I wonder if Ben is in his office. With the police interrupting me, he would have had enough time to get back here after watching me at my apartment. My mind is flitting everywhere as the past few days fill my head. I need my stream of mixed-up thoughts to shut up before I explode so I take a deep breath.

'Miss Baxter. Why do you want to see Mr Forge?' She speaks louder this time, like she's losing patience with me.

I clear my throat. 'I'm a financial adviser and I've been working for Mr Forge. I need to discuss these files with him before I hand them back over.'

'Oh, I remember him mentioning you now. Unfortunately he's not here. He said he had to meet a client about two hours ago and he hasn't returned yet. I have no idea when he'll be back. He comes and goes often and as he pleases. Can I give him a message?'

Two hours ago, that could put him at my apartment, lurking in the dark while he watched me. 'Yes, tell him these are all the files he's given me. I've emailed him everything I have and I've attached notes to each of the accounts.' I don't tell her that they're handover notes, he can read that for himself.

'I'll make sure he gets them.' She places them on a desk and walks back to me.

'Oh, they're confidential so they shouldn't be left out where the public may roam.' Here I am in a crisis, still making sure that I don't let my clients down.

She frowns. 'I'm sure they are and of course I know that! I'll put them in Mr Forge's office as soon as you leave.' The younger woman starts to photocopy a pile of papers and the man starts talking on the phone.

'Thank you.' I rush out of the door and back to my car.

Ben wasn't there. I stop the recorder on my phone and try to call him but he cuts me off so I leave him a message to contact me straight away. I tell him I know about his wife, about Justine and I know about him watching me. I need him out of my life and I need to know that Justine will be free of his unwanted attention too. Ever since he came into my life, everything has been going down the pan. A message pings up on my phone and I see it's from him.

Your apartment looks so lifeless without you in it, Marissa. Xxx

He has been watching me, I knew it but how did he know about my picture of the apple and how did he get it? He left it stuck to that lamp post for a reason. Pressure builds in my head and a flash of pain temporarily stuns me. There's got to be two people working together on sending me crazy; Ben and someone that knows all about my past. Had Ben and Dan been working together? Maybe Dan posted the first note and Ben posted the second after Ben had killed Dan. Maybe Ben is doing all this for my father. Could they be related? The answers are there, I just have to unlock my memories. I slam my hands onto the steering wheel and accidentally press the horn. It's then a flashback to water hits me again; for the briefest of moments. During one of my sleepwalks, I saw water. How? Why?

As I pull away, I glance back at the estate agency that Ben owns and the woman is staring right at me while talking on a phone. Maybe she's out to get me with Ben. I just don't know or trust anyone any more. I pull away and a car horn toots as the driver urgently swerves around me. Ben has finally shown me his hand. It's time to confront him and learn the truth. That text tells me that he's ready to talk.

CHAPTER FORTY-EIGHT

As I pull into my road, I stop and park a little way back. Staring ahead, I don't see anyone, in fact the whole road is empty. Although quiet and abandoned, the feeling that someone is watching me remains. I don't feel safe. I certainly don't want to park outside my apartment block. If I do, he will know that I'm back. I know he's watching me and I know he's waiting in the shadows.

Before I face what's coming to me, I'm going to tell Glen everything and if something happens to me when I catch up with Ben, I need him to call the police. Swallowing, I look away from my apartment. I feel slightly sick and jittery, which isn't me at all. It's like I've over-caffeinated except I've hardly had any. Maybe this is the inner me that I've been trying to suppress. That scared child is now bursting out of my skin and she wants to feel hurt, she wants to feel angry and she wants to grieve over her lost childhood. I'm ready for him.

My apartment block still looks abandoned. There are maybe a couple of lamps and some Christmas tree lights on behind some of the other windows in my block, but it looks like most people are out unless they are sitting in darkness. For a second, I consider popping back to my apartment, just to check everything, but I dismiss that idea. Ben could be waiting around that bend, sinking back into the trees that line the path, waiting for me. He's the one who's been trying to set me up for murder.

As I go to open the car door, a police car pulls into my road so I duck. As it heads towards the bend I hurry out in my stupid shoes and balance like Bambi as I cross over and buzz Glen. In such circumstances, I almost want to kick the wall and hurt myself as a punishment for being so thoughtless when picking them out to wear. I buzz again and swallow. My mouth is bone dry and my throat is slightly scratchy. Every time I inhale the icy air while the breeze whips around the back of my neck, it takes my breath away.

The intercom crackles for a second. 'Marissa. I wasn't expecting you yet. What a lovely surprise, come up.' I'm not going to be a lovely surprise when I tell Glen what's been going on.

'Hi.' I can't even force a smile and he knows that something is wrong. He's trying to make eye contact but I can't look at him.

He's wearing a thick jumper and a pair of cosy looking socks. His Christmas music is quite loud, maybe too loud but it's not a bad thing. It might just soften the blow of all the things I have to say to him about Simon and Dan, about the knife and the baubles and my sleepwalking. Who am I kidding? No amount of jovial sleigh bell tunes are going to make this better.

'Come in. I'll get you something to drink. Coffee? I have some good stuff. I've been shopping today.'

I shake my head. 'I need something stronger.' I find myself shouting a little to be heard over 'Santa Claus is Coming to Town'. I glance around and see that he's put a small Christmas tree up. It's only one of those that pops up, with its lights and decorations already in place but he's making an effort. I wonder if he's done this because I planned to come over. Even more effort on his behalf that is about to go to waste. I don't deserve to have someone like him as a friend.

He opens his cupboard to reveal a few bottles of spirits. 'I was saving these until Christmas but I suppose it has been a bad few days. Let's crack open the Courvoisier. Did you bring your diary, that's the main thing? We can't fix everything if you haven't started on the groundwork. We can sit down, have some food and work out what we do next.'

I shake my head and all the time my mind is on Ben. Glen can tell I'm not present.

'Oh, Marissa. I thought we were going to gather everything together and call the police. Whoever is following you can't get away with it. It's stalking and it's a crime. What if it has something to do with what happened to Dan and now this person is coming for you?'

'That's what the police thought too.'

'You've already called the police? That's a relief.' He pours two measures of Courvoisier and passes one to me. His kitchen spotlights reflect on the cut glass.

I take a gulp and almost choke on the burning liquid. I'm not sure I like it but I take another sip. Maybe it will calm my trembling hands down and slow my heart rate a little. 'The police came to see me. They wanted to talk about another recent murder and Dan. Did you hear about the murder of a man in his home about a mile from here? It has been on the news this week.'

'I can't say that I have. Did you know this man?'

I nod. There's no point hiding things now, not when I'm about to come clean. 'He was my uncle.'

'I'm so sorry. I didn't know you were going through a bereavement too.'

'He abused me as a child.' I blurt it out and pause, not knowing how to elaborate.

'I see.' Glen takes a huge gulp of his drink. 'I had no idea, well, I mean you've never spoken about your past. Do the police know anything?'

'No, but obviously they see a link. I knew both murdered men.' My voice is cracking under the stress so I clear my throat but this makes it worse. 'They also wanted to know if I'd seen anyone suspicious hanging around.'

'They must be worried that whoever murdered these men must be a threat to you. It's great that you're getting a grip on this. What did the police say about your stalker?'

'I didn't tell them. I said that I haven't seen a thing.'

'What?'

I take a seat at his table and sip the drink again. My head is beginning to feel a little fuzzy so I place the glass down. 'There's something I have to tell you.'

'Okay.'

'On the night that Dan and my uncle were killed, I'd been sleepwalking. I didn't want to keep the police at mine any longer until I'd told you, and I think I know who's stalking me, which is why I came straight here before going home. Before you jump to conclusions, I didn't kill them. Someone is trying to set me up and I think I know who. I just don't know why. I needed to tell you before all this comes out; because we're friends and I trust you.' A flash of a person runs through my mind but I can't see that person. It's like I'm looking at a rippling reflection in water. The water is back again. It's like my brain has just short-circuited.

'What? Did I just hear right? Say that again.' He coughs and places his glass on the worktop. I note that he hasn't come to sit at the table with me. I've scared him.

'I'm being framed.'

'How...'

'I don't remember either night. It's all a blur... actually, not even a blur. All I can remember is water. Before Dan's murder, I'd had a drink at yours and I woke up to find a bloodied knife in my bath. I don't remember how it got there. I can't remember anything, all I know is that the evidence against me was there when I woke up.'

Glen stares at me but he doesn't open his knife drawer. 'Shit.'

'I'm so scared. Thoughts whir through my mind. Ben, my stalker, knows my father, of that I'm sure, and he's watching my apartment now. I know that as he messaged me to tell me.' I can't bear to see Glen looking as worried as he is now. I bet he wished he'd never met me. I feel sick. I dash to his bathroom and lock the door in a sweat. The heat is radiating from my chest and my anxiety over this whole episode is making the room sway just enough to make me feel as though I'm on a boat in choppy seas. I lift the lid to the toilet and lean over the bowl. I don't want to be sick, I want to cry. My heart wants to spill, not my stomach.

He bangs on the door. 'Marissa, come out. You need to calm down and we can talk about this, work out what to do next. I will help you but only if you come out.'

Through my sobs, I manage to speak. 'I can't. I already know what I need to do. I need to go to my apartment, confront Ben and finally learn the truth. Then, I'm going to call the police, that's where you come in. If I don't call you within fifteen minutes of leaving here, I need you to call them for me and tell them everything I just told you. I know it's a lot to ask but can you do that? I need to clear my name first. I'm going to record our conversation on my phone.'

Glen doesn't answer.

'I think he was working with Dan. That's why you can't help me sort this. I can't even sort this. It's too far gone.' It rings true now. Dan was married to Petula. Maybe Dan had been privy to my case files at some point and maybe Ben approached him. He and Ben could have been friends. It's not the strongest of connections, but it's all I have.

'I'll help you in any way I can.' He pauses for what seems like forever. I rub my eyes and as I'm about to stand and open the door, he bangs on it so hard that it shakes the doorframe. 'Open this door now!' His tone has changed.

I don't want to open the door but I can't stay here forever. He's losing his patience with me, I know he is. He's probably wishing right now that he never invited me to his stupid residents' meeting and that we'd never met. I've done nothing but brought chaos and trouble into his life with my instability and now I tell him all this. 'I'm sorry, Glen. I'll try to explain myself better. I told you all this because I know who's behind the stalking. They've been playing games with me.' I halt back a sob. 'My father killed my mother when I was a child. I never knew who he was but I think Ben knows. That's another reason I need to speak to him before the police are involved. I'll never know the truth if I don't.' Tears slide down my cheeks. This isn't how I wanted to tell him about my mother, from behind a toilet door.

'Open up, now!' He's banging on the door. 'Marissa, you have finally found out who you are. Found your true self. Embrace it.' His voice is calm and low.

'What?' My eyes are drying up. My true self? What would he know? I realise we're friends but I've barely let him into my life. How would he know who I really am?

'Dan deserved everything he got and so did your uncle which is why you killed them, Marissa. Just come out so that we can talk.'

I shake my head and wipe my wet eyes with my sleeve. 'But… I didn't… I sleepwalked and saw the murderer and the murderer wants to shut me up. Ben murdered them.' I pause and my brows furrow.

'Marissa, just open this door. I don't want to have to remove the door handle and lock to get you out of there. I'm going to help you but you need to let me in.'

'I need a minute.'

'Fine, I'm sitting outside the door, making sure that you don't do anything stupid. You have one minute.'

I can't do this any more. Exhaustion is setting in and I can't see a way out of everything, not with Glen refusing to move and accusing me of being a murderer. I could take the same option that Reggie took. End myself forever, then no one else will get killed. I now see that there's no way back. I have reached my end. If I get out of this bathroom, I might have to consider my options.

I glance across at the scales, the small waste bin and my gaze stops on the laundry hamper. The sleeve of something dark hangs over the side. With trembling hands, I reach over and lift the lid as I stand and I see a dark hooded top. The hood is damp like it's been worn in the past couple of hours. I delve into the pockets and flinch as I cut my finger on something sharp. Pulling it out, I see that it's a shard of snowflake bauble. My heart hammers against my chest and I stare at it open-mouthed.

'Okay, if you're refusing to come out I'm fetching my tools and this door's coming off.'

I don't answer. I can't. I stare at the piece of bauble and the hoodie. Underneath it is a woollen hat and my eyes travel further across the floor and rest on the dirty black boots tucked up against the bath. Glen has been stalking me all along. Why has my friend been watching me? All this time, I trusted him. Am I sure it's the same hoodie? Sounding him out is the only way I'll get my answer. 'Glen, have you been watching me?'

'Marissa, open the door and we can talk at the table like adults. You're acting like a child.' He's angry. I've never heard him like this. An electric screwdriver whirs away against the door handle.

I open his mirrored cabinet and search for something. A razor blade, maybe. Kill myself or defend myself? I haven't decided yet. There aren't any and that safety razor would be useless. I throw it into the bath and begin to look for something else. I spot some sleeping tablets, some paracetamol and soap. Sleeping tablets? If he slipped those into my drink on the night of the meeting and when he walked me home before Dan was murdered, I would have been totally out of it. I knew I hadn't felt right. The door flies open and Glen stares at me. I go to push past him. 'I need to go, things to do. Sorry about your door.' A real sense of fear is radiating from my core and we both know that he isn't going to let me leave.

He easily grabs all nine stone of me, pinching my arm so hard his nails dig through my blouse and flesh. 'You're not going anywhere.'

I go to hit him but he's stronger than me. Trying to yank my arm free, all I do is send a jolt of pain through my shoulder. 'Let me go. Please, Glen.'

With a swift shove, I'm thrown into his lounge and I land so hard on my back, it knocks the wind out of me. As I gasp to regain my breath, I try to sit up but panic is taking all my energy. My arms are like lead and my trembling hands can't grip. The Christmas lights begin to flash and they muddle my mind, along with the ever-playing Christmas music. I want it all to go away, to turn off; to shut up. I can't think.

'Mistletoe and Wine' starts to play and I feel as though I'm living a nightmare. The need to escape is so strong in me yet he now has me pinned to the floor and unable to breathe properly. He's going to kill me, I know he is, so I close my eyes and wait for whatever he's going to do to be over but after a minute he settles above me, his legs and body firmly fixing me in place so that I can't move.

'Look at me.'

I don't want to. If I open my eyes with this song on while I'm pinned to the floor, I'll see Simon and I don't want to see Simon. 'No,' I cry. However much I try to force Simon from my mind, I can't. I'm in a living hell and there's no way out. Control is not a thing I possess right now. I'm at his mercy.

While straddling me, he grabs my chin with one hand, turning my head to face him and he prises one of my eyes open with his other hand, forcing me to look at him. 'See my nose, it's your nose, Marissa. You always did have your mother's beautiful skin colour but your lips. See, they're quite thin, like mine. I have always been there for you over the years, existing in the background and this time, I'm never going to let you go.'

It's then I realise. Caroline lied to me about my father's death. Glen is my father.

CHAPTER FORTY-NINE

'It was you who killed my mother…' I can't stop the tears from slipping down my cheeks and into the crook of my neck. 'I saw you at the apartment and the blood, what you did to her. How could you?'

'That question is yours to answer. You killed Dan and Simon. Tell me how it felt.'

I shake my head loose from his grip. 'I can't.' Maybe he's right. Like father, like daughter but I couldn't do that… could I? Maybe he's been trying to protect me all this time. The sleeping tablets, maybe they sent me funny, which is why I did those things in my sleep.

'You can. Tell me… Daddy knows everything. He always did. I'm so proud of you too. You showed those men, you really did.'

I'm choking on my words. 'No, this can't be happening.' I let him into my home and into my life and now he's going to kill me. I never imagined this day would ever come. Most fathers would be proud of their kid's achievements, maybe good exam results, a good job, a successful relationship. I have finally found my father and I'm sensing he's proud that I might be just like him. He wanted us to be alike all this time. He thinks only I can understand him but I don't and I don't understand myself and how I did what he's saying I did. I hate myself. 'We're not the same. You killed my mother. She didn't do anything wrong.'

'She took you away from me and she kept saying that I raped her. I didn't rape her, she wanted it. We got you. She refused to let me into her life so that I could see my little apple – that's you by the way, Marissa. That was so wrong and she had to pay. You were meant to be there when I came to the apartment. I was going to take you, had it all planned, but I wasn't going to kill her that day. Something came over me and I wanted to do it more than anything. Anyway, you understand. After that, it was going to be you and me in the log cabin in Scotland. I had a job lined up, new identification for the two of us.' His spittle hits my face.

I try to push him off but it's like he has the strength of several men and I am weakened by the few sips of brandy that I had. 'She was scared of you which is why we kept moving. You hurt her and stalked her and hit her. I heard you, when you found us at the cottage. Then when we moved again, you killed her and all she was doing was protecting me.'

'Yes, and I enjoyed it, every moment, just like you enjoyed killing Simon and Dan. People like us don't exist on the same plane as everyone else. I need you to see that. Only I could be the one to bring you up and look after you but you ruined it by not being there when I came for you.'

I was there when he killed her but I don't want him to know. I saw my mother's blood spill under our bed. My head is fuzzy. 'Why did you and Ben do this to me?'

His laughter makes my ears ring. 'You think you know it all, don't you? Well, I have another surprise for you, but we'll get to that in a minute, Answer this about Simon and Dan. Did you enjoy killing them?'

I can't answer him, I don't know. I can't remember anything. Again I see water and I don't know why. My mind flits to the notes I received. Similar notes to the ones that Reggie received with the red writing on them. 'You sent Reggie those notes, all those years ago. You took her from me.'

Glen shrugs as he keeps me pinned in place. 'She was a total waster dragging you into her world of risky behaviour. People like you, like us, need to stay in the shadows not stand on walls protesting for the world to see. She needed to go so I got myself a job covering on security occasionally. It helped me to get close to you both. Such a delicate personality Reggie was. I knew I could push her over the edge. I didn't expect her to kill herself. A nervous breakdown would have done the trick but, hey, what a result. You know, watching her breaking down was so satisfying. It took the game to another level. Everything I did was to bring you ever closer to me and when you moved to Stratford, I just knew the time was finally right to be in your life properly but it still took ages. I watched and I waited. Finally the time had come to make my move.'

Sobbing, I recall how I saw Glen at our first meeting and, though I'd been wary, I'd opened myself up to receiving his friendship. Only now do I see how I was played. 'You only sent out one invite to the residents' meeting, didn't you?' My bottom lip is quivering as I speak.

'Rumbled.' He lets out a sinister laugh. 'I was about to give up on that strategy after sending a whole twelve invites to you, but you can imagine how I felt when you walked through that pub door. I think the sinister note had something to do with it. Had you scared, didn't it? With your new neighbour and the notes, you had to do something.'

'You're sick!' I spit in his face but he just laughs and wipes it with his arm. I try to kick and wriggle but he's much heavier than he looks.

'I am sick but you are too. I kill, you kill. I hate, you hate. We're better than these people. I just had to help you see that.' He pauses. 'You can't deny yourself. You're my little apple. Your mother used to hate me calling you that. I loved the apple picture though, kept it close to my heart for years. It was all I had of you so I had to take it.'

I'm looking straight into his manic eyes and he's right, I see myself. His blood runs through me. I feel it and I see it as clear as day. This isn't how I want to be but sometimes we can't help who we are. Our inner nature is stronger than anything else and I know I have to tap into that inner nature to survive. 'I'm just like you. You're right,' I say in a broken voice.

As he loosens his grip, I don't try to run. This is like some dark game of self-discovery. I hope it's one of my nightmares and I'll wake up in an hour under my desk but right now, here, I've never felt so alive and I want to live.

CHAPTER FIFTY

'Are you ready for my surprise?' Glen loosens his grip on me.

I am ready but I can't speak, so I nod. As he helps me up, he leads me by the hand into the hallway. The front door is so close. Maybe I can kick him hard and make a run for it. I can see that the chain is on. By the time I reach the door, he'll have me pinned back to the floor. Will he kill me? I am after all his daughter. Does our unwritten code include not killing blood relatives? A part of me hopes so. I just want this to end. As soon as it does, I'm going to tell DS Brindle everything. I also want justice for my mother so I will tell Brindle what Glen did to her. I swallow and hope Glen is wrong about me murdering Simon and Dan but I can't prove otherwise. We will both have to pay for our wrongs when all this is over. It's time for the truth to come out.

Reaching into a bag by the door, he pulls Scarecrow out. 'I've tidied your toy up a bit. Look, his other eye is now sewn on. I remember Scarecrow well. You always had him gripped in your chubby little arms. You were such a beautiful baby. You know, your mother only let me see you twice then she ran away, but I found her. I found her every time. I knew I'd get you back one day so you can't possibly understand how happy I am right now.'

He goes to hand me the woollen doll and I snatch it. Scarecrow is precious to me. He was my mother's. I didn't want him fixed. He was perfect even with his flaws. 'Can I go now?'

'That's not the surprise.' The background music comes to an end and I hear a rustling sound. Glen points to the spare room door. 'Your surprise is in there.'

I almost choke as I swallow.

'Go on. Don't leave Daddy waiting. It's a gift.' He leans against the front door and I shake, knowing I'm trapped.

Swallowing, I pop Scarecrow on the floor against the skirting board and I press the handle. I have no choice but to do as he says. It resists me with its stiffness so I apply more pressure. Slowly, I push the door and it creaks before revealing a scene that will be emblazoned on my memory forever.

Ben is a whimpering mess. On seeing me, he starts fidgeting against the coarse rope that is tight against his stomach, wrists and ankles and the chair he is trapped in looks solid. The smell of urine and sweat is overpowering, so much so, I want to heave. Fear is radiating from his body. He makes squeaking noises from behind the gag and I'm transfixed. Stepping into the transparent plastic curtained box, I tread on the polythene underneath.

'Take your shoes off. You'll pierce it.'

Ben's eyes are stark and one is bloodshot. He shakes his head as I kick them into the hallway. Glen passes me a paper suit, a hair cap, latex gloves and foot covers. 'Put these on.' Glen starts doing the same.

I do exactly what I'm told. My gaze never leaving Forge's. I never imagined that I'd see Ben scared and right now as I think about what he did to his wife and Justine, a part of me is glad he's scared. I pull the hair cap on and tuck all my hair inside it. This isn't about Elizabeth or Justine or even Ben. I know that. It's about me. All of this is for me; a gift from my father. He wants me to be awake this time so that I can enjoy the whole experience. Another flash of a memory passes through my mind. There is a face blurred by rippling water. I shake that thought away. Glancing to the side of all the plastic, I see the photo of my mother and me. It's Blu-tacked to the wall, along with a collection of photos showing my whole life documented from afar. There's me with my mother; me at the farm. Me going into my shared house in Edgbaston; me with Reggie. A photo of Ben and me at the Drunken Duck. All these photos were taken without me knowing.

'Do you like your surprise?'

I snap on the gloves and glance back at Glen. 'I love my surprise.' Ben starts trying to make the chair jump in an attempt to escape. He seems to have given up on the binds as they look too tight. The chair is so heavy he's barely lifting it. He manages a little jump and then he yelps through his nose as the leg crushes the skin on the edge of his small toe. I know Ben didn't send me the last text, it was my father; the figure in the dark clothes. I nod at my father.

'He's all for you. You don't have to deny who you are any more. My love is unconditional and I hope you'll come to love me in the same way. We have the rest of our lives together.'

The gag slips slightly and I hear what Ben is mumbling. 'Please, Marissa. Please don't hurt me. I'm sorry about Justine and my wife. I've paid for what I've done. I'll leave Justine alone, I promise.' But I don't believe him. Can a person change who they truly are, deep inside?

I glance at Glen and then a flashback to the night of Simon's murder comes back to me and then there's another. Once they start, they keep coming. The ripple in the water is clearing and I can see through my blurred thoughts. Then I see Dan's face as the knife plunged through him.

Ben whimpers and shakes his head. He really is pathetic.

My father reaches down and slides open a small drawer then he presents me with a weapon. 'It's like your knife. I made sure it was a similar size. We all have our favourites.'

Slowly, I reach over and take the weapon in my hand. I stare at Ben's reflection in the metal and I'm no longer shaking.

'Why are you doing this?' Ben mumbles through the gag.

'Tell him.' My father casually leans against the door frame and smiles.

'You're a bad, bad, person, Mr Forge, and while you're around, women live in fear.' I pull the gag completely away from his mouth so that his voice is more than a mumble.

'I've changed, I really have… I thought we had something, Marissa. I was kind to you, wasn't I? Is this what it's all about?' His chin glistens and his nose is running.

I shake my head. 'It's not about you. That's the problem with people like you. Did you stop hurting your wife when she begged and pleaded?'

My father stands so close to me, I can feel his breath on my neck. The pit of my stomach is turning, over and over. Forge stares and shakes his head as I bend and prod the tip against his jugular.

'I'm sorry. I'm a bad person. Please don't kill me. I've been having therapy and it's helped. Justine was a slip-up. I'll apologise. I'll get out of her life. I'm not that person any more.'

My father places a hand on my shoulder. 'This will bond us forever, I promise. Go on, my little apple. Do it.'

I smile at him, knowing that he means it. He wants me to approve of him and love him. By now, Ben is sobbing and dribbling so my father pulls the gag back over his mouth. 'He's said enough. We both know people can't change. We are who we are. Go on, Marissa. Take what is yours. Take your gift.'

I smile as I stand and bring the knife up above my head then I plunge it directly into skin, feeling the point as it pushes through his clothing and fleshy layers. Ben's gaze is locked on mine and I can see the panic in his eyes as I send my father tumbling to the floor. I bend over and pull the knife back out of my father's side. His eyes are pleading and his mouth opens as he grabs the plastic sheeting, dragging the frame down with him.

'I remember everything now.'

CHAPTER FIFTY-ONE

As my father wrangles with the plastic, blood spurting from his side with every move, I know I don't have much time. That stab was bad but he's tough. Reaching over Ben, I use the knife to cut his gag and then the rope around his feet.

'Thank you, thank you so much.'

I finally free his hands and he stumbles from the chair where he grabs his shoes and jacket from the back of the room before walking back and kicking Glen.

'Leave him alone!' I push Ben away. 'Get out of here. Call the police and ask for DS Brindle and DC Collins. Tell them to come now.'

As Ben starts to fumble with his shoes in the hallway, I sit next to my father. 'Sorry, Dad. I am not you. I know you killed Dan and Simon. You drugged me on those nights, didn't you? Those pills in your cabinet...'

'I needed you to see.'

I clench my fists and seethe. 'See what?'

'You're just like me.'

'But I'm not. I didn't kill Dan or Simon. You knowing about my knife proved that you'd rummaged around and you could have only done that if you knew I wouldn't wake up, but I did, didn't I? I wasn't fully conscious but the memory was there, locked in the back of my mind. All it needed was triggering. You had to have left my apartment on the latch, then you came back later, that's the only way you could have done it. You found my little knife. What made you go looking?' I shrug. 'Maybe you knew it was there, after all, maybe I am a bit like you but I kept that knife where it was to protect myself, not to kill people. Then you killed Dan. I remember now, stumbling while half asleep to the bathroom. It feels like a dream really. In the bathroom, I was running the tap, looking at the rippling water and failing miserably at splashing it on my face. Then just after, I saw a blurred vision of you through the spyhole. *You* were going into Dan's flat to kill him, not me. Then at Simon's cottage, you were in his house. I sleepwalked there or maybe you drove me there; I don't think I'll ever know how I got there and woke outside my apartment block. It doesn't matter anyway. What matters is that I know you killed them. I must have half woken at one point, outside the cottage, because I have a picture of you in my head as you closed his curtains. You were purposely trying to send me crazy and for that, I will never forgive you. The baubles were a nice touch, you'd seen them at my mother's all those years ago and when you took them from Simon's tree, you hoped they would mess with my mind.'

'Marissa, please.'

I could hear Ben fighting with the chain on the door so I leave my father lying in his own bloodied mess to see what is happening. 'I'll tell the police what I heard. Thank you, Marissa. Thank you for saving me.'

Reaching over and removing his shaking fingers from the chain, I take over. 'If I ever find out that you've hurt another woman, or you go anywhere near Elizabeth or Justine ever again, I will come for you and that's a promise. I'm not a killer but you heard my father, maybe we're more alike than I think.'

I scratch an itch on my arm with the tip of the knife, not believing what I've just said for a minute but if it keeps Justine and other women safe, I'm happy for Ben to understand that as a threat. 'Also, if you repeat what I just said, I'll deny it.' I open the door and watch as he runs to the stairs, half falling down them as he calls out. I know the police will arrive in a matter of minutes now, he's already causing a commotion with his screaming and shouting. But right now, it's time to spend some quality time with my father. We have a lot of catching up to do.

CHAPTER FIFTY-TWO

He's dragging his body through the spare room door by his elbows. Mouth open, he's crying out in pain, leaving a blood trail as he goes. This time it's me on top as I turn him over. I'm now in control of this situation and I will show him exactly who I am. 'That surprised you, didn't it?'

He coughs and splutters and a few flecks of blood come from his side. 'You're a remarkable young woman but you stabbed the wrong man.'

I bite my bottom lip and shake my head. 'No, you are not turning me into a killer and you're going to pay for everything you did.'

'So make me pay.' He grins and grabs my arm. I allow him to gently guide the knife to his throat where the point leaves a small dent in his skin. 'Everyone will now know I'm the killer. You can get away with my murder. It would be self-defence. Mr Forge will back you up.' He laughs louder until he's shrieking. 'Go on, I'm yours to take and I know how much you want to do this. After all, your first time should be special.'

'No, I don't think I want or need to kill you. What I need is for you to rot in prison for murdering my mother. She deserves justice and so do I. If she hadn't been killed by you, I'd have never been sent to Simon and Caroline's. You were watching me while I was there. You must have got wind of how cruel they were to me back then and you did nothing.' I sneer at him. It feels good to finally be able to lay blame in its rightful place.

'I did. I killed him. I did it for you.'

'You did it for you. You just said you kill because you enjoy it, therefore it was for you. If you wanted to be there for me, you wouldn't have killed my mother or driven my best friend to kill herself.'

He laughs again. 'It's all a game. Life is a game. Now you've started playing, you are in it until the end. It will chew you up if you don't give into this urge, right now. You can have me, go on. Say I attacked and you had to stab me with my own knife.'

Shaking my head slowly, I squat and stab the tip of the knife through the plastic into the wooden floor. 'Goodbye, Dad. I am not your little apple. Never was and never will be.' The sound of the police bursting through the communal door makes him flinch and I know this is the worst punishment ever for him. He'll get to go to prison and the truth in its entirety will now come out. I feel a few tears erupting from the corners of my eyes. It's over. I stand and leave him there and I wait on the landing, ready to be taken to the station where it was going to be a long few days explaining everything. Just before they come up the last flight of stairs, I glance at my reflection in the landing window and I see that the collar of my white blouse is covered in blood spatter, my father's blood; my blood. Me being here dressed like forensics personnel is going to take a lot of explaining but Ben knows the truth and he owes me. I saved him and he really didn't deserve it but I'm not here to dish out justice, I just want my life back. I want to get drunk with Justine, do my work and keep saving for my cottage. All I want is for things to go back to normal.

'Stand back.' I don't need to turn around, I recognise DS Brindle's husky voice and the smell of smoke that follows her.

CHAPTER FIFTY-THREE

One month later

For hours I sat in that cell wearing standard issue track bottoms while DS Brindle interrogated me but Ben's statement was enough to get me out. A search of my father's apartment threw up enough forensic evidence to prove that he killed Simon and Dan. Eventually the forensics results came back and my father, however clever he thought he was, had left his DNA at both scenes. Just a hair at Simon's and a slight bit of skin under Dan's fingernail.

Christmas came, Christmas went. I hate Christmas. From now on, I'm going away on holiday for every single Christmas. I don't need to be reminded of murders or suicides. I see why it's often spoken about as being a depressing time of the year.

I still worry about myself, my sleepwalking and the things I struggle to remember, but I'm working through my issues with the help of a good therapist. Years of abuse and the grief I've carried around after losing my mother and Reggie are hard to let go of. I will never forget them and I hate Glen for what he's done. He took them both from me but I need to heal which is why I'm happily back in therapy.

That's the packing nearly done. All boxes filled and the removal people are due in the morning and I'll finally leave this apartment, ready for a fresh start. Of course, I can't go too far as I'm the prime witness to my father's crimes. Ben also tried to call me a few times but I don't want to speak to him. He's not blameless in all this. After all, he's just another abuser. Thank goodness for women like Elizabeth who make it their mission to get the word out about men like him. I've since spoken to her and I like her. I think we can be friends.

When my father gave me the opportunity to kill him, I knew I had to show him that we weren't the same in any way or form. I am not a killer, I'm a victim of his gaslighting and further mental abuse. Every little part of me hates him for what he's done.

Lastly, I place Scarecrow and my apple picture in the final packing box. I know why my mother had stared at this picture in a less than delighted way when I showed it to her. With what my father called me, she didn't need a reminder of his little apple. However, I still need a reminder of her, which is why I'll keep it. It's the last thing I ever did for her before she died and it will stay with me forever.

Cat, as I call him, winds himself around my ankles, meowing for food. I haven't had him living with me for long but his coat is already shiny and his eyes are bright. Lifting him up, I kiss his head. He purrs, melting my heart like Riffy once did. 'It's you and me against the world, Cat.'

Heading to the front door, I place a scattering of marbles down and make sure my feet are bare to ensure that I don't sleepwalk my way out of the apartment. This is how I have to live from now on. I can never risk losing my mind again. I'm not a murderer but I am a sleepwalker and I never want to have to question my own sanity again. The fire door bursts open. I peer through the spyhole. Two noisy men in their mid-twenties walk through. They joke, laugh and swear, then another two men follow behind holding a box of beer. I smile. I'm leaving tomorrow and I couldn't be happier. Let them party the night away.

CHAPTER FIFTY-FOUR

Eleven months later

It's Christmas Eve and a whole year has passed. I finally feel like I belong. I have roots and friends. 'Trixie,' I call to the little dog as she snuffles at a lamp post, then I give her a slight tug. I can't believe how attached I've become to this bundle of fur. She wags her fluffy piggy tail and continues along the icy path. I take in all the inflatable Santas in gardens and the fairy lights framing bay windows and porches, then I stop outside the cottage – my cottage – where Cat sits on the windowsill licking his paws.

This is where I live now and I love it. Checking my watch, I realise I don't have long until my visitor arrives. I also have lots to do before I meet Justine later at a new club in town where we are going to dance the night away without worrying that some creep is stalking either of us.

A twinge of sadness fills my heart as I begin walking back towards my cottage. I repeat that phrase again. My cottage. Simon did something right by me in his life. Maybe the guilt of what he took from me haunted him so he put me down as his next of kin. Without any children or siblings of his own, he left what he did have to me in his will; including the cottage. I don't know why and I'll never get to ask him. I see it as compensation for all he put me through, although no amount of money will ever take away the pain that lurks deep inside.

I reach my cottage and I see a happy home. Everything that was Simon's has gone and I've replaced it with my own furniture. I have a feature wall in the lounge, a fireplace and some candles and Christmas ornaments; but none of them are blue with snowflakes on them. Cat has a scratching post and a litter tray. I've bought yellow tartan curtains and a cosy rug. Sometimes, I leave a pile of clothes on my bedroom floor and toast crumbs on the worktop. Finally, I'm home. I found more photos of my mother amongst Simon's possessions so I've had them framed. There was also one of Riffy that I adore. Seeing my mother around the house that we were always meant to live in means so much. If she was still alive, I imagine she'd come here to live with me and we'd be happy. I feel as though she's always around and I like to think of her often. Scarecrow sits on the chair, next to my scatter cushions, and I like to see his cheery face.

Later, I'm going to visit Reggie's grave and leave her some flowers, then I'll come home and read the last letter she sent to me, again. I've taken to sitting on her grave and talking to her. I know she can't hear but it makes me feel better. Working on my happiness has been an ongoing trial but I persist every day, finding the positives in the small things, like cooking something new, or enjoying a long soak in the bath. It's the little things that make me happy now.

A few drops of rain begin to fall and Trixie shakes her fur up my leg. I bend down and stroke her. I'm only looking after her while Alice goes on a shopping trip today but I love having the little dog around.

My father continues to write to me from prison. Several life sentences were awarded after the enormity of his crimes came out. He gave a full confession to the police for the murders of my mother, Dan and Simon. On top of all that, there were murders I had no idea of. Two men and three women, all random and at different times in his life. He'd kept small tokens of his crimes, in one case a necklace, another, a shoe. There was a randomness to these things too. I guess that he did have a killer's instinct. It was always in him. And I guess, because I haven't killed anyone, it's not in me. I'm not like him and I never will be. The fact that he calls me his little apple in his letters, tells me that he still believes there is hope for me to follow in his murderous footsteps.

I shake my head and smirk. That's not me though. Who am I now? I wear a variety of clothes but still I love my grey trousers. Ben still sends me work and that's good as I get to keep an eye on him. I like him to think that I will hurt him if he upsets any more women. Between me and Elizabeth, we let him know that we're always watching him.

As for my apartment, I rent it out to a young couple. I'll struggle to sell it as the management company issues are still ongoing, but it's paying for itself so I pretend that it doesn't exist any more. It's merely an investment that I choose never to visit again. Too many bad memories.

Alice, my new neighbour, has been making her cherry cupcakes again and I quite often sit with her for afternoon tea. I really like Alice. She has been my friend, the grandmother I never had and my confidante all in one. After what happened with Glen, I thought I'd never trust again and I'll admit, trust still doesn't come easy, but I trust and care for Alice so I let her into my heart and my life. She's now one of my best buddies.

I have changed. Glen has faced up to his crimes. Simon paid for his. My mother and Reggie got justice, and I'm finally healing properly this time.

My father's voice rings through my mind. *Your blood runs through mine. You can't run and hide from who you are, my little apple*, and I disagree. I was never like him and I never will be.

I see Petula pull up outside the cottage and I give her a little wave as she steps out of the car. Her red hair is vibrant and her smile is full and warm, just like it always is. I go over to her. We hug and say our hellos and she follows me into the cottage.

'Shall I take my boots off?'

'No, don't worry,' I reply, as Trixie bounds in treading mucky paw prints everywhere.

She follows me through to the kitchen. 'How are you keeping, sweetie? It was good to bump into you last week and even lovelier to be invited to your new home. Your cottage is beautiful. Are you happy?'

'Yes, I feel as though I've finally found home.'

'And who is this little beauty?' Trixie snuffles at her feet.

'I'm dog-sitting. She belongs to my neighbour, Alice.' Cat runs in and begins to compete with Trixie for attention. I pick Cat up.

Petula drops her over-filled handbag on my kitchen table before bending to stroke the dog. I see a letter poking out and I recognise the writing. It's my father's. Grabbing it, I tear it open. She stands bolt upright and snatches it back. 'What are you doing going through my bag?'

Shaking my head, I step back. Another image flashes through my mind. I'm back there at my apartment glancing through the spyhole in my semiconscious state on the night of Dan's murder and in the background I see a shadow too. 'My father was your new man, wasn't he?'

'It's not what you think.' Her lips quiver and she bites them.

'What is it then?'

'He and I… I love him and Dan was so horrible to me… Glen helped me.'

'Did you know that he is my father?'

'No, honestly, Marissa. Not until that night…' She tails off, fear in her eyes.

'There was another person at Dan's apartment on the night he was murdered. It was you. You and my father killed your husband and tried to make me think I was losing my mind.'

'Please don't say anything. I didn't want to involve you…'

'I trusted you. I always trusted you and this is what you do. Get out!'

'Dan hurt me, Marissa. We did it for you…'

I grab her bag and thrust it into her arms. 'You and my father; all you both say is "I did it for you." Get out.'

'Please, Marissa…'

'Get out.' She puts the letter back into her bag and backs away slowly, clearly scared of me. I don't know why, she and my father are the killers. She's scared that I'll tell, that I'll blow her life apart and she deserves it. I could grab her and hurt her right now after all she's done to me. She left me with Simon and Caroline. She and my father almost ruined my life. I could do the unthinkable, just like my father said I was capable of. If I prepared my spare room just like he showed me, I could finish her and no one would ever know.

I'm sickened by my feelings. Glaring into her wide eyes I smile at the thought of taking her life. Maybe she's the real gift in all this, a gift to my father from me.

She starts walking backwards towards the door as if she can sense what I'm thinking. 'I didn't kill anyone, Marissa. I'm only guilty of falling for Glen. Please believe me. I got swept up in things I shouldn't have and I have to live with that. Simon and Dan were bad people.'

My stare intensifies. She turns and runs, shaking as she bursts out of the front door and darts to her car. For now, I let her go.

The glint of a knife on the draining board catches my attention. *You are not a killer, Marissa.* Is that so?

About Petula… polythene room or call to the police. Which should it be? That very much depends on who I am now.

A LETTER FROM CARLA

Dear Reader,

As always, I'm massively grateful that you chose to read *What She Did*. I hope that you enjoyed my standalone thriller as I really enjoyed taking the time to explore Marissa as a character. I wanted to delve into her traumatic past and develop a plot which saw that past coming back to haunt her. I also wanted to explore the condition of sleepwalking in adults.

If you enjoyed *What She Did* and want to keep up-to-date with all my latest releases, just sign up at the following link. Your email address will never be shared and you can unsubscribe at any time.

www.bookouture.com/carla-kovach

It's probably no surprise to you, after reading *What She Did*, that I'd been a little bit obsessed with sleepwalking. I didn't realise until I delved deeper into somnambulism, how many people, including a lot of adults, are sufferers. The possible reasons are broad but in some cases it can be down to emotional stress; and combine that with drinking and possible drug taking, it could be a recipe for disaster and I wanted this to be central to my plot. Also, it's quite scary to know that sufferers can straddle between being asleep and awake – this definitely sounds scary for a sufferer. I too have had some weird sleep issues and the confusion on properly waking is like nothing else. My sleep issues haven't been quite so dramatic. I mostly have false awakenings and I've always remained in bed, which is a relief. I don't know how I'd cope if I woke up in the street.

I then got on to researching what people have actually done while in this state and it's quite disturbing when coming across extreme cases. People have jumped out of high storey windows, drowned, ventured out for a drive or even committed an act of violence resulting in homicidal somnambulism. But – don't panic – most cases are totally harmless.

For all the points above, I found this to be an exciting book to write. As mentioned before, I wanted my main character to be caught in a struggle with her past, one where stressing about it made her sleepwalk.

Whether you are a reader, a tweeter, a blogger, Facebooker or a reviewer, I really am appreciative of everything you do and as a writer, this is where I hope you'll leave me a review.

Again, thank you so much. I'm an avid social media user so please feel free to contact me on Twitter, Instagram or through my Facebook page.

Thank you, Carla Kovach

CKovachAuthor

CarlaKovachAuthor

carla_kovach

ACKNOWLEDGEMENTS

As always, writing a book takes a team effort so I have many people to thank as I couldn't do it without everyone involved.

Firstly, I have to say a humongous thank you to my editor, Helen Jenner. She really did work hard on this book and I'm immensely grateful for her input. I always say I love working with her and I mean it.

I love the amazing book cover so here's a big thanks for Lisa Brewster who worked on the cover for *What She Did* with Helen. This is the first thing that people see and knowing I'm in such good hands is fantastic.

Huge thanks to Peta Nightingale too. It's always a pleasure to hear from her with updates and contract information.

Kim Nash, Noelle Holten and Sarah Hardy are amazing at what they do. They are the best publicity peeps around and I appreciate all the work and energy that this takes. They always make me feel special on publication day, too, so thank you to them.

This is when I'd like to express my gratitude to the brilliant bloggers for giving up their time to feature me on their blogs. They do all this for the love of books and reading and it means so much that they chose to blog about my book.

I also need to mention the Fiction Café Book Club, a group on Facebook of which I'm a member. Their admins and members are such book lovers and supporters. I'm thrilled to be a part of their community.

The other Bookouture authors are incredibly supportive and I love being a part of this huge happy family. What an amazing group of people.

My beta readers, Derek Coleman, Christel McMullan, Su Biela, Brooke Venables, Anna Wallace and Vanessa Morgan, are amazing. Receiving their early feedback always makes me feel less nervous about publication day. I also know what busy lives they lead with their own work, family and writing. I really do value the time they give me. I also referenced Vanessa Morgan's book in my café chapter, *Birmingham Murder & Crime*.

Last, but definitely not least, thank you to my wonderful husband, Nigel Buckley. The cups of coffee, the encouragement and the support keep me going. It's been wonderful celebrating my achievements with him.

Printed in Great Britain
by Amazon